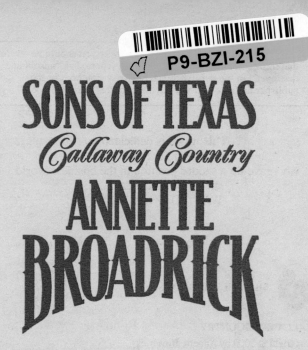

SONS OF TEXAS
Callaway Country
ANNETTE BROADRICK

Silhouette Books

Published by Silhouette Books

America's Publisher of Contemporary Romance

This novel is dedicated to
Dr. L. J. Moore
who gave up a secure position in the business world
to follow her dream....
WAY TO GO, LINDA!!

SILHOUETTE BOOKS

CALLAWAY COUNTRY

Copyright © 2000 by Annette Broadrick

ISBN 0-373-48407-0

Visit Silhouette at www.eHarlequin.com

Printed in U.S.A.

WHO CAN RESIST A TEXAN...
OR A CALLAWAY?

Clay Callaway was suddenly facing his biggest challenge—the one woman who haunted his midnight memories. Pam might have gotten the last word all those years ago, but Clay's heart was forged with steel now. And things would be different *this* time around....

Pamela McCall *never* would have agreed to take on this case if she'd known her partner would be the one man who despised—and secretly aroused—her. She'd loved him long ago, but in one bittersweet moment she'd been forced to let him go. Maybe this time she'd hold on...forever.

Katie Callaway was a model mother, an unforgettable woman—and a killer? Suspicions swirled around the disappearance of her evil ex-husband and fingers were pointing at her! This Callaway damsel needed a man who believed in her....

Lieutenant Colonel Sam Carruthers always put duty before desire. But no one had ever tempted him with such passion. Could this military hero unravel an intricate revenge scheme and save Katie...the woman he *loved?*

"Annette Broadrick's one terrific writer."
—Award-winning author Diana Palmer

ANNETTE BROADRICK

believes in romance and the magic of life. Since 1984, when her first book was published, Annette has shared her view of life and love with readers all over the world.

In addition to being nominated by *Romantic Times Magazine* as one of the Best New Authors of 1984, she has also won the *Romantic Times Magazine* Reviewers' Choice Award for Best in its Series for *Heat of the Night, Mystery Lover* and *Irresistible;* the *Romantic Times Magazine* W.I.S.H. award for her heroes in *Strange Enchantment, Marriage Texas Style!* and *Impromptu Bride;* and the *Romantic Times Magazine* Lifetime Achievement Awards for Series Romance and Series Romantic Fantasy.

Fascinated by the complexities found in all relationships, she continues to write about life and love, joy and fulfillment, and the bountiful gifts that are bestowed upon us as we travel along life's path. Readers have enjoyed over fifty love stories penned by this talented author. Annette currently lives in the hill country of her native Texas.

CALLAWAY FAMILY TREE

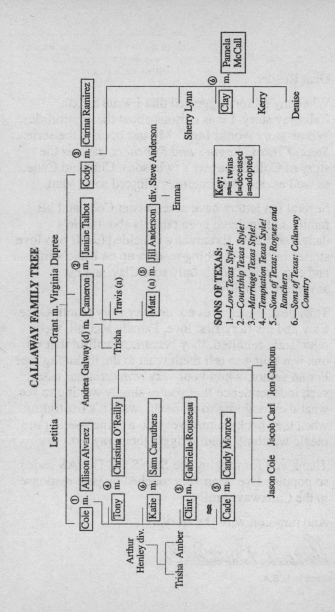

Letitia — Grant m. Virginia Dupree

Andrea Galway (d) m.

Cole m. Allison Alvarez ①

Cameron m. Janine Talbot ②

Cody m. Carina Ramirez ③

Clay m. Pamela McCall ⑥

Arthur Henley div.
Trisha   Amber

Tony m. Christina O'Reilly ④

Katie m. Sam Caruthers ⑥

Clint m. ﹦ Gabrielle Rousseau ⑤

Cade m. Candy Monroe ⑤

Jason Cole   Jacob Carl   Jon Calhoun

Trisha

Travis (a)

Matt (a) m. Jill Anderson div. Steve Anderson ⑤

Emma

Sherry Lynn

Kerry

Denise

Key:
﹦ = twins
d=deceased
a=adopted

SONS OF TEXAS:
1—Love Texas Style!
2—Courtship Texas Style!
3—Marriage Texas Style!
4—Temptation Texas Style!
5—Sons of Texas: Rogues and Ranchers
6—Sons of Texas: Callaway Country

Dear Reader,

When my editor suggested that I write a sixth Callaway story, I was curious about the possibilities. Whose story would I tell? My last book in the series, *Sons of Texas: Rogues and Ranchers,* gave us the story of Cole Callaway's twin sons, Clint and Cade, as well as one of Cameron's adopted sons, Matt.

Several fan letters have asked about Cody and his family. Others have been curious about Cole's daughter, Katie. Eventually I decided to tell two love stories in one—catching readers up on Katie's life and exploring Cody's only son, Clay, and his adventure with love.

This, dear reader, was not an easy story to tell. Once Clay and his fiery first love, Pamela McCall, were reluctantly reunited, they became so willful that no one was going to tell them what to do, including me! For an author, when your very own creations assert such independence that you're simply waiting to see what they're going to do next…well, it's frustrating when they back themselves into a corner—and pure magic watching them wriggle their way out.

Thank you for making the SONS OF TEXAS series so popular. I've been very touched by your response to the Callaway family.

And now…on with the story….

Annette Broadrick

Prologue

Racing black clouds streamed across the sky, blotting out the little light that came from the sliver of moon. A moisture-laden silence hung over the small Texas border town, occasionally interrupted by the desultory bark of a bored dog.

The narrow streets were empty of traffic. No one stirred outside the tiny houses clustered along the bluff overlooking the Rio Grande, the river that separated Texas from Mexico.

A sudden explosion ripped through the somnolent atmosphere, shattering the sleepy peacefulness of the small community. Fire tore through a huge factory-warehouse on the edge of town. Flames colored the night with an orange glow.

The people poured out of their homes and raced to see what could be done to save the only business in town, a business that had kept the local population from starving. They soon realized there was

nothing they could do but watch the business, along
with their futures, go up in billowing clouds of black
smoke.

At the same time that the factory on the border
was destroyed, other explosions occurred—in an office building in downtown Dallas, on an offshore
drilling rig in the Gulf of Mexico, and in an oil
equipment warehouse in east Texas.

There was only one thing these locations had in
common—they were part of Callaway Enterprises,
a conglomerate owned and operated by members of
the Callaway family.

The message was clear. Someone had declared
war on the Callaways.

Chapter 1

When the family decided to throw a party, they went all out, Clay Callaway thought as he paused just inside the doorway of the Grand Ballroom of the Anatole Hotel.

It was the Texas way, after all.

Everything glittered, from the giant chandeliers with their dazzling crystal pendants to the multitude of diamonds and other precious gems draped around the necks and wrists of the glamorous women who were attending the gala benefit in Dallas, Texas.

This little shindig would let the world know that there was solidarity in the family. Whenever trouble struck, the Callaways circled their wagons and unloaded their arsenal.

Tonight was the first salvo.

The melody from the song "We Are Family" kept running through his head as he spotted various members of the clan strategically placed at tables around the mammoth room, brushing elbows with the nationally elite in social, business and political circles. There were more than a few famous faces from the entertainment field, as well.

Clay wasn't supposed to be there, but someone with a great deal of clout had managed to get him pulled off his overseas assignment with his Special Forces unit. Yesterday, he'd received orders to come to Texas and to be available for this evening. He'd barely managed to get here in time for the benefit and was a little annoyed at the abrupt change in his assignment.

It wasn't that Clay didn't want to help out whenever and wherever he was needed. Once he'd been informed of the problems the family was having, he was willing to do whatever he could to resolve the problem.

What ate at him was the fact that circumstances had conspired against him, forcing him to return to his home state. He'd successfully managed to avoid the area for years. Too many memories were triggered whenever he returned home, memories he'd been able to avoid until now.

Clay mentally acknowledged his cowardice in making certain that he did not arrive at the party alone.

"Quite a collection of friends your family has," his date laughingly said in a seductively low voice.

Clay glanced down at Melanie Montez and grinned. She had no idea how grateful he was that she'd accepted his last-minute invitation to meet him in Dallas tonight.

She was one delectably sexy woman without any effort on her part—and her efforts tonight had his body humming. Granted, he'd been without a woman for much too long, but Mel would have a monk questioning his celibacy vows…and he sure wasn't a monk.

She glowed with excitement and anticipation. He wished he could feel the same way. Although his appearance tonight was a command performance, he had to admit that Mel would be an enticing consolation prize at the end of the evening.

Clay had met Melanie two years ago in Istanbul during one of his weekend liberties. She'd been there because she'd had a small part in a movie being shot in Europe that summer. They were staying at the same hotel. Once they discovered they were both Texans far from home, the two of them had struck up a conversation that had evolved into a friendship he'd grown to treasure.

Because his available time was limited—as was hers—it was a rare treat for him to be able to see her. As soon as he'd read his orders, he'd called her agent to find out where she was. After he'd finally managed to track her down, he'd been relieved that she seemed eager to be there.

The public who knew her image would never believe that Melanie could have a platonic relationship with a man. She had made it clear to him from the very beginning that she wasn't interested in a casual affair. She had no desire to live up to her public image in her personal life.

He enjoyed her company—her intelligence, her dry humor and her ability to laugh at her public persona while at the same time using her sexy image to build her career.

He hadn't been interested in a casual relationship,

either, and his spare time when not on duty was too limited to be able to offer any woman a stable relationship. However, when he'd offered to get them a suite at the hotel for the weekend, Melanie had readily agreed to stay with him, which was a first.

Clay knew that he was finally ready to take this relationship a step further. He took her presence there to mean that she wanted to move forward, as well.

"I wouldn't have missed this for the world, you know," she added, her eyes sparkling.

"Glad I could tempt you into coming," he responded with a grin.

She turned and stroked his cheek. "You're all the temptation I've ever needed, something I should never admit to you. You're cocky enough."

He took her hand and brought it to his mouth, then carefully kissed each fingertip, nibbling on the smallest one.

Something caught her attention and she looked past him. "Isn't that Cole Callaway?" Melanie whispered, nodding toward the tall, silver-haired man greeting new arrivals near the door.

Clay was amused at the awe in her voice. His uncle had that effect on people. "Yes, ma'am, it certainly is. Uncle Cole is the head of the clan. The petite lady beside him is his wife, Allison."

"*That* is Allison Alvarez, the famous sculptor? She looks too young to have made such a name for herself for so many years."

"She'll be pleased to know you think so," he replied. He took her hand and led her over to the line of people waiting to be greeted.

Melanie's infectious laugh rang out, causing a few

people to glance their way. "Don't you dare embarrass me by telling her, Clay. You promised to be on your best behavior!"

Clay attempted his innocent look but knew she wasn't buying it. "You are aware, are you not," he drawled, "that you will be meeting my parents tonight? My father will definitely demand to know your intentions toward me."

She blinked her wide green eyes, her long lashes quivering, and replied in a throaty voice, "Well, honey, I'll just have to explain to him that they are—and always have been—very dishonorable." She almost purred the last word, which caused him to burst into laughter.

The couple just ahead of them moved away and Clay was face-to-face with Cole. His uncle grinned. "I'm pleased to see you're already enjoying yourself, Clay." He shook his hand. "Glad you could make it tonight."

Clay nodded in response. "Oh, I don't think there was ever a doubt about that, was there?"

He had no idea how his uncle had managed it, but Clay had no doubt the man in front of him had something to do with his being there tonight.

Cole smiled. "We need to get together a little later this evening—if you can spare the time," he added with a sidelong glance at Melanie.

"Of course, sir. I'm looking forward to it." He drew her closer to his side and said, "I'd like you to meet Melanie Montez. Mel, my aunt and uncle, Cole and Allison Callaway."

Allison smiled and took Melanie's hand. "I'm delighted to meet you. I believe I read that you're originally from Texas, is that right?"

Melanie nodded. "Yes, from a small town in south Texas that nobody's ever heard of."

"I'm so pleased that you were able to join us tonight," Allison said. "I understand you have a new movie coming out in a few weeks."

Clay watched as his aunt managed to charm yet another person into opening up and sharing her life. Allison never ceased to amaze him. Cole was lucky to have her.

He slid his arm around Mel's bare shoulders and said, "I'm starving. Let's find a table somewhere and hit the buffet."

Allison chuckled. "I believe your mother expects you to sit with them tonight," she said, nodding to a table across the room from the entrance.

"Great," he said, slowly moving his hand along Melanie's shoulders and down her arm to her hand. Taking it in a firm grasp, he said, "Let's go meet the folks, gal. Hope you're up for this."

He started across the crowded room with the sound of Allison's laughter ringing in his ears.

Melanie said, "If I didn't know you better, I'd think you were nervous about seeing your folks tonight."

"Not nervous, exactly. It's just that they've been trying to get me to come back home for years and I've never made it until now. I generally meet up with them somewhere during their travels."

"Ah. So they're going to be surprised to see you here tonight?"

He knew his laugh sounded a little hollow. "It seems I'm the only one who's surprised," he said, glancing back at Cole. "Sometimes I forget the kind of power this family can wield."

Cody, Clay's father, stood when he spotted them approaching the table. His grin lit up the room. "Glad you could make it, son," he said, grabbing Clay in a bear hug. "Somehow I expected you to show up in your uniform."

"I took time to shave and change into my tux at the airport. You wouldn't have wanted to see what I looked like coming off that plane this evening." Then he leaned over and hugged and kissed his mother, Carina. "I swear, Mom, you get younger-looking every year."

He introduced Melanie to his parents.

Carina said, "Clay's sisters will be thrilled to death to meet you, Melanie. They should be arriving any time now." She gave Clay a quick glance that spoke volumes. "We had no idea that Clay knew you."

With commendable poise, Melanie chuckled and said, "I'm just one of his many deep, dark secrets, don't you know?"

Clay thought it was time to change the subject. "Have you two been to the buffet yet?" he asked his parents.

"Actually, we thought we'd wait until the line thinned down a little," Carina replied.

"Obviously you haven't skipped as many meals as I have getting here," Clay said. He looked at Melanie. "How about it, Mel? Think you can force yourself to eat something?"

She held up her fist in a mock threat before turning to his parents and saying, "Let's see if feeding him will calm this unruly beast, shall we?" She led the way to the buffet, giving Clay the opportunity to admire her figure, showcased in a flaming red dress that clung to every curve.

As soon as they reached the line in front of the buffet Clay caressed the small of her back. "Have I mentioned how exotic you look in that dress?" he whispered in her ear.

She leaned against him slightly and glanced over her shoulder at him. "I was beginning to think you hadn't noticed," she replied with a saucy grin.

"I may be suffering from severe jet lag at the moment, but I'm not dead."

She shifted her weight from one foot to the other, causing her body to enticingly rub against him. "Mmm. So I notice."

He laughed outright. "How long has it been since I last saw you?"

"Not that I'm counting, but it's been close to eight months...four days...and, oh, six-and-a-half hours?"

"Unfortunately it's going to be several more hours until I can get you alone, I'm afraid. I have no idea how long this meeting will last tonight."

"It must be important for him to have it this evening."

"Oh, it's important, all right. Otherwise he wouldn't have gone to the trouble to get me here."

The line moved ahead of them, and Melanie straightened and picked up a plate. "I'll be waiting for you whenever you can get away."

He smiled at her, placing his fingertip lightly against her bottom lip. "I'm counting on it."

Pamela McCall sat at one end of the ballroom watching the milling crowd, wishing she were anywhere else but at this big benefit bash. It felt a little strange to be back in Texas socializing with many of her father's constituents. She'd made a point of avoiding the political life he'd embraced for years.

However, she'd responded to the invitation out of a sense of loyalty toward the Callaways, particularly Cody and Carina Callaway. Her childhood would have been dismally lonely if Carina hadn't stepped into her life and filled in the empty space left when Pam's mother had died.

Pam knew that it was time for her to attempt to repay part of the debt she owed them, despite her personal feelings in the matter.

Ostensibly the party tonight was a benefit to raise money for various charitable causes, but anyone who knew the Callaways was aware this gathering was a bold statement made by the family: Don't Tread on Me.

Her father, a U.S. senator from Texas, had sent one of his staff members, Adam Redmond, to be her escort for the evening. Pam had made her own way in life and jealously guarded her independence from her domineering father, but she saw no reason to be rude to Adam, who was a nice guy. He was tall, dark, handsome and charming…and only those close to him knew that he was gay.

He was also a dear friend.

She glanced at Adam and smiled. "I'm so glad you're here, Adam. I can't imagine anything worse than coming to something like this alone."

Adam looked around the room before he said, "I thought you knew some of these people, especially the Callaways."

"Oh, I do. In fact, I was practically raised with

Cody and Carina's children from the time I started grade school. Their daughters are like sisters to me." She continued to scan the room. "Speaking of whom, I haven't seen them yet. I—oh, no," she murmured.

"Is something wrong?"

Pam tried to make light of the moment. "Not really. I just hadn't expected to see *him* here tonight," she said, deliberately turning away from the room and facing Adam once more.

Adam chuckled. "Him? He doesn't have a name?"

She attempted to hang on to her sense of humor as well as her emotional balance. "Sorry," she said with a forced smile. "His name is Clay Callaway, the only son of Cody and Carina."

"Why wouldn't you expect him to be here? You're the one who pointed out earlier that the Callaways had turned out in force tonight."

She shook her head. She didn't want to discuss Clay Callaway with anyone. Not even with a man as understanding as Adam. She should have expected him to be here, but as the years had passed without hearing anything about him, she'd managed to put him out of her mind. Or so she had told herself.

The twelve years since their last meeting seemed to have vanished as she noted the changes in him.

He'd been a nineteen-year-old boy back then.

He was all muscular, mature male now. She closed her eyes briefly. Seeing him again after all this time would not be a problem. She would not let it be a problem.

When Pam didn't say anything more, Adam asked, "Which one is he?"

She nodded to the buffet table. "See the man standing next to the blond bombshell in red? That's him."

"Hmm. They make a very attractive couple," Adam said amicably enough.

She watched Clay and his date leave the buffet line with loaded plates and thread their way through the crowd to a table she hadn't noticed before. Cody and Carina were there, which meant she'd have to go over there some time tonight to say hello.

She took another sip of champagne and decided to postpone that particular meeting for as long as possible.

"Are you ready to get something to eat?" Adam asked several minutes later.

With a renewed determination to enjoy herself, Pam smiled gratefully at him and said, "Sure, let's go."

After eating more than was strictly comfortable, Clay could feel himself relaxing into a mellow mood. The drink that kept getting refilled also contributed to his overall sense of well-being. He and Melanie danced several times before someone came to the table to ask her to dance.

Clay smiled his acquiescence and moved over a chair so that he was now next to his mother, who had just returned from the ladies' lounge.

"You look upset," he said in a low tone. "Anything wrong?"

She shook her head. "Oh, not really. I just get so angry sometimes at the way things work out."

"Such as...?"

"I happened to see Katie in the lounge. You know that louse, Arthur Henley, is still giving her a bad time, even though the divorce has been final for over six months."

"Are you talking about Cole's daughter, Katie?"

"Yes."

"I hadn't heard about the divorce. What happened?"

"She finally found out about all his extravagant spending, the other women, his many mistakes at work. Once she filed papers against Arthur, Cole fired him because so many of his management decisions had ended up costing the company a bunch of money.

"Arthur blamed Katie for losing his job, of course. I think he considered himself invincible, from the way he liked to live, throw his weight around, and in general be totally obnoxious. Your dad said the joke in the company for several years was that Arthur was only a divorce away from bankruptcy. I guess it never occurred to him that eventually Katie would get her fill of his behavior and toss him out on his ear. From what she was telling me just now, he's doing anything he can either to harass and annoy her or to play on her sympathies."

"Why'd she marry him in the first place?"

Carina smiled. "You know Katie. With her exuberance for life and her need to take care of everyone she meets, she fell headlong into the idea of helping Arthur meet his full potential. Let's face it, the man is very charming when he wants to be, as well as highly intelligent. He played into her need to be needed, portraying a courageous man working to overcome his impoverished background. I swear he wanted to make Katie feel it was her fault that he'd come from such a poor family. I remember how she used to make all kinds of excuses for him, based on his miserable childhood. Eventually, even our optimistic Katie had to give up. I say that, sooner or later, a person has to take responsibility for himself, instead of looking for others to blame.''

''I've lost track of time. How old are Trisha and Amber now?''

Carina's face softened. ''They're five and absolutely adorable. They remind me so much of Katie when she was at that age...so full of life.''

He glanced around the room. ''Where's Katie now?''

Carina looked around. ''I think she's sitting with her folks tonight. I found her crying in the lounge. I guess Arthur dropped by just long enough to upset her and try to ruin her evening, then left. Being Katie, she was fighting mad that she'd allowed him to get to her that way.'' She spotted Katie making her way through the tables across the room and nodded. ''There she is now.''

Clay excused himself from the table and wound his way through the crush of people to his cousin.

He hadn't seen her in years. Her hair had darkened from the reddish-blond color he remembered to a soft auburn, and her beautiful eyes had lost their sparkle. He'd never met Arthur Henley but decided on the spot that the man should be horsewhipped for making Katie miserable.

''Hi, cuz', how about a dance?'' he asked as soon as he was close enough to be heard.

Katie, looking his age rather than the ten years

older he knew her to be, glanced around at him in surprise. "Clay? My word, I can't believe it! You grew up on me when I had my back turned."

He led her out on the dance floor. "It's good to see you again, Katie. Where are you living these days?"

"In Austin."

He was surprised when he took her in his arms to discover that she was tiny. Because of the age difference, he'd always remembered her as being one of the "big kids" in the family. Time certainly had a way of changing a person's perspective. She barely came to his shoulder, even though she wore high heels.

"You're looking smashing tonight. Black definitely plays up your beautiful coloring," he said. It was true. Her fair skin, amber eyes and dark red hair were all enhanced by the midnight color of her gown.

Her eyes filled with tears. "You're good for my ego, Clay," she whispered, and looked away.

"I can't believe the twins are already five. I remember hearing about their birth. Guess I've been away for longer than I realized. Maybe I'll get to see them while I'm home this time."

She glanced at him in surprise. "Don't you have to get back to your assignment right away?"

"Actually, I'm on a thirty-day leave, so I'll be hanging around for a few weeks."

She brightened. "Well, then. Why don't you plan to come see us next week? I know the girls will be delighted to see their handsome cousin."

He wanted to ask her about Henley but decided not to bring up a subject that would be a reminder of all she'd been through. Instead, he kept the conversation lighthearted and teasing. By the time the dance was over, she was laughing with a hint of the old sparkle in her eyes.

He escorted her to the table where her parents held court, bowed over her hand and thanked her for the dance with suitable intensity—causing her to laugh again—then returned to his own table.

Once again, Melanie was dancing. Since his dad was in deep conversation with someone Clay didn't know, he held out his hand to his mother. "Would you like to dance?"

She grinned. "Taking care of all us neglected women, are you?" She hopped up and took his hand. "I'd love to." He swung her out onto the dance floor. "Do you know how long you'll be here?" she asked after they circled the floor once in silence.

He glanced at her and shrugged. "I'm officially on leave for thirty days, but I understand there's more to my being here than that. I'm to meet with Cole later tonight and will probably find out what's expected of me."

"They're all really worried, Clay. And they aren't certain who they can trust. Whoever was behind those attacks has money and power. Your dad feels they probably already have their fix in with those in authority."

"I wonder what they think I can do to help?"

"Your dad says you've developed useful skills during your stint in the military that would assist in the investigation to find out who's behind the assault. Once we have that, Cole will be able to handle it from there."

"I'll do whatever I can. You know that. I'm curious why he didn't ask his own son? Clint's working in clandestine operations and has more experience in that type of investigation than I do."

She smiled. "I don't know. You'll have to ask Cole."

Clay turned them around on the crowded dance floor so that he was now facing in another direction. His attention was drawn to a woman dancing nearby. She was tall and held herself proudly. The high-necked, long-sleeved silver dress she wore was provocative in its simplicity, subtly drawing the eye to her sleek lines. She wore her blond hair drawn up in a classic style that emphasized the pure, aristocratic planes of her face.

She looked like a princess to Clay.

Suddenly she looked his way and he got a glimpse of her eyes. He'd only known one person with eyes so blue they were almost purple. His worst fears had just been confirmed. She had shown up for the benefit. On some level he must have known that he would see her there tonight. However, nothing had prepared him for the sight of her after all these years.

She'd been an attractive teenager. She'd become a stunning-looking adult.

"What is Pamela McCall doing here? I would have thought she'd be too busy with her social life in Washington." He looked around the room. "Is her father here as well?" He studied the man dancing with her. He was as dark as she was fair. They made an attractive couple.

Not that it mattered to Clay, of course.

"I don't think the senator was able to come. Allison mentioned that he sent his regrets."

"And his daughter. Is that her husband?"

Carina glanced around. "I don't think so. I don't believe she ever married."

"Now, why doesn't that surprise me?" he muttered, turning so that he was no longer facing in Pam's direction.

"All of that happened years ago, Clay," his mother said in a gentle voice. "Don't you think it's time you forgave her? You're both different people now."

He could feel his heart pounding at the sudden shock of seeing her after all of these years.

"You're right," he agreed smoothly, fighting to control his reaction. "She means nothing to me."

"She and Kerry have been friends since they were small girls. I know how hard it was for you to—"

"It's all right, Mom. Really." He turned once again before he said, "So tell me what you and Dad have been doing since I saw you last November." For the rest of the dance he concentrated on his mother's conversation and ignored the other people on the dance floor.

When the dance was over, Clay escorted Carina back to the table. Melanie had returned moments before. He sat down and draped his arm on the chair behind her. "Having fun?" he asked, leaning over and playfully nipping at her ear.

She chuckled. "Actually, I am. This kind of party has all the ingredients of some of my childhood fantasies. To be rubbing shoulders with all the rich and famous families of Texas is something to be savored."

He straightened. "Ah, now I know why you

showed such an immediate interest in me when we first met.''

She coyly batted her lashes at him and gave him a simpering smile. ''But of course, sugar. My attention was in no way swayed by your sexy good looks and fantastic bod. It was only the name Callaway that appealed to me and fed all those girlish fantasies.''

''That's good to know. I wouldn't want to think we were taking this relationship to a new level of intimacy for any other reason than to fulfill your fantasies.''

Her laugh rang out, full-bodied and infectious. ''Gee! And all this time I thought you were hanging out with me to get your face plastered across all the tabloids as the mysterious male in my bed and in my life.''

''Darn. My secret is out.''

He heard a slight rustle behind him and glanced up to see his mother smiling at someone behind him.

Carina held out her hand and said, ''Pamela. Come join us and give us a chance to catch up. Kerry was here a few moments ago. She and Connor should be back shortly.''

Clay fought to remain expressionless as Pam eased past him and sat down in the empty chair between him and Carina. ''Hello, Mama Cee,'' she said in her husky voice. A wisp of a floral scent wafted around him from her passing. ''It's so good to see you again.'' She slowly turned her head and said, ''Hello, Clay.''

He noticed that she didn't add how she felt about seeing him again. At least she wasn't being a hypocrite.

Clay nodded. "Pam, I'd like you to meet Melanie Montez." He turned to Melanie and said, "This is Pamela McCall, the senator's daughter. She's been a friend of the family for years."

Pam smiled at Melanie. "Hello. I feel a little tongue-tied at meeting you in person. I've really enjoyed your work."

Clay watched Melanie's face as she quickly took in the woman's appearance. He wasn't sure how Pam managed to look classical as well as seductive, all without baring any part of her body. Melanie smiled at Pam and said "Thank you" without losing her poise.

He hadn't realized it until right now, but there was a strong physical resemblance between the two women—both blondes, both tall, and both with eye-catching figures. He hated the thought that he might have been attracted to Melanie because of her resemblance to Pam.

He turned to Melanie. "I haven't had a chance to dance with you in a while. Shall we?" he asked smoothly, standing.

Melanie took his hand and rose. She looked over at Pam and said, "It was nice meeting you," before following Clay out on the dance floor.

Once dancing, Melanie asked, "What was that all about?"

Clay pulled her closer so that their bodies touched from chest to knees. "I don't know what you're talking about."

She leaned back in his arms and looked into his eyes. "Now, that's interesting. You've never been evasive with me before. One of the things I've most admired about you is how you are so direct with me.''

He sighed. ''I don't know what you want me to say.''

''I want to know what's between you and Ms. McCall. The tension between the two of you was undeniable. If it's none of my business, just say so, but don't pretend you don't know what I'm talking about.''

''You're right. I was avoiding answering you because she isn't one of my favorite people. However, my family thinks the world of her. She grew up as part of our household. She probably spent more time with us than at her own home.'' He moved slowly across the dance floor before adding, ''And the truth is, we used to date in high school until she made it clear she was no longer interested in a relationship with me.''

''Ah. You must have been quite serious about her or it wouldn't still bother you today.''

''I was just a kid back then and it doesn't bother me to see her today. Not really. I haven't thought about her in years.'' He knew that was a lie as soon as it came out of his mouth. He'd worked hard not to think about her and most of the time he'd succeeded. Determined to put his past where it belonged, he added, ''I'm much more interested in the future than I am the past.'' He knew that statement to be a hundred percent true.

''She's very attractive,'' Melanie said musingly, as though discussing a painting.

He nibbled on her ear. ''Maybe, but I've only got eyes for you, sugar.''

* * *

Pam watched them dance together for a moment before turning to Carina. "He's changed a great deal, hasn't he?" She knew the regret she felt was echoed in her voice.

Carina patted his hand. "First loves are always hard to get over. He managed, just as you did. It was a tough time for you both."

"But he's never forgiven me. That's obvious." Pam didn't know why she should feel so much concern after all these years that she had made an enemy of Clay, but the truth was that it hurt. She'd been such a child back then, so caught up in her own pain and turmoil, that she hadn't faced what her behavior had done to him.

Carina nodded her head toward Clay. "He's done very well, you know, and loves his career, working in the Special Forces unit of the army. I don't think he has any regrets. It was just a surprise to see you here when he wasn't expecting it."

Pam watched him in silence for several minutes before she said, "I want him to be happy. I figured his ego might have been bruised for a while, but I suppose I hoped that eventually he would realize I saved us both from a serious mistake."

"Waiting until the night before your wedding to tell a man that you no longer want to marry him takes its toll, honey. Yes, you were both too young. I thought so at that time, but no one was listening to what I had to say then. But it was very hard for Clay. He dealt with it the best way he knew how." Carina studied her for a moment before briskly saying, "Let's put all of that in the past where it belongs, all right? What I want to hear from you now is how you're enjoying your job with the FBI, not to mention hearing about that delectable-looking young man you're with.''

When the music stopped, the band announced a short break. Melanie paused in the middle of the dance floor and asked, "Do you have any idea how much longer we need to stay? I'm really tired."

Clay glanced at his watch. "In that case, why don't you go on upstairs? I've got that meeting with my uncle and I don't know how long I'll be, but you don't have to wait around for that."

"If it's really all right with you, I think I *will* get some rest," she replied, leaning against him.

He gave her a quick kiss and said, "I seem to have gotten my second wind, but when this last rush of adrenaline is gone, I'm going to be ready to collapse, myself. I can't remember the last time I managed to get more than a nap during the past few days."

"If you're sure you don't mind..."

"No, you go on. Oh! And you'd better tell me the room number. I never thought to ask when I called you from the lobby." They walked out of the ballroom during their conversation and paused in the hallway outside.

"It's a suite," she said, "just as you requested. It's really very nice. Number 973. Keep knocking so I'll hear you, in case I fall asleep."

"Better yet, I'll get another key at the desk." He kissed her again, this time with a little more heat. "I'll enjoy waking you up once I'm lying beside you."

Clay watched as Melanie walked down the hallway toward the lobby. He wished he was going with her now, but she was the reward he had to look forward to once he was through with this meeting.

He turned and went back into the ballroom, determined to concentrate on the future he hoped to build with Melanie and erase the past from his memory.

Chapter 2

By the time Clay returned to the ballroom, Pam was no longer at the table where his mother and dad sat with two of his sisters and their husbands. He felt the tensed muscles in his neck and shoulders relax as he returned to his family's table.

Well, he had finally seen Pam after all this time. He was irritated to have to face the fact that most of his reluctance to return to Texas had been due to the memories of her that surfaced whenever he came home. They were adults with other interests now. The fact that she wasn't married didn't surprise him. She'd made her opinion of that hallowed institution clear a long time ago.

He was greeted with warm welcomes from his sisters when he sat down with the family and explained that Melanie had decided to call it a night. He lost track of time while he caught up on family news and was surprised some time later when Cole stopped by the table and said, "Carina, I hope you'll forgive me for borrowing your husband and son for a short while."

She smiled. "Not at all, Cole. I would say the evening has certainly been a success. You had a great turnout."

Cole looked around the room. Although many people had left, there was a solid group of dancers who showed no sign of stopping. "Allison is pleased. Frankly, I've decided I'm too old for this sort of thing. All I want to do is find a comfortable bed for a few hours."

Clay and Cody followed him across the ballroom.

"Sorry it took so long to have this meeting," Cole said. "The man heading up the group just arrived. We could have waited until morning but he was eager to meet with us for a few minutes, and since you were still here, I thought we could get the deal going."

He paused in front of a door and opened it, standing back so that first Cody, then Clay walked through.

Two men stood at the end of the room talking. Clay immediately recognized his uncle, Cameron Callaway, who was second in command of Callaway Enterprises. However, it was the other man who made him stop in his tracks.

Cole closed the door and walked to the small conference table. "Sit down, everyone, and let me introduce you to Lieutenant Colonel Sam Carruthers, who is here to explain the reason for this meeting." He glanced at Clay and smiled, as though amused by the look of shock that Clay figured must have registered on his face. "As well as your presence here, Clay," he added.

Cole nodded to the man dressed in casual clothing and said, "Sam, these are my brothers, Cameron and Cody." With a deliberate pause, he added, "I believe you know Clay."

Even though neither of them was in uniform, Clay fought the reflex to salute a superior officer. He vaguely heard Cole say, "I'll let you take over this meeting," to the colonel.

Sam Carruthers was a wiry, tough-looking man of medium height. There was nothing about him to draw attention. Clay knew that was intentional. What in the hell was Colonel Carruthers doing there?

Carruthers looked around the small room and said, "Sit down, gentlemen, let's get down to business. I'll try to make this meeting as brief as possible."

Each of the men quickly found a chair and sat down.

"First of all, I want to apologize for my delay in getting here. I've just come from a meeting with the deputy director of the CIA; the deputy director of National Security; and General Allred, head of Army Intelligence. We're all concerned about the recent trouble you've had with several of your installations."

He looked around the room, making eye contact with each man. "For the past five years, one of your companies has been working on a top-secret fuel for the military. As you've discovered, certain oil wells here in Texas have a tendency to develop a very high-octane fuel that the government has been interested in testing in our rockets and missiles, as well as possibly developing for tank and jet fuel.

"The recent attacks on your various facilities around the state have us very concerned, gentlemen. I've been assigned to head up my own team to investigate." He looked at Clay. "When I was going through the roster of possible men to choose for this particular mission I came across your name. I remembered you from our training sessions at Fort Benning."

Clay would never forget his training in Georgia, or the fact that Colonel Carruthers was the toughest of all the instructors he'd had.

"I decided to make you a part of our group," Carruthers continued. "It was easy enough, given the circumstances, to arrange to send you home. I figured you'd want to be in on this mission since it affects your family. Am I right, Captain?"

"Yes, sir!" Which was the truth, of course, but they both knew there was only one correct answer to the colonel's question.

Carruthers permitted himself a brief smile. "That's what I figured. Of course, that leaves us with the dilemma of why you're back home. We certainly don't want it known that you're on temporary assignment."

"I'm on leave, sir. I was overdue for one and was told that I had no choice but to take it now."

Carruthers nodded. "That will work for us. It goes without saying that no one must realize that the government has a private investigation going. I'm sure all of you understand that we'll need to keep a very low profile. Therefore I'll be working this mission undercover as well, so you can start thinking of me as Sam for the duration of this investigation."

"Yes, sir. Uh, Sam." Clay felt like a fool when the other man smiled slightly.

"I don't happen to agree with the government's position on this, Colonel," Cole drawled. "Our security has been too tight on the fuel testing. Outside of the offshore drilling rig and its oil exploration, none of these explosions had anything to do with our government ties. I'm hoping that your investigation will also include a check for someone with a grudge against the family or some other kind of personal vendetta."

"Yes, your theory was brought up at the meeting today. As thorough as you are, I take it you've done background checks on all your employees."

Cameron spoke up for the first time. "We've had that system in place for several years, sir. This isn't the first time our family has been the target of terrorism. I doubt it will be the last."

"I understand your point," Sam replied, meeting each man's gaze. "As it happens, I decided to borrow one of the FBI's best investigators to run a series of profiles on anyone who might be interested in harming the family. Pamela McCall informs me that she knows the Callaway family and she has the added bonus of having lived a large portion of her life in Texas. She said she's looking forward to working on this project."

He turned to Clay, who felt as though he'd just been slugged in the middle of his chest with a fist. The air seemed to have been knocked out of him with the colonel's words.

"Clay, you and Pamela will be paired off on this

mission. Our other man won't arrive until early tomorrow morning. I'll arrange a meeting for the whole group once he arrives. In the meantime, I think we could all use some sleep." He looked at Cole. "On behalf of the government, we want you to know that we appreciate your concern and cooperation in this matter and we intend to get to the bottom of it quickly."

"We appreciate the help, Sam."

Carruthers nodded and stood. "Thank you for your time, gentlemen. Sorry to have this meeting so late, but as I said, we do what we must." He shook hands with the three older men before turning to Clay. "I'll call you in the morning and arrange a time to meet for breakfast. I take it you're staying in the hotel?"

Clay had taken in little of the conversation after Pam's name had been mentioned. When he realized the colonel was speaking to him, he forced himself to focus on his question.

"Uh, yes, sir." He paused to recall the room number Melanie had mentioned earlier in the evening. "It's room 937, sir. I'll wait to hear from you."

Clay left the room, his mind reeling. Sam Carruthers had requested him for this assignment. He still couldn't believe it.

Carruthers had made a name for himself in Special Forces. Clay had the greatest admiration and respect for the man. Carruthers didn't suffer fools gladly, and Clay was grateful he'd never been at the receiving end of one of Carruthers's tongue-lashings.

He also knew that he would not make any points

with the man if he asked not to work with Pam. However, he couldn't fathom being paired with her for the duration of the investigation. So what in the hell was he going to do?

He glanced at his watch. He didn't want to go back to the ballroom, so he headed for the bar. He ordered a double bourbon, then took it to a back corner and slid into a chair.

Pamela McCall.

With her appearance here tonight his past had reared up before him and slapped him in the face. Surely the intervening years would help him to deal with the present situation. He'd been tested by everything the army could throw at him, and he'd survived. In fact, he'd thrived. He enjoyed what he did. He served an important function in the military, dealing with terrorists. It made sense that these attacks fit that category.

He was honored that the colonel had asked for him, and he wanted to show him that his trust had not been misplaced. Between now and tomorrow morning Clay had to come to terms with his feelings regarding Pamela McCall.

Part of the problem was that she had been a part of his life for as far back as he could remember. By attempting to erase her from his memory, he'd also blocked out years of warmth and laughter that he'd shared with his parents and sisters. He'd realized earlier tonight how much he'd missed, such as his sisters growing up and marrying without his being there. The periodic visits with his parents hadn't been adequate, as he'd faced tonight.

He'd associated his family with Pam's presence in their midst. While he'd been in grade school he'd treated her as a kid—as a nuisance, in fact—the same way he'd treated his sisters. He'd spent his recreational time hiding from all of them back then, considering all girls to be pests.

Clay's mind drifted back over the years, back to the time when he'd been a young boy with three sisters determined to make his life a living hell....

Clay successfully eluded all the females around his house and headed toward the grove of trees a few hundred yards from the hacienda-style home where the family had lived since he was born.

He climbed to the top of one of the huge live oak trees, then settled into a comfortable position straddling a massive limb and raised his dad's binoculars to his eyes.

He could see for miles and no one knew he was watching.

Boy, was he tired of females bugging him. At twelve, he'd discovered that he had to stay alert not to get in trouble when his sisters were around. Sherry Lynn wasn't too bad. She was two years older and ignored him most of the time. But Kerry and Denise, ten and nine, always wanted to know what he was doing in his room, or they'd follow him around when he went outside.

But not today. Today they were playing with Pam, who'd shown up about an hour ago with her suitcase and a sad face. Her dad had to go out of town again because he was a very important man and he was needed to help run the country.

It was always easy for him to spot Pam when she played with his sisters. All of them had dark hair

like Mama and her family. Pam's blond hair made
her look very different.

Clay lost track of time as he scanned the hills,
watching deer feeding as well as cattle and sheep.
When he paused to get a drink out of the canteen
slung over his shoulder he saw furtive movement
near the house.

He immediately raised the glasses and saw Pam
standing very still next to the house. While he
watched, she carefully looked around the corner,
then ran across the driveway to the barn, slipping
inside and out of sight. He drew back to get a wider
angle and saw her leave the back of the barn and
follow the trail to the creek.

Where was she going? Whenever she came to
visit, Pam stayed with Kerry, sleeping in her room,
playing dress-up and other dumb games. He looked
back at the house. No one stirred. He looked back
at the path. She'd disappeared into the trees.

Clay decided to follow her. He crawled down out
of the tree very carefully, making sure he didn't
damage the binoculars since he didn't exactly have
permission to use them. Of course, his dad didn't
need to know he'd borrowed them if he put them
back where they belonged before Dad got home tonight.

Once on the ground, he pretended he was tracking
game, moving silently along the path. He stepped
off into the underbrush when he reached the creek
and stealthily lifted his binoculars to scan the area.

When Pam's face suddenly filled the viewer, he
jerked, startled to see her so close. He peered over
the brush and saw that she had stopped at the edge

of the creek. She'd found a large rock to sit on and sat staring into the stream.

He figured there was no reason to hide from her. He peered into the high-powered glasses once more before stepping out on the path. That's when he realized she was crying. Silent tears slid down her face while she stared into the creek bed. The water wasn't all that deep, but he wasn't sure if she should be alone out there. What if she slipped and fell? Maybe hit her head and was knocked out? Then maybe she would drown and nobody would know.

He convinced himself that he needed to find out what was wrong before he went back to looking for wildlife.

She didn't hear him until he was a few steps away. By then it was too late for her to hide the fact she was crying. She quickly scrubbed her face and said, "What are you doing here?"

He noticed that she'd changed clothes since she'd arrived at the ranch. When he'd spotted her getting out of her father's car, she'd been wearing a dress. Now she had on shorts and a T-shirt with sneakers. The only thing that looked the same was her expression. She still looked sad...as well as irritated that he'd shown up.

He could certainly relate to that. Clay started to leave but he hated leaving her out here alone like that. So he came closer and said, "You wanna look through these binoculars?"

She turned and looked at him, her face still streaked where she'd hastily dried her cheeks. "Does your daddy know you have them?"

He shook his head. "So now you can get me in trouble if you want."

She looked surprised. "Why would I want to do that?"

He shrugged. "How should I know, but that's what Kerry and Denise seem to enjoy doing the most."

She looked away, then back at him. "I know you get mad at your sisters but you should be glad you've got them."

"You think so? It's obvious you don't have sisters or you wouldn't say that. They're always messing up my things, tattling, getting me in trouble. You're lucky you don't have to put up with all that."

Whoa. That had obviously been the wrong thing to say, he decided. Tears started rolling down her cheeks again.

"Why are you crying?" He knew she'd probably get mad at him for mentioning it, but it was dumb to pretend he hadn't noticed.

"Why don't you just go away?"

He sat there for several moments, trying to think of something to say. Something smart alecky, maybe, or offhand. Nothing came to mind. So he decided to try the truth.

"Because I hate to see you so sad. And I thought that...well, maybe talking about it might help."

"Talking about it doesn't change a thing," she said angrily, refusing to look at him.

"Don't you like coming out here to see us?" he finally asked, trying to figure out what had her so upset.

"It's not that. Not really," she finally replied softly.

"You miss your dad?"

A sob escaped. "I just wish I had a family like yours. You don't know how lucky you are. I see how your mom and dad are around each other, laughing and teasing, and the way they are with you and your sisters. And it makes me hurt inside."

"Do you remember your mom?"

She shrugged. "I was six when she died. And she'd been sick for a long time. I never heard her laugh, or my dad joke with her. Now he's gone so much. Paulette tries to do things with me, but she's just the housekeeper. She and Carl are paid to live there and look after things. They don't do it because they like to."

"You can be a part of our family, if you want."

"Not really. I don't look anything like you. Nobody would believe I'm a Callaway."

"You don't have to look like us. Some of our cousins have your color hair, or close."

She almost smiled. "Just what you need, Clay. Another sister."

He thought about that for a while. "Well, maybe that would be okay. I mean, we could talk about things—like we're doing today. And I could show you some of the places I've found on the ranch that I've never told anybody about—an old log where I found a nest of raccoons once. And some caves that I think coyotes live in. You could pretend I'm your brother, couldn't you? Someone to talk to when you're upset or mad or something?"

She thought about that for a long time. "I don't care what Kerry says about you," she finally said. "I like you, Clay."

"Well. Good. I like you, too, Pam. And I'm glad

you stay out here on the ranch with us. Heck, you're practically family already.''

After that day, he made a point to keep an eye on Pam, both when she was visiting the ranch and at school. As he grew older he found it easy to talk to her and tell her about things at school, fights he had with his sisters, and the time he got sent to the principal's office.

She in turn told him about her teachers and things she liked to do and the classmates she worked hard to avoid. He learned to trust her...and she trusted him.

He could still remember his junior year in high school when he'd successfully intercepted the pass for the winning touchdown. Pam had been the first one there when he walked off the field, fighting her way through the other players to reach him. She'd thrown her arms around his neck and given him an enthusiastic kiss that rocked him back on his heels.

Until that moment, Clay had considered Pam a very special friend who patiently listened when he discussed his frustration with other girls, his struggle to bring his English grades up, and what he wanted to do in college.

Now he found his arms wrapped around a delectable female. He discovered that he didn't want to let go of her. Instead, he responded to the kiss with wonderment, only letting go of her when his teammates started making catcalls and whistling.

Nothing was ever the same after that.

For the next two years he and Pam were a pair. His parents were amused, remembering his grousing as a young boy about all the girls at home. Now he didn't mind it a bit when she stayed over at the ranch for a weekend or longer, when her father was gone for long periods of time.

By his senior year he'd decided to join the Corps of Cadets at Texas A&M University. The corps was the largest uniformed body of students outside military academies. Organized like the military, it was a student organization and it provided cadets the opportunity to receive a commission in the United States Armed Forces.

Pam had another year before graduating from high school, and she was already planning to go back east to one of the universities there.

It was the night before Clay left for college that everything changed between them once more....

"Where would you like to go tonight?" Clay asked as soon as he picked Pam up in his ancient pickup. He was nervous and on edge. Of course he was glad to be going off to college. It had been his dream for years. What he hadn't counted on was this hollow deep within him at the thought of not seeing Pam every day.

She looked down at her hands, clasped in her lap. With a small shrug, she said, "I don't care."

"Well, gee, you don't have to sound so enthusiastic about seeing me tonight."

She turned and stared at him in the shadowed interior of the truck. "Well, excuse me for not being excited about the fact that you're leaving!"

He slid his hand beneath her hair and rubbed the nape of her neck. "I know, honey. But this is hard on me, too."

"How can it be? You've got a whole new life to

look forward to. I'm the one who has to keep going to school in the same place, only without you."

He pulled her closer and softly kissed her. "I'll be with you, don't worry. I'll always be there anytime you want me."

She threw her arms around his neck and hung on to him. "Oh, Clay. I'm sorry for ruining your last night home, but this is so hard for me! You've been my very best friend for years and now you'll be gone."

"You know I'll come home every chance I get. It isn't that far. Just a few hours. And you can come see me."

She sighed. "I know. I've known I'd have to face this day for months. It just got here too fast."

He chuckled. "Fair enough. So why don't we watch some funny movie, then get the richest concoction of ice cream and syrups made and forget about tomorrow for a little while?"

"Something with chocolate ice cream…and chocolate syrup."

"Man, you drive a hard bargain, but okay."

It was barely eleven by the time they got back home that night, but Clay was pleased to see that Pam had enjoyed the movie and the huge, custom-made banana split.

As soon as he pulled up in front of her house, she said, "It's too nice a night to go inside. Why don't we sit out in the gazebo for a while, unless you need to go?"

"Sounds good." He helped her out of the truck, took her hand, and together they wandered into the large backyard of the McCall family home. The gazebo could not be seen from the house, giving them the illusion of being alone in a night filled with stars.

"You promised to write," she reminded him.

He made a face. "Or call. You know how much I hate writing letters."

They sat down on the padded cushions of the gazebo. Pam began to tell him about her memories of growing up with the Callaways. They laughed at some of the silly things that had happened—the water pistol fights, playing dress-up with the old clothes found in the attic, telling ghost stories late at night. Finally, she said, "I hate to think what my life would have been like if I hadn't known all of you."

He hugged her to him. "Well, just think about this time next year when you'll be the one leaving, going out of state. Time seems to fly by so fast."

He kissed her. He loved kissing her, loved the way she gave herself up to him, returning his kisses with enthusiasm. Only tonight their kisses had to last for weeks and weeks. When he realized that his control was getting away from him, Clay straightened and pulled away from her.

"Don't leave," she whispered.

"I have to," he replied, his shaky voice revealing how much his body trembled.

But he didn't. Even now, so many years later, Clay couldn't remember exactly what had caused them to lose the control that had always been in place before. They'd been innocent kids, dreading the idea of not seeing each other for a while, wanting to express the love they each felt for the other.

By the time he left her that night, they'd made love—awkward, fumbling, terribly uncertain, neither of them knowing what to expect. He'd been scared, and later worried about the fact that he hadn't used any protection.

They'd lucked out, and from that time on, he was never without protection. For the next year, whenever they could be together, they explored this new realm they had discovered. They learned what gave each of them pleasure and they talked about the time when they would marry—after both of them finished college and were settled in their careers.

Their futures were planned...until the night Senator McCall found them together in the gazebo wearing nothing but moonlight, and demanded an immediate wedding.

The rattle of ice against the glass brought Clay back to the present. He glanced at his watch and was surprised to discover it was almost two. He had actually forgotten about Melanie waiting for him upstairs. What did that tell him about his frame of mind? He shook his head. He'd been awake too long, had crossed too many time zones, and had had too much to drink.

It was time to go upstairs; even though at the moment the most appealing aspect of the idea was that he could get horizontal for a few hours and pass out.

He left the bar and checked at the concierge desk for his bag. Once he had his belongings, he stopped at the front desk and asked for a key to the suite.

He was given a card that was programmed to unlock their room and took the elevator to the ninth floor.

At this time of night, very few people were stirring. His footsteps made no sound as he walked down the hall and paused in front of his room. He let himself into the suite without making any noise. Faint light glowed at the windows and he spotted the open door to the bedroom without need of further illumination.

Melanie had no doubt been asleep for hours.

He couldn't help but be relieved. Too many things had happened to him tonight to be able to deal with his feelings for Melanie. If anyone had asked him yesterday, he would have said that he was ready to make a commitment to her. However, at the moment he was battling ghosts from the past that weren't fair to bring into their relationship.

He probably should get another room for the night, but the truth of the matter was, he was too tired to go many more steps without some sleep. Melanie would be perfectly safe with him tonight. He'd make his apologies tomorrow and go from there.

By the time he reached the doorway to the bedroom he'd already removed his jacket and tie. His shirt and belt soon followed, leaving a trail of clothing into the darker room. He felt his way to the bed and gingerly sat down on the side.

Melanie didn't stir.

He quickly removed the rest of his clothing except for his briefs, then slipped between the covers with a silent sigh. The pleasure of feeling a bed beneath him was all he needed to drift into a deep sleep.

He and Pamela were in the gazebo. It was dark, with only a sliver of a moon to cast a soft light over the area. This wasn't the Pamela he remembered from his teenage years. This was the Pamela that he'd seen in the ballroom...still wearing the shimmering silver dress.

"I didn't expect you to be here," he said, reaching out to touch her hair.

"How could I not come, Clay? I wanted you to know that I..." *Her voice trailed off.*

"What, Pam? What did you want me to know?"

"That I didn't mean to hurt you. I've never wanted that. I've loved you for years and years. You were my first love...my only love."

She shivered and he slipped his jacket off and draped it over her shoulders. "I find that hard to believe, given the circumstances," *he replied.*

"I wish I'd been better equipped to explain. How does an eighteen-year-old find the words, the maturity, to tell you that she's fighting for her life? There was so much I wanted to accomplish before we were ready to discuss marriage."

"Yeah, and that was my fault. I couldn't keep my hands off of you."

"It was what we wanted, Clay. It wasn't just you. Once I'd actually made love to you that first time, all my fantasies were about doing it again."

"We were such kids back then. I thought my dad was going to kill me for touching you."

She stroked his jaw. "We're adults now, Clay. No one will interrupt us."

He stared at her in shock. "You want to make love with me?"

She reached behind her back and caught the zipper that slid down her spine. The dress fell away

*from her, leaving her standing in a lacy, see-through
bra and matching panties. "Very much."*

*"I don't know, Pam. So much has happened to
both of us since those days. We can't just—" Somehow he couldn't keep his mind on what he was saying as she unfastened his pants and slid them down
his legs.*

*As soon as she touched him, his body responded.
She cupped him, crooning her admiration and satisfaction.*

*He scooped her up and laid her on the padded
bench, rapidly disposing of the remaining items of
clothing they both wore. He slipped his hands
through her hair, removing hairpins until it fell like
a veil around her head.*

*"Do you have any idea how many dreams I've
had of you, dreams of making love to you, dreams
of you looking at me in just that way?" he whispered.*

*"Show me, Clay," she responded, placing her
arms around his neck and pulling him down to her.*

*He knelt between her legs, resisting the urge to
plunder. Instead, he wanted to take his time and
explore her. He leaned down and licked the hardened tips of her breasts, one after the other, smiling
when she shivered.*

"Are you still cold?" he asked.

*"No. Oh, no. I feel as though I'm burning up in-
side, waiting for you to take care of the fire."*

*He rewarded her honesty with a kiss that repre-
sented all the years of missing her, loving her, griev-
ing for the loss of her in his life. Then he began a
trail of kisses down her body, wanting to memorize
her with his mouth and tongue.*

She cried out when he touched her through her thick curls. He savored her for a moment before trailing kisses down her inner thigh and the back of her knee. He glanced up at her as she lay with her eyes closed and her neck arched slightly, her body glowing in the dim light from the moon.

He moved to the other knee and began his slow way back up, pausing once again at the apex of her thighs, giving her the pleasure he denied himself.

She groaned out his name, her breathing uneven. No longer able to lie quiet, she undulated, silently begging him to enter her.

He could no longer ignore her plea. In one long stroke of possession he moved inside her, fighting to maintain his control until he brought her to the very peak they both sought.

She wrapped her legs around him, holding him tightly against her, and met each thrust with her own. She chanted his name with each movement, placing hot kisses on his mouth, his cheeks and his jaw.

It had been so long—too long—but he could no longer hang on to his control. Instead, he increased his pace, moving faster, his rhythmic movement driving them both onward. He felt her tension increase until her involuntary spasms signaled that she had gone over the edge, taking him with her.

When he felt his own body release he cried out her name as he tumbled into the darkness of oblivion once more.

The persistent br-ring of a nearby phone drifted into Clay's consciousness, forcing him out of an almost unconscious state. Without opening his eyes he fumbled for the receiver and pulled it to his ear. "H'lo," he mumbled.

"Rise and shine, Callaway. We've got work to do." Sam's rumbling voice was like a shock of cold water.

"Yes, sir," he responded automatically.

"Meet me downstairs at the coffee shop in twenty minutes." Sam hung up the phone.

Clay let the receiver drop back into the cradle with a groan. He felt as though he'd just fallen into bed. He forced his eyes open to a squint in order to see his watch. It was almost eight o'clock. He hadn't gotten to bed until after two, but he was thankful to have gotten at least a few hours of rest.

He rolled over onto his back and only then remembered that he was sharing the bed with Melanie.

Melanie. Had he made love to her last night? Or had he dreamed it? He couldn't remember what was fatigue-induced fantasy and what had actually happened. He definitely recalled dreaming at one point, but not about Melanie. He'd been dreaming about—

He sat up in bed and pushed the covers away. He had to get downstairs right now. This was the day he was officially assigned to work with a woman he'd hoped never to see again.

He glanced over his shoulder and met the horrified gaze of the woman in bed with him.

He closed his eyes, convinced he was hallucinating. Melanie's eyes were a gorgeous black. The eyes staring at him were a pansy-blue. There was only one woman he'd ever known with eyes that color.

Pamela McCall.

Chapter 3

Clay stared at the woman in his bed in complete and total shock.

"What are you doing here!" they both said in unison.

Clay leaped off the bed as though he'd been stung by a swarm of hornets and then realized that he was buck naked.

Son of a— He didn't finish the thought, but he knew he was in trouble, big-time. He had gone to bed wearing his boxer shorts. There was only one reason for him not to be wearing them now.

The dream he remembered was a hell of a lot more real than he wanted it to be.

He flipped the sheet back on his side of the bed and scrambled for his shorts, almost groaning out loud as he discovered them at the bottom of the bed.

He jerked them on before he turned back to her. She sat up in bed, her hair tumbled around her shoulders, clutching the sheet to her chest. Pam looked thoroughly loved and sexy as hell. Her eyes, however, told a very different story.

"I want to know what you're doing in my room," she said grimly.

"I—uh, well…" He shoved his hand through his hair. "Damn it, I don't know! I thought this was *my* room. You don't think I deliberately came here last night to—" He spluttered to a halt, unable to put into words what had happened.

"I don't know what to think, Clay. You practically looked through me all evening and then you—you—well, you crawl into my bed and…" She paused, apparently unable to give voice to what had happened.

"I know we need to talk about this," he finally said when she didn't say anything more, "but frankly, I don't have the time right now. I've got to get downstairs." He almost told her why, but if she didn't know about the planned meeting and that he was going to be working with her, he did not want to be the one to break the news to her. The situation was volatile enough as it was.

He hastily gathered his clothes from the floor, retracing his trail from the night before. Hell, he scarcely remembered coming into the room, much less undressing and getting into bed.

How could he have made such a stupid mistake?

He found his bag, opened it and pulled out the first clothes he could find, which happened to be underwear, a pair of well-worn jeans and a faded knit shirt. Without looking toward the bed, he retraced his steps and went into the bathroom. He quickly showered before getting dressed.

He returned to his bag and grabbed a worn pair of running shoes and put them on. Then he left the room. What in the hell had he been doing in Pam's room? Hadn't Melanie told him room 937?

He stopped in the middle of the hallway and rubbed his aching head.

Or had she said 973?

Damn.

He must have gotten the room numbers confused. And of all the people that he might inadvertently end up spending the night with, why did it have to be Pamela McCall?

When he spotted room 973 on his way to the elevators, Clay impulsively paused before the door and knocked. Within a short time the door opened. Melanie stood there in a filmy negligee, her expression puzzled.

For a very good reason.

"Good morning, Clay," she said, taking in his casual dress, a far cry from the tuxedo he'd been in the last time she'd seen him. Instead of commenting on his clothes, she lifted an eyebrow and drawled, "When you said you were going to be late getting to bed, you weren't kidding."

He leaned his hand against the doorjamb and scrubbed his face with his other hand. "This has been one hell of a get-together. I'll explain everything after I get back from another meeting." He straightened, trying to think of something to say, something believable, something—forgivable?

"I know when you hear my story, you'll be able to see the humor in it, but right now—" He shrugged. "I'm already late for a meeting and—"

"Your meetings are definitely getting in the way

of our reunion,'' she replied, eyeing him with a wary look.

"As soon as we're through, I'll be back to see you. I promise."

"It's a good thing I haven't been holding my breath for you to keep your promises, Clay."

He shook his head. "I can't tell you how sorry I am,'' he murmured, aware of the terrible truth of that statement. He gently squeezed her hand. "I'll be back as soon as I can." He hurried to the elevators and pushed the button. He glanced over his shoulder and watched as Melanie closed the door.

The pinging sound of the elevator caught his attention. He stepped inside and pushed the lobby button, glad that at least for the moment he had the car to himself.

What in the world was he going to do? How could he possibly explain to Melanie what he couldn't fully explain to himself? Plus, he still had to face Pam.

The doors opened and he crossed the lobby in long strides toward the coffee shop. He spotted Carruthers at the last booth, sitting with his back to the wall, as soon as he stepped inside the room. Clay wondered how the man could look so polished and alert in his casual clothes this early in the day. Sam wore a light blue T-shirt the same shade as his piercing gaze. Clay walked past the row of booths and paused at the last table. Another man sat across the table from Sam.

The two men stopped talking when he approached. Sam glanced up at Clay, picked up the carafe near his elbow and poured coffee into a third cup on the table.

"Sit down," he said with a half smile. "You look like you could use this."

The other man moved over and Clay sat down beside him. He propped his elbows on the table and dropped his head into his hands. "You have no idea," he muttered, wishing he could redo the past twenty-four hours.

Sam cleared his throat and said, "Clay Callaway, I want you to meet Joe Chavez. Joe's from Florida, one of the best reconnaissance men I've ever worked with. He kindly volunteered to help us out here."

Clay raised his head and looked at the man beside him. Dark eyes bored into him before Joe offered his hand. "How's it going?" Joe murmured politely.

Clay heard himself chuckle with a sense of disbelief that he could exhibit any sense of humor. "Believe me, you don't want to know." He briefly shook Joe's hand. "A volunteer, huh?"

"The colonel has a fine sense of humor," Joe replied with a deadpan expression.

"No titles here," Sam said. "We're on a first-name basis on this little party. No need to be too formal since we're supposed to be army buddies enjoying a little R and R."

Joe rolled his eyes, making Clay feel better by the minute. So he wasn't the only one commandeered to work this job.

Sam checked his watch. "I finally reached Pamela McCall. I left a message for her when I arrived last night but she didn't return my call. Since I didn't have her room number, I had the hotel put my call through a few minutes ago. She said she'd be down as soon as possible, but not to wait on her for breakfast."

The waitress came and took their orders. As soon as she left, Sam said, "Joe's been briefed on what's happened here recently. We're agreed that it would be a relatively simple matter to set explosives on land, but it took some tough professionals—someone trained as we were—to do the underwater demolition work on the offshore rig. So it's possible we're going to find that Uncle Sam trained whoever did this.

"My biggest concern was to pick investigators that I could trust absolutely in any given situation. That's why you two are here. You work well alone, you're damn good explosives men, and you can put yourselves in the perp's head to figure out how it was done.

"It's up to us to find out why, as well. We're going to do just that, which is why Ms. McCall is part of the group. She knows how to analyze records and do background checks, which will relieve us of that much."

"Does she know who she'll be working with?" Clay could no longer resist asking.

Sam shook his head. "Most of the time she'll be working alone gathering information. Clay, I'm assigning her to you because she may need to do some fieldwork. I know she's a trained operative, but most of her experience has been in the office. I'd feel better knowing you were with her in case we run into unexpected trouble. We're also going to need to set up a command post that's centrally located."

Clay said, "The families have condo units in Austin we could use. There are several of them in one building. There shouldn't be a problem with our staying there."

Sam nodded thoughtfully. "Sounds like a plan. I'll speak to Cole about that as soon as we finish here. Plus, we're going to need some transportation," he added, looking at Clay. To Joe, he said, "You've got the rental car you picked up at the airport for your use."

Once again Clay spoke up. "My dad has a couple of pickup trucks we could borrow."

Sam smiled. "I intend to rent a car, but I may wait until I get to Austin. Cole said something last night about having the company plane available for our use. He suggested we meet in the lobby at noon. By then, he'll have arranged transportation for us to the airport where his plane is located. I figure that's how we'll go to Austin." He looked at both of them and asked, "Do either of you have any questions?"

Chavez took a sip of his coffee. "What are the local authorities saying about this series of events?"

"They're scratching their heads," Sam replied. "I'm not much into trusting local authority. We're going to be working independently, and we're not going to be sharing anything we get with the locals."

Chavez nodded.

After a moment, Sam said, "We've got a man who'll get hired on at the offshore rig. He'll be able to report anything he finds there. We've got to know quickly if this was an inside job or not. Chavez, you're going to be covering the border area in south Texas, and your story is that you're looking for family members. It will be a good cover for asking questions." He paused while the waitress placed their orders in front of them. Once she was gone, he said,

"Callaway, you and Pamela will be working with me in the central Texas area."

He glanced past the men and stood. "Good morning, Ms. McCall. Glad you could join us." He held out his hand and shook hers before motioning for her to sit down next to him.

Clay reluctantly looked up. She wore a pair of soft green tailored slacks and a cream-colored long-sleeved silk shirt. She'd woven her hair into a single braid pinned in a coil at the nape of her neck. She looked pale this morning, which wasn't surprising, given the circumstances.

She also looked calm, very cool and ultrasophisticated.

"I want you to meet your teammates, Pam. This is Clay Callaway and Joe Chavez. Pamela McCall."

Clay had to give her credit. If he hadn't been watching her carefully he wouldn't have noticed the slight tightening of her facial muscles as she nodded to each of them.

"Gentlemen," she said quietly, sliding across the bench seat and folding her hands together on the table. Her gaze didn't quite meet his.

Sam filled the last empty cup on the table with coffee and handed it to her. She took it gratefully, lifting it to her mouth without looking at either of the men across from her.

The waitress returned to the table. When she looked at Pam for her order, Pam shook her head and said, "Coffee's fine for me."

Sam glanced at her and almost said something, then shook his head. The three men quickly made short work of the meal in front of them while Pam had a second cup of coffee.

After he finished eating, Sam refilled his cup and looked at Pam. "I was just telling them that we need to keep our cover story simple. Clay's on leave. I'm retired and visiting old friends. Joe is looking for extended family members. I was told that you know the Callaway family. I thought it would make sense to have you and Clay paired off. I doubt that anyone would think anything of seeing you together as a couple."

She cleared her throat. Without meeting Clay's gaze, she said, "Is that really necessary? My work doesn't call for me to interact with another person. My guess is that Clay will be needed more in the field."

Sam nodded. "That's true. But you'll need to stay in constant contact with each other. I don't want you sneezing without his knowing about it. This thing is going to take long hours because we're going to be thorough. If you have a problem working with Callaway, you need to tell me now."

Pam darted a quick glance at Clay. He smiled at her, daring her to tell the colonel about their shared past. He knew he sure as hell wasn't going to mention it.

"Whatever you want to do is fine with me," she replied, absently nibbling on her bottom lip. Clay was immediately reminded of his erotic dream last night—the dream that had become immensely real. He remembered touching her soft lips. He remembered doing all kinds of things he now wanted very much to forget.

"All right," Sam said. "Here's what you need to know about my background. I'm from Virginia. We met some years back. I'm retired from the army—

currently keeping an eye on the family farm. I'm here visiting friends.'' He looked at Clay. ''You heard I was in town and invited me to visit you.''

''Uh, yes, sir. And my reason was…?''

Sam's lips quirked. ''You wanted to see me again, perhaps? Maybe renew our friendship?''

Clay leaned back in his chair and looked at Sam. ''I guess that works,'' he replied. He looked at Pam. ''Is that what we're doing…renewing our friendship?''

Pam glanced quickly at Carruthers before replying, ''It doesn't really matter, docs it? The most important thing is to get to the bottom of this situation as quickly as possible and get on with our lives.''

''Exactly,'' Sam said, nodding. He looked around the table. ''Any other questions?'' When no one answered, he said, ''Then that should do it for now. Chavez, you'd better take off. You've got a long drive ahead of you.''

''Yes, sir.''

Clay stood to let Joe get out of the booth.

Sam continued. ''You've got the number to my cell phone. Call me any time and we'll get onto a secured line.''

Chavez nodded and walked away.

Clay turned to sit down when he heard a feminine voice behind him say, ''I thought that was you.'' With the way his luck was running this morning, Clay froze and apprehensively glanced over his shoulder.

Katie Henley paused beside their table. ''Oh, I was hoping I could join you for breakfast, but it looks like I'm too late.''

Clay, wondering what to say, glanced around at

Sam and was startled by the look on Sam's face. He was staring at Katie as though the Christmas tree angel had come to life right before his eyes.

Sam had immediately stood as soon as Katie first spoke. "By all means, join us," he said with a warm smile. Clay stared at Sam, amazed at how his warm expression thoroughly changed his looks.

Clay allowed Katie to slide into the seat recently vacated by Joe before he sat down again. He introduced her to Sam, and using their new cover explained that they had met a few years ago when Sam was still in the army and that he was visiting the area.

Katie smiled at Sam. "It's a pleasure to meet you," she said, before allowing her gaze to rest on Pam. "It's so good to see you again, Pam. I never managed to get over to your table last night to say hello." She leaned against Clay and playfully nudged his shoulder. "It's wonderful to see you two together again."

Sam quirked a brow. "Again?"

Katie looked a little uneasy, suddenly realizing she might be putting someone in an awkward position. "Clay and Pam grew up together. In fact, I think at one time there was talk about a marriage, but they were so young back then—still in school. I guess it was called off..." she finished.

Clay was glad his talkative cousin had caught herself before the hole she was digging for him buried him alive.

Sam looked at him with speculation in his eyes, but came to his rescue nonetheless. "If I'd known that Clay had a cousin as beautiful as you, I'd have come to visit him long before now," he said, his eyes gleaming.

Katie actually blushed at Sam's compliment, Clay noticed with surprise. She was much more animated this morning than she'd been last night. This was the Katie he remembered when he was growing up. He was glad that meeting Sam had been able to put some color back in her cheeks. He could almost forgive her for bringing up the past at a very delicate time.

"You're very kind," she managed to say.

Sam chuckled. "Me, kind? I'm sure Clay would agree that that description doesn't fit me at all."

Memories of some of the situations this man had dreamed up for the recruits flashed in Clay's mind. No. *Kind* was not the word that first came to mind when he thought of Lieutenant Colonel Sam Carruthers.

He knew there would be no more discussion in front of Katie. Taking a chance on irritating his superior officer, Clay said, "If you will excuse me, I've got some errands to take care of before heading out of here."

Katie laughed. "Don't let me run you off, Clay."

Pam spoke up. "Actually, I need to go as well." She looked at Clay. "I believe we need to finish that discussion we started earlier, don't you?"

Clay glanced at Sam, who moved so that Pam could get out. "I'll stay here and visit with you," Sam said to Katie, "if that's all right. No sense in you having to eat alone."

Katie looked up at Pam and Clay before glancing uncertainly at Sam. "If you need to go, of course I'll understand."

Sam shook his head. "I'm in no hurry." He nodded at Clay and Pam. "I'll see you guys a little later, I'm sure."

As soon as they left the coffee shop Pam said, "Did you arrange this, Clay?"

He glanced down at her. "What? Having Katie show up?"

She shook her head. "No. That Sam would have the two of us work together."

"Don't flatter yourself. I didn't know until last night that you worked for the government or would have anything to do with this assignment."

"Oh."

"How long have you been with the FBI?" he asked as they crossed the lobby to the elevators.

"Five years. Why?"

"No reason. What were you doing before then?"

"Getting my education. I spent some time working overseas with a humanitarian group before I returned to the States and applied for the position I now hold."

They reached the elevators and stepped into the open door of one.

"Which floor?" she asked.

"Ninth. I need to get my bag out of your room."

"By the way, what happened to your date last night? Does she know where you ended up spending the night?"

He looked at her without smiling. "I'll deal with Melanie. Don't worry about me."

She looked away without speaking.

When the elevator doors opened they stepped out together and came face-to-face with Melanie Montez.

* * *

Sam Carruthers sat across the table from the vivacious Katie Henley, feeling like a middle-aged fool. The truth was, he'd never had much time for women. At forty-two, he had long ago decided that his bachelor status would stay intact indefinitely.

The last thing he'd expected was to come to Texas on an assignment and turn to mush because of a killer smile and expressive, extremely vulnerable golden eyes.

He scarcely noticed when Clay and Pam left the table. They'd finished their meeting for now. Katie held his attention to the exclusion of all else. Had a terrorist burst into the coffee shop, he doubted that he would have noticed.

Katie gave her order to the waitress before she said, "Thank you for allowing me to join you. Are you sure I'm not keeping you from something?" she asked, her gaze dropping as though struck by a bout of shyness.

He grinned, feeling lighthearted. "Not at all. Tell me, do you live in Dallas?"

She shook her head. "Austin. In fact, I'll be leaving for home as soon as I finish breakfast and check out of the hotel."

An alarm suddenly went off inside his head, and he quickly glanced down at her hands...and her bare fingers. "I, uh, suppose a woman like you is married," he muttered, feeling completely out of his depth.

Her smile faded and her eyes no longer sparkled. "I was, Sam. I've been divorced for about six months."

The surge of relief he felt at her admission made

him pause. What the hell was going on with him, anyway? He'd just met this woman and he was already damned possessive of her. His stomach knotted at the thought—much the same way it did before he made a jump.

Not a good sign.

When he didn't say anything, she continued. "I have five-year-old daughters who manage to both help me keep my sanity as well as convince me I'm on the verge of losing it." Her smile widened. "Do you have children?"

"Uh, no, ma'am. I've never been married."

"Really?" She tilted her head and looked at him as though trying to solve a puzzle. "Don't you miss having a family?"

He smiled. "Oh, I have a family. I was the oldest of several kids. We had a tough time surviving on the farm. I did whatever I could to make sure we all had enough to eat. I figured no woman would be willing to live that way if she could help it."

Katie looked down at her hands folded on the table. "I suppose you have little use for people like me, who never had to go through something like that."

He grinned, amused by her attitude. "Not at all. I don't wish that kind of life on anybody." He knew he needed to get going, but he hated to leave her without getting some kind of signal that she might want to see him again. Since he didn't have a clue how to do that, Sam continued to sit there feeling helpless, staring at her.

The waitress soon returned with her order. Sam sipped on his coffee while she ate. He asked her casual questions, hoping to learn more about her.

She mentioned a much older brother—almost sixteen years' difference in their ages—plus twin brothers three years younger. He got her to tell him about growing up in Texas, about meeting her husband while she was in college and getting married not long after her graduation.

Before he knew it, he was also answering questions about his early life. She seemed to be sincerely interested. So he told her what it was like being the oldest of six children, about losing his dad when he was nine, and doing what he had to do to hang on to the farm and make sure his mom and the children were taken care of.

He didn't tell her that his biggest reason for joining the army was to be able to send his money home to the family.

When Katie glanced at her watch and announced the time, Sam was surprised to discover how long they'd been there.

"I really need to be going," she said with what he hoped was regret coloring her voice. "Thank you for letting me join you this morning."

He picked up her ticket. "Let me get your breakfast for you."

"Oh, you don't have to do that," she said, obviously flustered.

"I want to, Katie. I hope to see you again."

"Are you planning to come to Austin?"

"As a matter of fact, Clay invited me to spend some time at the family's condos in Austin."

"Oh!" She smiled with obvious delight, causing him to swallow hard. "Well, in that case," she said, digging into her purse, "Let me give you my phone

number. Be sure and call and I'll have you out to
my place for dinner some evening.''

"A home-cooked meal sounds like something I
only dream about.''

Katie laughed and handed him a card that she'd
hastily written on. After he took it, carefully insert-
ing it in his pocket, he stood with her, took her hand
and shook it, causing her to blush.

He felt as if he'd received an electric shot, himself. Reluctantly he let go and watched her turn
away. She gave him a little wave before she hurried
out of the restaurant.

Sam tossed some money on the table for the waitress and went up to the cashier to pay for the meals.

Melanie looked at the two of them as they stepped
off the elevator. The smile she greeted him with fal-
tered when she saw that he wasn't alone.

"I think I'm beginning to understand about all of
these so-called meetings you've been having, Clay,''
she said, her gaze flicking over Pam. "What I don't
understand is why you bothered to invite me here at
all.''

"Uh, Melanie, we need to talk,'' he began, while
she stepped past him to hold the elevator.

"Yes, that's what you said to me earlier. Just
where did you spend the night last night?'' she
asked.

Clay knew he looked guilty as hell—because he
felt that way—as he tried to think of something to
say…to explain…that wouldn't make the situation
worse.

Melanie stepped into the elevator. "Never mind.

I can guess without too much strain on my intellect."

"No! Wait a minute. Please, we just need to take the time to—"

She ignored him and looked at Pam. "Was he with you last night?"

Clay groaned. He couldn't help it. He heard Pam's voice softly answer in the affirmative.

"I got the room number confused," he hurriedly said. "I don't know how it happened and I'm really sorry."

"Uh-huh. Well, that tears it as far as I'm concerned," Melanie said, pushing the down button on the elevator. The doors closed inches from his face.

Clay turned to Pam. "You could have helped with an explanation, you know."

"Since I have no idea why you were in my room, I'm afraid I can't make any excuses for you. I have to admit that getting the room numbers confused is a dandy story. What are the odds of that actually happening, Clay?"

She looked at him as though he were something that had only recently crawled out from under a rock. "I think you would do anything to humiliate me. I had no idea you were still carrying a grudge after all these years. This is going to be quite an assignment," she muttered, turning on her heel and striding down the hallway to her room.

Clay started after her, then stopped. He had to find Melanie and try to get her to understand. He jabbed the elevator button and waited impatiently for the next car to appear.

Grateful that one showed up quickly, he rode down to the lobby and scanned the area. He let out a sigh of relief when he saw Melanie waiting in line to check out.

He walked over to her and said, "Damn, Melanie, please don't leave like this," in a low voice.

She spun on her heel as soon as he spoke and stared at him. "I don't know what little game you're playing, Clay, but I don't like the rules and I'm opting out. I thought we had a friendship that could be relied upon or I would never have met you here. It's obvious to me that any friendship was on my side. So, what was the purpose of my being here? To make your little girlfriend jealous?" She looked around the crowded lobby. "Be very glad," she said, carefully enunciating each word in a low voice, "that we are in a public place. The unfortunate effect of being known on sight is that my behavior is under constant scrutiny. If we were alone, rest assured I would kick you where it would hurt the most. I must have been out of my mind to think that we could ever have more than a casual relationship. Damn it, you had me believing you last night when you told me all that stuff about missing me and wanting me..." Her voice broke and she scrambled in her purse for a handkerchief. As though talking to herself, she said, "I am not going to make a fool of myself over another guy, so help me God."

Melanie lightly touched the soft material of the lacy handkerchief to the corners of her eyes.

"I didn't plan it, damn it!" Clay said. "It was a stupid accident. I reversed the numbers of the room, that's all. It could have happened to anybody!"

She lifted her head and met his gaze. "Are you saying that you did not make love to her?"

"I thought she was you! Of *course* I—" He suddenly decided he didn't want to finish that particular sentence.

"A family friend, huh? Well, that's damned friendly, I'll give you that. Now, if you'll excuse me, I have a plane to catch."

"Let me take you to the airport, at least."

She gave him a withering look. "Please don't do me any favors."

He watched as she moved up to the counter. There was nothing more he could say at the moment without causing a scene, which he certainly didn't want. He remembered that he had left his bag in Pam's room. Whether he liked it or not, he had to face her again.

Chapter 4

Pam quietly closed the door of the suite behind her and wearily sank into a nearby chair. She absently noted that her hands were shaking as they rested on her thighs.

She felt nauseated and knew that she should have forced herself to eat something while she was at the coffee shop, but she'd barely been able to sip on the coffee placed in front of her.

She'd scarcely recovered from the shock of finding that Clay had spent the night with her when she'd received the call informing her of a breakfast meeting downstairs. There had been no way for her to prepare for the additional shock of discovering that she would be forced to work with Clay on this assignment.

What in the world was she going to do? She rubbed her hands over her face and sighed. What more could possibly happen to her than what she'd gone through these past twenty-four hours?

First of all, she'd been given no choice about whether to take this assignment or not. She'd been told that the orders had come from much higher up than her immediate supervisor. She'd thought she was tapped for the assignment because she knew most of the players. Never had it occurred to her that Clay Callaway would be anywhere in the picture.

Much less had she imagined—not in her wildest dreams—that she would end up in bed with him her first night back in Texas. She didn't even want to think about what had happened, what *must* have happened last night.

She'd been exhausted when she'd left the party, having spent the past three days and nights clearing her desk so she could take on this new job. All she'd wanted to do was to fall into bed for a few hours of oblivion.

She hadn't been surprised that she dreamed of Clay. He showed up with alarming regularity in her dreams—particularly the more erotic ones.

Her dreams had definitely been erotic last night. The horrible truth that she could no longer avoid was that she hadn't dreamed making love with him. After all of these years, she had ended up in Clay's arms again.

As if all of that wasn't enough to face in a few short hours, she'd discovered an alarming sense of jealousy toward Clay's date. She had—for a very brief moment—been glad that he hadn't been with the other woman last night.

So what did that make her? Of course she had no

interest in Clay. None whatsoever. So what difference could it possibly make to her who he was seeing or sleeping with?

She'd obviously been working too hard. Either that or she must be losing her mind.

The phone rang beside her and she listlessly picked it up. "H'lo?"

"Pamela, this is Cole Callaway. I've just spoken to Sam Carruthers. I understand that he's planning to base his operations in Austin. I have the company jet at the Addison airport, so I'll be taking all of you back with us today. Think you can be ready to leave by noon?"

She glanced at her watch. It wasn't quite ten o'clock. Dear God, look at what had happened to her all in the space of a few short hours. The day stretched out ahead of her with alarming prospects. Considering all the things that had happened to her by midmorning, there was no telling what else might occur before this day was over!

Cole was waiting for her answer. She hastily replied, "Uh, yes, sir. Shall we meet in the lobby?"

He laughed. "Sir? I thought I was Uncle Cole to you, missy."

She could feel herself blushing. "I was a child then, and didn't really know better."

"Then make it Cole, honey. And yes, I'll see you in the lobby."

She hung up and rubbed her forehead where a nagging headache had begun to make itself known. She reached for the phone again, this time ordering food from room service. She needed to keep up her strength. She also needed to figure out how in the world she was going to be able to work with Clay on a daily basis for the length of this assignment.

While waiting for her order to arrive, Pam went into the bedroom and gathered her clothes. While she packed, she went over the details she'd learned about this particular job. If she could stay focused on what she needed to do, maybe she would survive.

She'd spent the previous day getting lists of all the employees of all the different companies affiliated with Callaway Enterprises. The stack of printouts was the size of a metropolitan phone book.

She'd also set up several programs to group them together in terms of seniority, background and experience. Sooner or later she knew that something would show up that didn't belong in a profile. The work took time as well as a well-developed sense of looking for patterns that others may have overlooked.

Pam was in the bathroom gathering up her toiletries when she heard the tap on her door. She quickly dropped them into her bag and hurried into the other room. She swung the door open, saying, "Thank you for being so—" She stopped when she saw Clay standing there.

"For being so...? What, Pam? What were you going to say?" he asked, stepping around her and into the room.

"I thought you were room service. I was expecting..." She let her voice trail off.

He raised an eyebrow. "Why didn't you eat downstairs?" he asked, slipping his hands into the back pockets of his tight-fitting jeans.

She spun away from him. "What are you doing here?" she asked, striding back into the bedroom and emptying out the last drawer of clothes—which happened to be her lingerie. She jammed them into her bag as Clay strolled into the room behind her.

"I told you. I needed to get my bag." He sat down in one of the chairs and propped his feet on the end table. "You made sure you got your last dig in, I noticed."

She stopped and stared at him. "What are you talking about?"

"With Melanie."

"What? You wanted me to lie for you?" She looked at him with contempt. "I'm not to blame for your showing up here last night, Clay, and you know it."

"I'm not blaming you! But the truth is that we *are* here for business reasons—"

"Except this is a covert operation and telling your honey about it wasn't part of our instructions."

"Damn it, she isn't my honey, as you put it. We're friends."

She laughed. She really couldn't help it. He sounded so disgruntled and so very misunderstood. My God, the man was unbelievable. "Yes, I noticed just how friendly you were with her last night at the party. You were practically making love on the dance floor!"

He slouched down into his chair a little more. "So?"

She threw up her hands. "Why are we having this conversation?" she asked, looking toward the ceiling as though for divine intervention.

"To avoid talking about what happened last night," he muttered in a low voice.

She sank down on the edge of the bed and looked at him.

He returned her gaze.

Those eyes of his had always gotten to her. As far back as she could remember she had loved his black eyes with their thick fringe of lashes. Even now, as irritated, as humiliated, as nauseated as she was feeling at the moment, Pam recognized that this man's gaze could still mesmerize her.

"All right," she replied quietly, forcing herself to meet his steady stare, "let's talk about it."

He straightened in his chair, his feet falling to the floor. He leaned his elbows on his knees. "First of all, I owe you an apology. It doesn't matter how I ended up here, it was my fault and I'm sorry."

What was she supposed to say to that? That it was all right, that she forgave him? That because of his actions the past twelve years of her life seemed to have disappeared and she felt like an insecure teenager once again?

She looked down at her hands and realized that she was clenching them so tightly they actually ached. She forced herself to let go of her death grip and slid her fingers along her thighs.

Without looking at him, she said, "I'm sorry, too."

What more was there to say, after all?

The silence grew in the room as they sat there. Finally, Clay said, "I would never have consciously taken advantage of you, Pam. Please believe that. I was dreaming and then I realized I wasn't dreaming, but by then, it was too late."

"Besides, you thought you were with Melanie," she said to her hands.

"It was your name I called out," he said quietly.

She remembered that. That was the problem. She remembered each and every detail far too well. The shock had been how easily she had accepted his presence in her dreams—and in her bed.

He cleared his throat. "We have one other problem we need to address," he said just as she heard a knock on the door in the other room.

As though escaping from some unknown threat, she hurried to the door. This time she was relieved to find her breakfast had arrived. She stood back while the waiter rolled the table into the room and made certain everything was there. She found her purse and tipped him, then closed the door behind him.

Clay walked out of the bedroom. She could feel her stomach tighten, which was what his presence had done to her at the coffee shop. If she let her reaction to him dictate her eating habits, she'd soon starve to death.

Doing her best to ignore his presence, Pam sat down and began to eat. She hadn't ordered much, but by the time she finished she was feeling a little better. More able to cope with the situation. Until Clay spoke.

"I need to know if you are using some form of birth control," he asked, as though merely waiting until she'd finished eating to bring up the subject. "Because if you aren't, we could have more problems than just having to work together."

Well, at least he'd confirmed that he didn't want to be around her any more than she did him. She wasn't certain why that hurt. She only knew that it did.

She carefully set the empty glass that had held orange juice down on the table before she looked at him. "No, Clay. I have no reason to be using birth control."

He rubbed his hand over his face. "I just thought that—" he shrugged "—well, I figured if you're dating that you..." He stopped speaking when he finally looked over at her.

She was so angry that she could hardly find the words necessary to respond to him. "For your information, I don't sleep with everyone I date, Clay." She bit off the words, forcing herself not to say anything more.

"I didn't mean it that way," he replied. "I just figured that you're going with the man who was with you last night."

Adam? He was implying that she and Adam had something going? And why not? Any woman would enjoy having Adam's attention. He'd been a very understanding friend.

"I'm not going to discuss my relationship with Adam with you, Clay."

He sighed. "I'm not handling this at all well," he said.

Now, there was something they could agree on, she thought to herself.

"The fact is," he continued doggedly, "that you may be pregnant because of last night."

No. Not that. Let's don't even go there.

She suddenly got a mental image of an ostrich with its head in the sand.

Pam rubbed her forehead, where her headache had suddenly returned with throbbing intensity. She took a few slow, deep breaths before she finally looked at him—at those unforgettable eyes of his—and said, "There is that chance. Yes."

He'd been looking out the window while she ate, but now faced her, watching her as though trying to read something in her face. She struggled to keep her expression calm.

After a moment he walked over and sat down across from her. "We need to have a plan, just in case."

She glanced at her watch, pleased to see that it was close to noon. "That may be true, but we don't need the plan right at this moment. And your uncle is expecting us in the lobby in a few minutes." She got up and went into the other room, not stopping until she reached the bathroom.

Pam closed the door behind her and weakly sank against its firm support. A baby. She could be pregnant with Clay's baby.

Wasn't it the fear of a pregnancy that had caused her father to insist on her marrying Clay all those many years ago? She could just imagine what her father would do with this bit of information.

She pressed her open palm against her stomach, wondering what she would do, wondering what an unplanned pregnancy would mean in her life at this point. She was no longer eighteen.

Pam closed her eyes rather than face her reflection in the mirror. She had never in her life been able to imagine having a child by anyone other than Clay Callaway. Now there was a slight chance that she might have that child.

By the time she came out of the bathroom, Clay had their bags in the living room and was waiting for her.

"Get everything?" he asked.

She nodded.

He opened the door and said, "After you." She reached for her bag, but he shook his head and said, "I'll get it."

When they arrived in the lobby, the whole clan seemed to be gathered. Clay walked over to his mom and dad while Pam paused by Sam Carruthers, who was in conversation with Katie Henley. Pam blinked in surprise. She certainly didn't know the man well, but it was plain to anyone that he was very attracted to Katie.

Cole spotted her waiting to speak to Sam and moved closer. "Cody and Carina are going to take some of us out to the airport. As soon as Allison gets back, we'll be heading out there ourselves."

Sam turned at Cole's words and said, "I really appreciate your offering us the ride."

"It's the least I can do," he said, his face lighting up as he caught sight of his wife moving toward him.

Pam felt a moment of envy and loss, knowing that there was no one who had ever looked that way when she came into view. She'd always been on the outside of family groups, looking on, wishing for a family of her own.

She knew that none of the Callaways would understand. They took their close family ties for granted. She had destroyed any opportunity she might have had to be a part of this family when she'd walked away from Clay and their planned marriage.

She'd refused to let the past bother her until now. It was just being here in their midst that made her feel so vulnerable and so very unsure of herself.

Carina walked over and said, "It was so good to see you again, Pam. Clay tells me you are going to be working with him." She took Pam's hand and gently squeezed it. "I am so pleased. I've always felt that the two of you belonged together. It was just the timing that created such a turmoil."

Pam was horrified to feel tears in her eyes. She looked upward, trying to keep them from falling. "I, uh, it was good to see you, too. Please don't think that just because we're working together that Clay and I could ever..." She couldn't think of anything else to say. Could ever be friends? Could ever be lovers? That rule could be tossed out the window. Could ever become a couple?

Carina smiled. "Twelve years is a long time, you know. Both of you have exciting careers. You've had a chance to be out in the world, to make a place for yourselves. It is time to make peace with each other, you know."

"I made peace with my decision a long time ago, Mama Carina. Given the opportunity, I still wouldn't change it. I never expected Clay to understand or to forgive me."

Cody joined them. "Why don't you ride with us, Pam? Cameron and Janine will take the others to the airport."

Pam glanced at Clay, who stood behind his parents. His expression gave nothing of his thoughts away. She smiled at Cody. "Thank you. I'd like that." She walked out to the car with Clay's parents on either side of her and Clay carrying their bags behind them.

She almost laughed at the absurdity of her situation. Laughter would be much better than the tears that lurked just beneath the surface.

Chapter 5

Clay helped the pilot load the luggage, gave his mom an extra hug, spent a few minutes speaking to Cameron and did everything possible to postpone getting on the plane. Cole finally signaled to him that they were ready to take off before he reluctantly stepped on board.

So he shouldn't have been surprised to see that everyone else had settled into seats awaiting takeoff. Of course his aunt and uncle were together. And he shouldn't have been all that surprised to see that Sam had chosen to sit next to Katie.

Clay had the choice of being polite and sitting down next to Pam or of being a complete boor and going to the back. The fact that he had to give the decision some thought pretty much summed up how he was feeling at the moment.

Seeing her again had been bad enough. The longer he was in her presence, the more agitated he became. It was one thing to deal with the fact that Pamela McCall was somewhere on the planet getting on with her life while he worked hard in his career. Having her in the confined space of the jet brought everything too close for his personal comfort.

Cole growled, "Light somewhere, will you?"

Clay nodded and took the seat next to Pam.

She leaned over and whispered, "If I didn't know better, I'd think you dislike flying as much as I do."

He glanced around at her in surprise while he buckled himself into his chair. "What have you got against flying?" he asked.

She closed her eyes and waited while they got clearance, then took off. He figured she didn't intend to answer him so he was surprised when she finally said, "Claustrophobia."

"Aahh." He leaned back in his chair with a smile. Now, there was something he'd never known about Miss Pam. His smile faded. Not that it mattered, of course.

"Do you know where we're going to stay?" she asked a little later.

"At the family's condos in west Austin. Cole has the largest one. We'll probably stay there, set it up as command central. Once we get some leads, I'll be on the road checking them out, while you and Sam work on gathering data."

"What about transportation?"

"Dad's bringing me my truck from the ranch tomorrow. I understand Cole intends to lend Sam one of his cars."

"What about me?"

"You won't need wheels. If you go anywhere, you'll be with me."

She rolled her eyes. "Whose idea was that?"

"It certainly wasn't mine," he replied firmly. "You made your opinion of me quite clear some time back."

"No, I didn't. What I told you was that I couldn't marry you."

He hit his forehead with the heel of his hand. "Oh! That's right. I forgot. You didn't mind having sex with me, as I recall, but I shouldn't have considered that it meant anything more to you than a momentary kick."

She glared at him before looking around the interior of the plane to see if anyone had heard him. He knew that with the noise of the plane and the obvious absorption in their own conversations, the others weren't paying any attention to them.

"You're being obnoxious."

He settled back into his chair and closed his eyes. "Just one of my many charms."

By the time they landed at the private airfield near Austin, all Clay wanted to do was to get settled into the condo and get this assignment under way. When he stepped off the plane he noticed two automobiles waiting.

"Whose car?" he asked Cole, pointing to the low-slung sports car.

Cole grinned. "That's one of mine. I thought Sam might enjoy using it while he's here. I think there's room for you and Pam to ride along. You don't have far to go. Didn't Cody say he was bringing you a truck tomorrow?"

Clay absently nodded, still studying the car. The only way he and Pam were going to fit into that car with Sam was if she sat on his lap.

If he didn't know better, Clay would swear there was a family conspiracy going on.

He watched as Sam shook Katie's hand, then stood with his gaze fastened on her while she followed her mother to the larger town car waiting for them. Cole handed the keys of the smaller car to Sam.

"Here you go. It might be a tight fit for the three of you with all your luggage, but I think you can manage. Keep in touch," he said with a wave as he strode across the tarmac to his wife and daughter.

Sam studied the glistening sports car in silence. "Interesting choice," he finally said.

Clay grinned. "The Callaways delight in doing the unexpected."

Sam looked at him thoughtfully. "Thanks for the warning." He picked up his briefcase and bag while Clay gathered the other luggage. Pam followed them over to the car, her eyes widening when she looked inside.

"There's no back seat."

"Nope. Plenty of luggage space, though," Clay replied, opening the trunk and loading it.

Sam opened the driver's door and looked over the top of the car at Pam. "You don't mind sharing the seat with Clay, do you?"

Clay waited to hear her protest. He could see the silent struggle, but she finally shrugged, saying nothing, and walked over to the passenger side of the car. Clay sat down first and waited while she settled herself on his thighs.

"Isn't this illegal?" she asked with obvious irritation.

"Undoubtedly," he replied, already uncomfortable with the feel of her soft curves pressing against him.

"Do you know where we're going?" Sam asked, starting the engine.

"It's not far." Clay rattled off directions, slid his arms firmly around Pam and pulled her snugly against him. Recognizing her obvious discomfort went a long way toward alleviating his.

The condominium high-rise was located west of the downtown area overlooking Lake Austin. It was a quiet neighborhood away from the main traffic arteries.

Sam pulled into the underground garage and found a parking space. "Nice place," he said.

"Yes," Clay replied. "It was built by one of the family businesses. As I recall, by the time the members of the family bought in, the place was more than half-sold before they ever broke ground."

"How does it feel to be a part of a family like the Callaways?" Sam asked once they got out of the car with their bags and headed to the elevator.

Clay looked around for Pam and saw that she had paused by the car and seemed to be going through some kind of breathing ritual. He glanced back at Sam and replied, "That's a tough question. I'm not sure I have an answer. It would be like asking how you feel about being born into your family. I don't have anything else that I can compare it to. The family is quite close. They visit among one another all the time. They work together, shop together, baby-sit for one another's kids. What can I say?"

Sam pushed the button for the elevator and asked, "Why didn't you go into one of the family businesses?"

Pam finally joined them. Clay gave her a quick glance. She appeared to be lost in her own thoughts. The elevator arrived and opened. They stepped inside and Clay pushed the top button. "I'm too restless to spend my days locked away in offices. My dad's the same way. He ran the family ranch south of San Antonio for years. Then they decided to move into San Antonio, so my cousin Cade took over the ranch. Mom says I'm very much like my dad." He glanced at Sam out of the corner of his eye. "I consider that a compliment."

They reached their floor and the doors opened.

Pam stepped out first and looked around without commenting.

Sam followed her and said, "I would, too. I envy you your relationship with your parents. I never really had that. I was too busy looking after my mother, brothers and sisters to think about what it would be like to have someone look after me."

Clay paused in front of the door to Cole's condo. "Here we are. I think the key is part of the set Cole gave you."

Sam looked through the keys, tried one and opened the door. Once again the men waited for Pam to enter first.

Clay had been to the condo enough to appreciate its effect on first-time visitors. He waited and followed the other two through the door.

His aunt Allison's artistic talent had never been better displayed than through her choice of furniture, drapes, oil paintings and her own sculptures.

She'd also worked with the architect when he'd designed the building, so each room was open and spacious. Because it was on the top floor, the apartment had cathedral ceilings and arched windows.

"I don't believe this," Sam muttered, halting in the middle of the mammoth living area while Pam silently continued across the room until she reached the windows. "How big is this place, anyway?"

Clay grinned. "I don't know the square footage, but it has four bedrooms, five baths, with a separate dining room as well as kitchenette for smaller meals." He glanced over at Pam, who was looking out at the lake. "You haven't had much to say, Pam. Do you think you can be comfortable here?"

She glanced around. "Who couldn't?"

Sam turned and looked at him. "You grew up taking places like this for granted. You have no idea how fortunate you are."

"With all due respect, Colonel, I was raised on a working ranch and that means exactly what it sounds like. I was never pampered. None of us were. You, better than most, know the training I've been through since I joined the army. And yes, I'm fully aware of how fortunate I am. Not because my family seems to have a knack for making money, though. I have a family who loves me, who is always there for me no matter what. My family is the most important thing in my life, sir."

"I stand corrected," Sam replied with a nod and a grin. "Of course you're right. I was jumping to conclusions based on what I see. But I helped to train you. I know exactly what you went through. A pampered man would never have survived."

Sam walked into the dining room and set his

briefcase down on the table where twelve people could easily be seated. "We'll set up in here." He pulled out his laptop computer and a stack of files.

Clay paused in the doorway. "Do you want to assign bedrooms?"

Sam turned and looked at him in disbelief. "Excuse me? This isn't being treated like a military operation within our group. Grab whatever rack you want." He sat down and booted up his computer.

Whatever softening effect Katie had had on the colonel had worn off, Clay decided with a shrug. He grabbed his bag from the living room and walked down the hall. He chose the first guest bedroom he reached, tossing his bag beside the bed. When he turned around, he found Pam hovering in the doorway.

"The colonel doesn't seem to be in a very good mood," she said quietly.

"On the contrary, this *is* his good mood. Better get used to it. Have you decided on a room?"

"Uh, no. Not really. I don't suppose it matters."

"The master suite is at the end of the hallway."

She shook her head. "Oh, I wouldn't want that." She looked through the other doorways along the hall. "Actually, one of the guest rooms has been set up as an office. That's just what I need."

"Is there a bed in there?"

"A daybed, which is fine."

"Callaway!" Sam called. "I need you to explain this map to me. It doesn't give me much in the way of topography."

"Yes, sir!" He turned to Pam. "Hope you're ready to start your day."

She glanced at her watch. "At four o'clock?"

He nodded toward the front of the condo. "He won't be in bed until after midnight. He's a tough bird."

She straightened. "The sooner we get going, the faster we'll be out of here." She picked up her bag and disappeared down the hall.

Clay looked away. She meant nothing to him now and he needed to stop watching her every move, her every expression.

He had better things to do. Right now, he needed to answer the call of his commanding officer.

Chapter 6

Sam rubbed his hand down his face, feeling every one of his years. He'd been pushing himself, as well as his team, hard in the past three days. He glanced at his watch. It was after eight o'clock.

Pamela was in her room, working on her background checks, while he'd spent the day going over the reports made by the Bureau of Alcohol, Tobacco and Firearms in their investigation and forwarded to National Security. They'd taken a short break for food that he'd had brought in, then both had gone right back to work.

No one at ATF would know that he was independently investigating the explosions, but it helped him to see what they had discovered in case he wanted to do some more probing in certain areas.

Clay had left before dawn this morning to check out the east Texas site. Pam had given him a list of the personnel. Clay had shown that he had a good grasp of the fieldwork needed. Because he looked more like the Ramirez clan, his mother's family, rather than the older Callaway brothers, Clay had chosen another identity as a cover for his nosing around. He promised he wouldn't arouse suspicion among the authorities already working in that area.

Sam could only hope that was true. They weren't there to create an embarrassing situation among the various arms of the government presently investigating the case.

He'd been concerned when Katie had mentioned that Clay and Pamela had been an item once upon a time, until Clay had assured him in no uncertain terms that there was nothing about their relationship to distract him now.

Sam had accepted the explanation, since he'd been wrestling with his own conscience because he couldn't get Katie Henley out of his mind.

He'd been thinking about her off and on since he'd last seen her on Sunday. The fact that this was Tuesday and he'd actually been congratulating himself because he'd managed not to call her before now told him that he was in serious trouble.

His behavior was totally out of character and he knew it. He'd long ago given up the idea of having a relationship. Marriage and family demanded too much time. He was content with his life. So why had the memory of the bubbly woman with the beautiful eyes kept him company ever since he'd arrived in Austin? He'd awakened this morning with the annoying knowledge that he'd been dreaming about the woman.

He was being absolutely ridiculous.

Sam reached into his pocket and took out the

phone number she'd given him. It wasn't all that late to call her tonight. She'd probably wonder why he was calling her, but after all, she had been the one to suggest it.

Besides, he didn't want to go to bed until he'd spoken with her. He saw no harm in checking in to say hello.

Rather than use the wall phone in the kitchen, Sam went back to the bedroom he'd chosen—the third guest room. He hadn't been comfortable with taking over the master bedroom. Since all of the bedrooms here were larger than his quarters at the base, he was quite comfortable. A man could get spoiled living with this much luxury on a regular basis.

He sat down on the side of the bed and called the number she gave him. The phone rang several times.

She probably wasn't home. A woman like Katie no doubt had a busy social life. After all, she—

Someone picked up the phone.

"Hello?" a young voice said.

He grinned. "Hello. Is your mother there?"

"Yes, she is, but she can't come to the phone right now. Who's this?"

Sam knew his disappointment was uncalled-for. What had he hoped would happen, anyway? "Oh. Tell her that Sam called, okay?"

"Mommy!" the young girl yelled into his ear, causing Sam to jerk the phone away in dismay. "It's Sam and he wants you to know he called."

Sam could hear voices in the background, then the little girl said, "She says can she call you back 'cause she's having to cut Amber's hair 'cause Amber got gum in it.'' Her disgust came across the line loud and clear.

''That would be fine. Remind her I'm at her dad's condo in Austin.''

''You're in Austin? Cool,'' she said, causing him to blink.

''Where did you think I was calling from?''

''Oh, I don't know. But you're not far away at all. We live in Lakeway. Do you know where that is?''

''I'm afraid I don't. I'm just visiting and this is my first time here.''

''Do you have a little girl?''

''Uh, no, I'm afraid I don't.''

''A little boy?''

''No. I'm not married.''

''My mommy's not married, either, but she still has two girls.''

''Well, yes, I can see how that could happen.''

''Our daddy doesn't like us. He never comes to see me and Amber. Not in a long, long time.''

''What's your name?''

''Trisha.''

''What a pretty name.''

''Thank you.''

Sam heard someone speaking in the background and Trisha started talking, but he couldn't make out what she was saying.

The next voice he heard wasn't Trisha's.

''Sam?'' Katie said, sounding breathless.

''Hi, Katie. I'm sorry I called at a bad time.''

She gave her delightful laugh. ''Oh, Sam, if you only knew! Things around here are *always* hectic!''

''Would you like to call me back?''

"Oh, yes, that would be wonderful. As soon as I can get the girls down for the night. In the meantime, be thinking about coming for dinner tomorrow night. That is, if you don't have anything else planned."

"Sounds great. I'll wait to hear from you for a time and directions."

"Thanks for calling, Sam. You have no idea what a boost it is to my morale to hear from you."

"The pleasure is all mine, believe me." He hung up the phone and happened to get a glimpse of his expression in the mirror across the room. He was grinning like an idiot. And his heart was racing as if he'd just pulled off a ten-mile run.

He shook his head in exasperation and went back to the dining room. Pam was waiting for him.

"Here's some information you might pass along to Joe," she said, handing him several pages. "Some of the workers in the factory on the border have aliases. That may not mean much, but I would guess that it needs to be checked out."

Sam nodded.

"I gave Clay a similar list before he left this morning that covers the warehouse personnel. There were a couple of questionable items in one man's file that he'll check on."

"Thanks. You're doing a great job."

She smiled. "You're welcome. Actually, I'm enjoying it. No interruptions, no phones ringing. At least, not for me."

"Actually, I, uh, am expecting a call a little later. I'm going to be gone tomorrow evening. Are you going to be okay with staying here?"

"Clay left me his truck. He said it was too easily traceable, so he took a rental car. I'll be fine."

Sam nodded. He looked down at the stacks of printouts spread out on the table. "Surely we're going to find something in all of this."

"Or lose our eyesight trying," she replied with a grin. "I think I'll call it a night, though. We'll hit it again tomorrow."

She turned away and walked out of the room. She was a lovely woman, Sam thought. If she had been engaged to Callaway at one time, it must be tough on him having to work with her again.

He was curious why Cole Callaway had been so insistent that she be a part of the team. Not that she wasn't carrying her part of it with style. There had to be more than her skills involved. Cole Callaway hadn't gotten where he was by being stupid, so he must have figured they would manage to work together all right. He was just curious what else Cole had in mind.

At five-thirty the following afternoon Sam pulled up in front of Katie's Lakeway home. She'd given him excellent directions on the phone the night before and he'd had no trouble finding the place.

The house was on a rise overlooking the street, with several columns supporting a second-story balcony. It called to mind cotton fields and southern plantations.

He decided to pull into the circular driveway since the street was narrow. He didn't want anything to happen to Cole's sports car. He stopped the car in front of the brick steps leading up to the veranda and double-door entrance.

He stepped out of the car and walked up to the door. He paused, then rang the doorbell, startled when he heard it chime the first twelve notes of the song "Dixie."

A treble voice yelled, "I'll get it!" just as another one said, "No, I'll get it!" The sound of running feet echoed behind the door. Next came the brief sounds of scuffling before the door finally opened to reveal two young redheaded girls—one with hair considerably shorter than the other.

"Hi, you must be Sam!" said the one with the longer hair. "We talked on the phone last night."

He nodded. "Hello, Trisha. I'm very pleased to meet you." He turned to the other girl. "And you must be Amber."

She rolled her eyes and said, "Must I?"

Her sister nudged her with her elbow. "Don't be rude."

"I'm just being honest. That isn't rude." She looked up at him. "I don't like the name Amber. If I was going to be named after a color, I much prefer Scarlett."

"Like Scarlett O'Hara," Trisha explained.

Sam didn't know what to say. He hadn't been around children since he'd been one himself. Certainly he'd never been around little girls quite so self-possessed.

He heard a sound and looked up in time to see Katie round the corner near the stairs and start toward the front door.

"Do you intend to leave our guest standing on the front porch?" she asked politely, smiling at Sam as though sharing the joke with him.

Later he would look back on this scene and be

able to describe it in detail—what the girls wore, the way Katie's hair curled around her ears, her smile of welcome, the way the crystals in the chandelier in the foyer created a dazzling display upon the scene. He would look back and realize that it was at this very moment in his misspent life that he fell in love for the first time.

"Did you have any trouble finding us?" Katie asked as each girl grabbed one of his hands and pulled him into the house. He was tempted to say yes—that he'd been looking for her for years, but knew that wasn't what she meant...and he didn't want to come across as too forward.

"You give fine directions," he answered, knowing that he wore a very foolish grin on his face. He didn't care.

"It looks like you've met Trisha and Amber," Katie continued.

"It has been my pleasure," he replied, wondering when the twins intended to let go of his hands. Obviously not any time soon as they continued toward the back of the house and entered a large family area. The room appeared to be the hub of the house, with its television, a piano, fireplace and comfortable-looking sofas and chairs. Several windows revealed the back lawn, with its swimming pool and tennis court.

"Nice place," he said, reminding himself that she was, after all, a Callaway. There was no reason not to enjoy the fruits of the family's success.

"I like it. Actually, it belonged to my parents. They built this back when I was a little girl, before my twin brothers were born. When they talked about selling it, I asked for it. Mother wanted something without so many stairs to climb, but I need the exercise.''

There must have been an unseen signal because the girls appeared to be through with their escort duties at the same time. With a whoop they released his hands and raced for the door that led into the backyard.

''Such energy,'' he said, once the door slammed behind them.

Katie smiled, watching them greet one of the dogs waiting impatiently for them. ''Yes. I'm glad they have each other.'' She looked back at him. ''I missed having a playmate when I was growing up. I had the twins but it wasn't the same. They really didn't need anyone else. They had each other.''

He had a flash of what she must have been like as a little girl—energetic like her daughters, but alone. On impulse, Sam took the necessary steps to her side. Unable to resist touching her in some way, he took her hand and said, ''Thank you for inviting me here tonight. I feel like a shameless beggar, unable to say no to a home-cooked meal.''

She laughed and squeezed his hand. ''Don't be silly. I'm so pleased to know you're staying in Austin. I hope to see more of you before you have to return home.''

He'd given her the cover story because it had been necessary. As usual on an assignment such as this, everyone was considered to be on a ''need to know'' basis. He'd never felt hampered by those restrictions before. Now he found himself wanting to tell her about his military career, the loneliness and how well he understood what that felt like.

Katie said, ''I'm as bad as the girls, keeping you

standing here instead of offering you a drink and a place to relax. What may I get you from the bar?''

"I'm a bourbon man, if you have it. Over ice."

"A man after my own heart," she replied lightly, turning away and going over to the wet bar. "I have a theory about the type of people who prefer bourbon to Scotch."

"Oh?"

She paused in dropping ice cubes in a glass and glanced up at him, her eyes sparkling. "I'd have to know you much better before I would share my theories."

"That can certainly be arranged."

She flushed, which delighted him. Her saucy banter wasn't quite as easy for her as it appeared.

She brought his drink as well as a glass of red wine for herself. He waited for her to sit down before he chose the chair across from her. She took a sip of her drink, then glanced at him. Her cheeks were still flushed and she quickly looked away when she discovered he'd never taken his eyes off her.

"I—uh—I thought we might eat outside on the patio, if that's all right with you," she said, sounding a little breathless.

"Sounds great."

"I should have told you to bring a swimsuit. You might have enjoyed a swim later."

"Next time, if I can coax another invitation from you."

"Well, of course! What I mean is, I would enjoy having you—" She paused, took a deep breath and sighed. "It's been so long since I've tried to do any entertaining, that I feel very clumsy and inept."

"Maybe next time you'll allow me to take you

and the girls out for dinner. You just name the place.''

''Well, there is a wonderful place on the lake where you can sit and watch the sunset that's quite popular with visitors to the area.''

He grinned. ''Great. Let's do that tomorrow night.''

Her face lit up. ''Really? I mean, so soon? I'm sure you have things you want to do....'' She left the sentence hanging as though unsure of herself.

''I'll be around for a while, but I don't know how long, exactly. So I don't want to waste an opportunity to spend some time with you.''

Katie looked down at her drink as if trying to find the words she wanted to say. Without looking up, she murmured, ''You're very good for my ego, Sam. I'm afraid it has taken a beating this past year or so.''

Her ex-husband was obviously an idiot to have let her go and a fool for making her feel so insecure. For whatever time he had here in Texas, Sam vowed to himself that he would do what he could to keep that sparkle in her eyes and her beautiful smile flashing.

Dinner had been over for several hours. Sam waited on the patio while Katie put the girls to bed. He glanced at his watch, amazed to see that it was almost ten o'clock. He'd been here close to five hours. How was that possible?

The girls had kept him entertained throughout dinner with their outrageous stories. They were a couple of imps who seemed very well-adjusted, con-

sidering what the family had gone through the past
several months.

He recalled Trisha's statement on the phone last
night. She didn't believe her daddy liked her because he never came to see them. He'd found the
statement painful to hear, partly because she'd
sounded so matter of fact.

As soon as Katie returned, he would take his leave
of her. He heard the door to the house close quietly
behind him. "Sorry to take so long," Katie said.
"As usual they were full of questions as well as
long-winded stories. Anything to prolong and postpone bedtime."

As soon as he heard her, Sam stood and turned.
The only light came from the house, placing both
of them in shadows. He saw her in silhouette, moving closer to him.

He wanted to say something light, to respond in
kind to her comments, but he'd lost his ability to
speak. Instead, he drew her into his arms and carefully enfolded her as though she was a precious
prize that needed careful handling.

With a sweet innocence that completely undid
him, she lifted her face to him, allowing her eyes to
close in a gesture of utter trust.

Sam realized he was trembling in an effort not to
sweep her off her feet and place her on the chaise
longue nearby, where he wanted to slowly—with a
thoroughness he'd never before considered—touch
and caress her from the crown of her head to the tip
of her rosy-painted toes.

Instead, he kept the kiss very circumspect.

But not for long. A brief taste of her created an
instant craving for more. He kissed her more deeply,

delighted when she sighed and slipped her arms around his neck, her breasts pressing against him, immediately triggering his arousal.

She opened her mouth to him and he accepted the invitation to tease and explore, taste and enjoy, memorize and claim.

He eased his hand up her side and under her breast, feeling its weight, fighting the hunger that was sweeping over him.

The distant melody playing "Oh, I wish I were in the land of cotton" drifted around him. It took him a moment to realize it was her doorbell. He reluctantly eased away from her. "You've got company," he murmured wryly.

Katie's eyes slowly opened. She blinked, and then his words seemed to register. "Oh!" She turned away and hurried back into the house. Since he needed to leave, anyway, he followed her inside. He'd loved the look of her in that moment when he'd stepped back from her. Her rosy cheeks, her slightly swollen and moist lips, her slumberous eyes.

Damn. He'd better get his mind on something else before he stepped inside the house. No need to advertise his condition to whoever had arrived—he glanced at his watch—at eleven o'clock at night.

Once he quietly let himself inside, he could hear voices—Katie's voice sounding strained and a deeper, masculine voice. Sam heard the man say, "Don't give me that, Kathleen. Remember me? I was your husband. I *know* what you look like when you've been making love. All I want to know is who you're keeping tucked in your bed these days."

Sam walked into the foyer and approached the couple, who still stood at the door. It was obvious from her body language that Katie didn't want the man here. If, as he gathered from the conversation, it was her former husband, he could certainly understand the awkwardness she might be feeling.

Neither one of them had noticed his presence at the back of the foyer. It gave him an opportunity to size up the other man.

Sam had to admit the man was damned good-looking. Movie star good-looking with blond hair boyishly tousled, a couple of curls falling on his forehead. He was more than six feet, at least a couple of inches taller than Sam. The suit he wore was obviously tailored to his broad-shouldered, slim-hipped physique. Compared to this specimen, Sam felt like a frog.

He cleared his throat and they both swung around to face him. Katie looked ready to cry, which infuriated Sam for some reason. she'd been so relaxed and happy during the evening. He hated to see her sparkle gone.

Sam walked over to the man and held out his hand. In his most pleasant voice, he said, "I don't believe we've met. I'm Sam Carruthers."

Sam could see the automatic charm kick in on the guy. With a smile that was an orthodontist's dream, the man said, "Arthur Henley." He took Sam's hand and gripped it in a childish test of strength. Sam refused to play.

"Here to see your daughters?" Sam asked with a hint of a smile. He glanced at his watch, then looked at Katie. "Thank you again for taking pity on an old army buddy of Clay's tonight, Mrs. Henley. I enjoyed meeting you and your daughters."

Henley's head jerked. "Army? You're in the army?"

Sam smiled. "Well, not anymore. That's where I met Clay, though, several years ago. He kept talking about Texas, so I decided to take my vacation here and see what all the bragging was about."

"I never had any use for you army guys. I was in the navy. Did my SEAL training there, but got sick of the nonsense and opted out of the service. Best thing I ever did was to come back to civilian life."

"You were a SEAL?" Sam asked, suddenly going into alert mode.

"I did some of the training. Never completed it. I learned all I needed to know to figure out I wanted no part of the military system."

Sam nodded. "I hear you."

"So what was your rank?"

"Lieutenant," he replied blandly, leaving off the rest of his rank.

"I'd forgotten Katie's cousin was still doing his duty for good ol' Uncle Sam." He glanced at Katie. So did Sam. She now looked pale and tired.

Sam reached for her and squeezed her hand. "Thank you again. I'll give Clay your regards."

"Yes," she replied, with a mere hint of a smile.

Arthur opened the door and waved him through. "Glad to meet you," he said airily.

Sam couldn't be that openly hypocritical. He gave them a short wave and went to his car.

Arthur drove a late-model BMW convertible, sleek and gleaming. Sam appreciated his less-flashy but equally expensive loaned vehicle more by the minute.

So Arthur Henley had trained to be a SEAL.

Sam decided to have Arthur's military records checked out as soon as he got back to the condo.

Chapter 7

Pam wandered into the kitchen some time after ten and decided to make some coffee. She was pleasantly tired. A pattern was beginning to form in all the reports she'd been studying. There was time enough to discuss all of it with Sam in the morning.

In the meantime, she would enjoy a cup of decaf coffee before taking a soaking bath and going to bed.

She heard the front door open and she called out, "I'm in the kitchen. You're just in time to join me in a cup of coffee." She got two coffee mugs out of the cabinet. With her back still to the door, she said, "So how was dinner?"

"I haven't had dinner," Clay said from the doorway.

Pam spun around in surprise and more than a little dismay. "Clay! I wasn't expecting you." He looked tired, and for a moment she felt an almost overpow-

ering desire to walk over to him and massage his
shoulders, which showed her how tired she must be.
Her defenses against this man must be weakening.

He pulled out one of the kitchen chairs and sat
down. ''Is there any food here?''

She turned away from him, ostensibly to pour the
steaming liquid into the coffee mugs. ''Some...''

He opened the refrigerator, removed the pizza,
placed it on a plate and set it into the microwave.

''What are you doing back so early?''

''I found out what I was looking for. The warehouse had only a few employees. Two of them
hadn't worked there long at the time of the explosion. They left a week later. Their background information didn't match—home addresses were
phony, listed relatives had never heard of them. That
tells me we have a couple of prime suspects to look
for.''

The microwave pinged and Clay removed the
heated pizza, picked up his cup of coffee and sat at
the table. Pam stayed where she was, as though the
distance between them might protect her from the
strong sexual response she experienced in his presence.

''Let me guess,'' she said. ''They were members
of a local militia group, right?''

Clay had just taken a sip of coffee when she
spoke. He set his cup down in an abrupt motion.
''No one went that far with explanations, but I
wouldn't be at all surprised to discover they were
members of some kind of underground group.''

She leaned her folded arms on the table, and said,
''What keeps occurring in my various runs is a series of employees who are dissatisfied with the pres-

ent government and are part of some kind of group that meets on a regular basis.''

"But what does that have to do with the Callaways, I wonder?''

She shrugged. "Possibly because you're part of the in crowd, so to speak.''

"So you don't think it's a personal attack, is that it?''

"I don't know. I found a group of employees who seem to have similar interests hating all politicians and large corporations. I'd like to show the list to you and Sam. They seem to have a connection with a well-known activist who currently resides in central Texas.''

He quickly demolished the remains of the pizza before saying anything else. When he did, his words surprised her. "You're really enjoying this, aren't you?''

She looked around the kitchen, then at him. "Enjoying what?''

"Looking for suspects, finding patterns, that sort of thing. Your eyes are sparkling despite the shadows beneath them.''

She nodded. "I'm pleased to have made this much progress so soon. You've confirmed that we're headed in the right direction.''

He stretched and yawned. "Well, I for one am going to call it a day. I'm beat.''

He stood and carried his plate to the sink. She turned to set her cup on the counter and found herself chest to chest with Clay. She took a quick step backward and came up against the refrigerator. He followed her, placing his forearms on either side of her head, leaving his face inches from hers. She couldn't seem to catch her breath.

"What do you think you're doing?" she asked faintly, inundated by the high voltage sensations he invariably aroused in her.

He pulled out the clips that held her hair away from her face, then slipped his hands through her hair, ignoring her question. "You are so beautiful," he murmured as though to himself. "No matter how many long hours you've put in, you still manage to look stunning."

She forced herself to breathe. How was she supposed to think clearly with him so close? "Clay? I—uh—"

"Shh," he whispered, lowering his mouth until his lips brushed against hers. "Just let me..." His mouth settled with alarming familiarity against hers, while he gently tilted her head up for a closer fit.

Pam knew that this was the last thing she wanted. The very last thing. They had to work together. They didn't need to be reminded of the volatile reaction that took place whenever they were in close proximity to each other. It was that strong sexual attraction that had gotten them into so much trouble as kids.

Her arms snaked around his waist and she held on to him with an intensity she hadn't felt in years. Never had she felt it with anyone else.

She moaned deep in her throat when his tongue slipped inside her mouth, teasing her with tantalizing, suggestive movements. He ran his hands down her spine to her hips, lifted and turned her so that she was seated on the countertop. Nudging her knees apart, he stepped into the V formed by her legs without ever breaking the kiss.

When he finally paused in his sensuous assault, it was just for a quick gasp of air before he claimed her once again. She frantically fumbled with the buttons on his shirt until she was able to push it out of her way. She wanted to feel his bare chest, her fingers exploring the muscled shape, searching for the tight little button-shaped nipples that were surrounded by soft hair.

Clay shoved at the silken T-shirt she wore, lifting it to expose her lacy bra and reaching for the clasp. She could feel the chills across his chest as she teased him. She anticipated the release of her bra, then the weight of her breasts snuggled into cupped hands. She arched her back, pushing against him, wanting him to—

They both heard the sound of the front door opening and froze. Clay took a step back from her, his eyes ablaze with passion, his mouth moist and slightly swollen, his arousal obvious.

Pam had a lightning-flash image of what she must look like sitting there with her hair tumbling around her shoulders, her breasts exposed. She was too stunned by what had just happened to move, but Clay reached over and pulled down her shirt and kept his back to the door.

They both looked through the doorway and watched Sam walk through the living room and into the hallway without glancing toward the kitchen. Neither of them moved until they heard his bedroom door quietly click behind him.

Clay let out a gusty sigh of relief and dropped his head on her shoulder. She draped her arms around him and held him in silence until she felt his shoulders subtly move beneath her arms. She leaned back to see his face. He slowly raised his head until his gaze met hers.

She was caught off guard by the fact that he was silently laughing.

Laughing? When they'd almost been caught necking in the kitchen like a couple of teenagers?

A couple of teenagers.

Omigod, this was a replay of dozens of times when they'd almost been caught at her place or his. Her eyes widened in recognition and acknowledgement of what had just happened. She covered her mouth with her hand, barely muffling a choked laugh.

"Are we insane?" she whispered. "What were we thinking?"

He ran his fingers across her cheek, down her throat, and rested his hand over her breast. "All I was thinking was how much I want to make love to you," he replied softly.

Pam wrestled with her conscience and her pride. Truth finally won out. "So was I," she admitted sheepishly.

As though her comment was all the permission he needed, he scooped her off the counter and into his arms, flipping off the kitchen light with his elbow on the way out of the room. He went into his bedroom and closed the door by leaning against it.

The room was dark.

"Clay—" she began.

"Don't think, Pam. Just feel."

He moved toward the bed in sure steps as if he could see in the dark and laid her on the bed. He straddled her, lifting her shirt over her head and tossing it along with the unfastened bra across the room. He leaned back and quickly unzipped her slacks, pulling them down over her hips, pausing only long enough to slip off her shoes before pitching the remainder of her clothing aside.

She'd already unbuckled his belt and pulled on the snap of his jeans, then shoved his shirt off his shoulders. She could feel him tugging off his shoes and jerking his jeans over his hips and down his long legs.

When they were both totally bare, he moved so that he was between her legs.

"My gosh," he whispered into her ear. "A bed. We've got an honest-to-goodness mattress beneath us and we're both wide awake. Will wonders never cease."

His mouth turned up at the corners as he began to kiss her. He trailed slow, very leisurely kisses from her mouth down her body and paused at the tip of her breasts, where he carefully licked the surface, then pulled the nipple of first one, then the other, into his mouth.

She almost came off the bed at the sudden sensation of his mouth moving over her, his tongue teasing her as it curled around her nipple, setting off a tingling sensation that shot through her like a sudden bolt of lightning. She wrapped her legs around his hips, holding him to her while she did some exploring of her own.

He continued a path of tender, loving kisses down her body, following a line along her thigh, knee and calf before switching to the other leg and tracing a route back to the apex of her thighs.

He paused and she could hear his heavy breathing that almost matched her own. She cupped him, feeling the rigid strength and the softer, more rounded parts. He groaned and shifted his weight. She heard a drawer open nearby and then he pushed a small foil package into her hands.

"Here. It may be too late, but…" his voice trailed off into another groan when she hastily ripped open the package and carefully worked the protection onto him.

He leaned down and kissed her on her cluster of curls, and she bit her lip not to cry out. Her body was shouting commands, demanding relief, yet all she could do was to ride out the wave of sensation that his meticulous attention to detail was creating.

"Oh, Clay, please," she begged, almost incoherent with need. "Please…"

He straightened and nudged her legs farther apart, then leaned forward and slowly and steadily filled her.

"Oh, yes, yes, oh, Clay, I, oh…" He began to move slowly, teasing her as if each stroke might be his last. She pulled his face down to hers and began kissing him—long, mind-drugging kisses that effectively caused him to lose his concentration and rhythm.

She lifted her hips to him, meeting every lunge, forcing him higher and higher, moving faster and faster until they were both gasping for air, their bodies damp with excitement.

Her keening cry of fulfillment was smothered by his deep kiss as he brought her to her climax, following her a few strokes later until they were both quivering with reaction and release.

He rolled to his side with her still wrapped securely in his arms. She was plastered to him, the heat and moisture creating a seal, bonding their bodies together.

How could she have ever given up this man for any reason? was her last thought before falling into a deep oblivion.

Clay held Pam in his arms long after he knew she'd fallen into an exhausted sleep. He was exhausted, too, but his mind continued to race. He couldn't believe what he'd done. How could he have acted on his blasted fantasies?

Here he was making love—again!—to the woman who had broken his heart. Didn't he ever learn anything? His brain seemed to shut off every time he was within arm's length of her.

He was honest enough with himself to know that it would happen again, over and over, if he had any say about it. They were like spontaneous combustion whenever they got near each other. The thing to remember was to protect his heart.

She obviously enjoyed making love with him. So why shouldn't they slip into bed now and then while they were on this assignment? She'd made it clear enough that her independence was more important to her than any commitment he might want her to make. So be it. He'd become a realist over the years. He'd learned to stop yearning for what he couldn't have.

Pam would never be his on a permanent basis.

He would take what he could get.

As often as possible.

For as long as possible.

Some time later he woke up with Pam burrowing against his chest, and he realized they'd never turned the covers back. He tried to pull away from her, but she clung to him with a tenacity that amused him. It took a while, but he finally pulled the covers loose and draped the sheet over them.

When she finally relaxed her hold and flowed onto her back, he leaned over and kissed her breasts, encouraged by their immediate reactions to his caresses. She shifted once again to her side, unerringly finding him with her fingers. She sighed, running her hand up and over his hardened length, then guiding him once more to her.

They continued to lie side by side facing each other. She placed her leg on his hip, giving them both a new freedom of movement with a heart-stopping angle that had him forgetting to breathe.

Their movements were lazy while they indulged themselves in long, leisurely kisses, their tongues intertwined, mimicking the movement of their hips.

Then, from one slow stroke to the next, Clay felt his body suddenly take over. His movements became quicker while his body began to tense and draw tighter, until he exploded with a mind-numbing intensity. Pam's response was just as cataclysmic.

He was drifting off to sleep once more, sated and relaxed, when he suddenly thought about how his life had changed in such a short period of time. He had survived so many dangerous assignments—but would he survive Pamela McCall?

The sound of a distant alarm set off warning signals in Clay's head. He forced himself to surface from a deep sleep and squinted at the clock beside the bed.

Not quite six o'clock. The colonel believed in early starts to his day.

The colonel.

The mere thought of the man brought Clay to an upright position in bed, effectively unveiling his bedmate of the sheet they had shared the night before. He scrubbed his hand over his face. Oh, boy. How did he find the words to explain this to the colonel?

Or did he have to? Was it anyone's business that he and Pam had slept together last night? Not that they'd gotten much sleep, come to that, but what had happened last night had certainly changed their relationship.

Again.

He looked back at Pam. She was turned away from him, her silky strands of hair draped around her bare shoulders, her face half buried into her pillow. Clay rubbed his chest, hoping the ache would go away. He was no callow youth pining for his ideal mate. There was no reason for him to feel a sense of grief that this woman was willing to go to bed with him but had no reason to commit to him.

But now was not the time to reflect on what the future might bring. He had a job to do and another day to face. He had to report to Sam with the information he'd obtained during his previous eighteen-hour day, and somehow he had to continue to treat Pam as nothing more to him than one of the team members.

He slipped out of bed and dressed, then left the bedroom. The condo was quiet in early-morning, but he saw a light shining from the kitchen, which meant that Sam was already up. He headed toward the beckoning scent of freshly brewed coffee.

He paused in the doorway to the kitchen. The colonel sat at the table with a mug of steaming coffee cupped between his hands, studying the liquid as though hoping to find answers to his weightiest questions.

"Mornin'," Clay mumbled, making a beeline to the coffeepot.

Sam glanced up in surprise. "What are you doing here? I thought you planned to stay for a few days."

Clay filled a cup and joined Sam at the table. "I think I found a couple of suspects, but since they'd left the area, I saw no reason to hang around."

Sam's gaze sharpened. "Who are they?"

"All I have are aliases, but I'm hoping Pam can trace them for me. Two men, claiming to be brothers, hired on a short time before the explosion. They disappeared soon after, so it makes sense to find them for a little talk."

"That information didn't turn up in any of the reports we received from the local authorities or government investigators. How did you get so lucky?"

Clay grinned. "Skill, Colonel. Skill. Actually, I lucked out. Ran into a college buddy of mine who was pleased to see a representative of the family had decided to check out the official version of the warehouse bombing. Since he already knew me, there was no reason to use a cover. He hired on into management not long after the place opened. I guess there's been some friction between the middle management and the guy running the place."

"Do you think any of them are in on it?"

"That's another thing I want Pam to check out. I tend to trust my source, but I'm willing to be proved wrong."

"Well, it makes sense that if it was a longtime employee involved he would prefer to point the finger at transients."

"Yeah, that's why I bought him lunch and sat and listened to all of his gripes and comments. His story checked out as far as I could go while I was there. I asked him not to mention who I was to anyone else. I don't know if being recognized worked for or against me, but I saw no point in hanging around after that."

"Good call. I would have done the same thing."

Clay's stomach rumbled and he rubbed it ruefully. "I think I'll make some waffles this morning. Sound okay to you?"

Sam's mouth quirked into a half smile. "As long as you're doing the cooking." He poured himself another cup of coffee, then asked, "What do you know about Arthur Henley?"

Clay found the ingredients he needed and plugged in the waffle iron while he considered Sam's question. "Only what my mom mentioned to me last weekend. Why? Are you interested because of our investigation or is there a more personal reason?"

Clay was surprised to see a flush appear on the colonel's tanned cheeks. *Oh-oh, this is getting more and more interesting,* he thought to himself.

"A little of both, probably," Sam replied with a candidness that Clay appreciated. "I had dinner with Katie and her daughters last night. He showed up rather late for no good reason that I could see other than to upset Katie. When she introduced us he mentioned that he'd been in the navy and had trained to be a SEAL.''

Clay carefully poured batter into the heated waffle iron and closed the lid. ''That's certainly news to me. A trained operative could do some serious damage if he wanted to.''

''That's what I was thinking,'' Sam admitted. ''Granted, I'd love to catch the bastard doing something illegal just to put him away where he couldn't upset Katie and the girls.'' He rubbed his forehead as though to wipe away the frown lines. ''Which means I don't really trust my judgment where he's concerned.''

''Have you talked to Pam about him?''

He shook his head. ''I came in too late last night to bother her, but I'll see what she can dig up on the guy this morning.'' He glanced at his watch. ''Plus I need to contact Joe. I expected him to call me before now.''

''You know...'' Clay said slowly, leaning against the counter with a fresh cup of coffee in his hands. ''Mom mentioned that Henley used to work for one of the companies and was fired when Katie filed for divorce. That would certainly go to motive if he wanted some payback.''

Sam nodded. ''Yeah, it does. I have to admit he's a smooth character. Looked like the answer to any woman's dreams.''

Clay grinned. ''According to Katie, all that charm and good looks did little to make him a decent husband and loving father.'' He moved the waffles to a plate, zapped some maple syrup in the microwave for a few seconds and set them on the table in front of Sam. "Eat while it's hot."

Sam looked at the food as if he'd never seen waffles before. "Hell, man, that looks good enough to eat." He picked up his knife and fork and cut into his breakfast.

"Yeah? Well, I'm just full of surprises." He started another waffle. "I wonder if I should call Pam. No reason for her to miss out as long as I'm cooking."

Sam glanced up. "How's it working out for you to be working with her? One of the reasons I sent you to east Texas was to ease the tension around here. There seems to be a pretty strong force field whenever you two are in the same room."

Clay chuckled. "Well, we'll see." He thought about the night before. A lot of his tension had certainly been worked off during the night! He'd slept better than he had all week. "I have to admit that it was a shock seeing her again after all these years."

"If you don't want to talk about it, I can understand. It's none of my business, and as long as it doesn't affect your performances, it's none of my concern, either."

"I don't know where I stand on any of my issues with Pam. After she refused to marry me, I did everything in my power to forget she ever existed. Now, years later, I'm faced with looking at what happened back then through the eyes of an adult. I always knew how important her education was to her. If I'd known that she thought she wouldn't be able to continue with her education after we married, I would have reassured her that there would be no reason for her to stop." He paused to take a deep breath. "But we weren't given the opportunity to talk about it because the senator was determined to get us married before there was a hint of scandal in the family. I suppose I figured we'd have all the time in the world to discuss school once we were married. The irony where the senator was concerned was that her calling off the wedding at the last minute created a minor scandal after all. Knowing how much she always wanted to please her father, and how difficult it must have been for her to challenge him on this issue, I can better appreciate the tremendous courage it took for her to stand up to us both." He sighed heavily. "At the time I was too wrapped up in my own hurt to give a thought to what she must have been going through. I've got to admit that I admire her for her determination. The senator is one tough adversary."

Sam cocked an eyebrow. "You speak as though from personal experience."

Clay laughed. "You got that right. There was a time when I thought he was going to kill me. I think he would have if he'd thought he could get away with it. I speak with total confidence when I say that I will never be one of his favorite people."

"Why? Because you fell in love with his daughter?"

Clay took his time removing the second waffle, refilling the waffle iron and gathering eating utensils before he answered Sam. He sat across from him once again, and while he cut up the waffle, he said, "Actually, for seducing his innocent daughter."

Sam tried to cover a laugh with a cough. "Hmm. Well, I could see where a man might be a little touchy about that."

Clay nodded. "We were both a couple of kids, neither one of us knew much about what was happening. We just enjoyed all those sensations we'd discovered when we were around each other, and one night we didn't put a stop to the explorations."

Clay noticed Sam's eyes going out of focus as though he was thinking about something other than the conversation. Presently he nodded and said, "Those are some pretty powerful sensations, no matter how old you are."

Clay ducked his head and continued to eat. He didn't want to know what memories might have been triggered for his commanding officer.

"Something smells terrific in here," Pam said, walking into the kitchen. "Mind if I join you?"

Clay stood and said, "You're just in time. That waffle's ready to come out and it has your name on it." He attempted to meet her gaze, only to discover that her smile was aimed at both of them and didn't actually reach her eyes.

He also noticed that she had whisker burns on her cheek, jaw and neck. Oops. He hadn't had much of a problem with that as a teenager.

While she poured a cup of coffee, he filled a plate for her and motioned for her to sit down at the small table.

The conversation quickly turned to the events of the previous day. At one point Pam went to her room for a notepad and pen to make notes. Her attitude was one of total concentration, a professional at work.

She didn't ignore him. Not exactly. She listened carefully to his report, took down names and asked insightful questions. But she never looked at him.

Her gaze was directed to his earlobe or at the V of his shirt.

He had to admit to himself that her attitude eased his jumpiness. She wasn't any more certain of herself this morning than he was. So she was ad-libbing. He had no problem with that.

The case was the important thing. He wasn't certain that he wanted her to define where they stood at the moment. It was enough to know that she was still as drawn to him as he was to her. That had to count for something.

Only time would tell exactly what.

Chapter 8

Sam reached Joe about midmorning. Joe answered with a brief, "Yes?"

"Are you somewhere you can talk?"

"Yes. I'm in my room."

"What kind of information have you gotten?"

"Very little, so far. People are accepting my story. They're friendly enough. The talk in the village is about the recent bombing. So I listen."

Sam nodded. "Good. Exactly what I was hoping for. Any theories?"

Joe chuckled. "Everyone has a theory—anywhere from the idea that it's a group of people wanting to claim Texas as a sovereign state to space aliens covering their tracks."

"Sounds like fun. Keep me informed. You have the number of the condo as well as my cell phone number."

"How's it going at your end?"

"We're following up several leads. There's no way of knowing at this point if anything will pan out."

"Well, at least you've got some. I haven't been able to spot anything here that appears to be out of the ordinary. No new hires, no sudden resignations."

"It might not be locals. Give it another couple of days. If you don't turn up anything, come to Austin." He smiled, thinking of the master bedroom sitting empty. "We've got a place for you to bunk here." He gave him directions to the condo.

"Okay. I'll see what I can do. I'll see you soon."

Sam disconnected and stared blindly at the papers in front of him. Clay and Pam were working in her office this morning. He was pleased to notice that the tension had eased somewhat between them.

Pamela McCall was a difficult read. He had no idea what she felt about anything, but she was damned efficient at what she did. At the rate they were going, things might be wrapped up in short order.

He'd return to the base and get back to his regular duties. His so-called vacation would be nothing more than a few memories.

Sam stopped fighting his urge to place another call and picked up the phone once again.

Katie answered on the second ring. "Hello?"

Just the sound of her voice caused him to immediately harden. Damn, but he had it bad. "Hi, Katie. This is Sam."

"Oh, Sam! I'm so glad to hear from you." Her voice suddenly had a lilt to it. "I owe you an apology. I figured that with my ex showing up last night I'd never hear from you again.''

"I can't be chased away that easily," he replied. If she only knew. "Besides, I don't have a problem with ex-husbands. They're out of the picture.''

She sighed. "How I wish that were true. He never showed any of us much attention during the marriage. Now he's always finding an excuse to call or come by at odd hours.''

"Trisha mentioned on the phone that her daddy didn't like her because he never came to see her.''

"Yes, she keeps saying that. I don't know which is worse, trying to make excuses for the man or letting my daughters feel they aren't important to him.''

"We can talk about it tonight, if dinner is still on.''

"That would be wonderful. I know the girls will enjoy it.''

"If you don't mind making reservations, I'll pick you up around six tonight.''

"I'll be glad to." She paused. "Thanks, Sam.''

"For what?" he asked.

"For being such a nice guy.''

He laughed. "Honey, if you knew me better, you'd know that the last adjective anyone would choose to describe me is *nice*.''

"Well, actually," she said with a hint of hesitation, "I could think of several others, but I might end up embarrassing both of us.''

He immediately flashed to that torrid kiss they'd shared before good ol' Henley showed up. "Uh, hold that thought. We'll explore some of those adjectives later tonight, okay?''

"You are very good for my ego, Mr. Carruthers," she replied with a chuckle.

He winced at the civilian title, a forcible reminder that he hadn't told her the whole truth about himself. Well, the sooner he got this matter cleared up, the faster he could explain everything to her. He felt certain she would understand.

"I'll see you tonight, sunshine," he said, and hung up.

With that call out of the way, Sam was better able to concentrate. He checked with his contacts in Washington as well as his man on the drilling rig, then followed up with a faxed status report to the men monitoring the progress of this investigation. He was pleased with what they were uncovering.

When he casually mentioned to Clay and Pam that he'd made plans for the evening, Clay was equally casual about mentioning that he'd invited Pam out for dinner and a possible movie.

He wasn't certain what there was about that statement that caused Pam to blush, but Sam had to admit the color was very becoming on her.

He was still smiling about her reaction when he pulled up in front of Katie's home that evening.

The first thing Katie said once he stepped inside the house was to suggest that they go to dinner in her larger sedan. Sam agreed. When she suggested that he drive, he smiled and said, "Since you know where we're going, why don't you drive?"

She looked at him in amazement. "It won't bother your male ego to let a woman chauffeur you?"

"I'm sure my ego will recover from the trauma just fine," he replied with a chuckle.

Trisha and Amber chattered nonstop during the ride to the lake restaurant. They were full of questions that kept Sam on his toes trying to answer. By the time they were seated at the table overlooking the lake, Katie had obviously reached her limit.

"All right, girls. That's enough. It isn't polite to monopolize the conversation."

"What's *monopolize*?" Trisha asked.

"Do all the talking."

"Oh. We was doing that?"

"Yes, you were doing that."

"Oh." She looked at Sam and gave him an angelic smile. "We're sorry."

He looked at Katie, unsure of what to say. She continued, "Now, then. Let's see what you would like to order before the waiter comes, okay?"

Amber spoke up. "This is my most favorite place to eat in all the world."

"Really? I thought your mother made a great meal last night," Sam replied.

Amber nodded. "Mommy doesn't count, 'cause she's the best cooker in all the world. But I like to eat here 'cause I can see the boats, an' watch the sky turn all kinds of pretty colors, and then the water turns the colors, too. It's neat."

Katie looked at Sam. "Amber definitely inherited my mother's love for color."

"I can draw like Granmama, too. She got me all these pretty sticks of colors and told me to have fun. Do you like to draw?" she asked Sam.

"I'm not at all sure I know how. I've not done much of it."

"It's easy," Amber assured him. "I could show you how if you want."

"Amber," Katie said in a warning tone. "Choose what you want to eat, please."

When the waitress came up, she smiled at them and said, "What beautiful children you have." She looked at Sam. "You must be quite proud of them."

Sam caught Katie's eye and grinned at her discomfiture. "Yes, we are," he said with a very deliberate glance at Katie. She turned a very appealing pink.

Amber said, "But—"

Trisha said, "Be quiet, Amber." She reached over and touched Sam's hand. "It's all right, you know. We don't mind."

The waitress looked confused. Sam could feel his heart ache for these little girls but could think of nothing to say. He listened as Katie ordered for the three of them, and acknowledged to himself how much he liked the idea of being a part of this particular family.

Hours later the girls were tucked into bed and Sam sat in Katie's den sipping coffee. Katie was beside him on the sofa with her shoes kicked off.

"So how did you spend your day?" she asked, her head resting against the high back of the couch, watching him.

He certainly couldn't explain anything about what he'd been doing, so he shrugged and replied with, "Doing as little as possible." Before he could gain control over his unruly tongue, he added, "And counting the hours until I could see you again."

She turned a bright pink at his words, and he could have kicked himself for being so blasted forward. His lack of social graces had never been so evident.

"I'm sorry," he said, "I—"

She chuckled. "You're sorry for counting hours?"

It was his turn to feel embarrassed. "Not that, just for—"

"Being honest?"

He sighed. "I do have a tendency to blurt out whatever thoughts I'm having whenever I'm around you."

"How refreshing. I'm used to not having a clue about what Arthur was thinking or feeling. It's nice not to have to wonder."

"Are you still in love with him?"

She looked at him in surprise. Then she gave a brief shake to her head. "I've never been asked that one before. Everyone has been feeling so sorry for me, metaphorically patting me on the head like a schoolchild for losing such a charming, intelligent, handsome man. When the truth is, there is very little substance to him once you get past the physical attributes. So, no. I'm no longer in love with him, and because he's the father of my children, I'm dealing with enormous amounts of guilt because of my lack of feeling for him."

"What did he want last night?"

"To point out all my shortcomings as a woman, a wife and a mother. This is his current litany whenever we come into contact with each other."

"Could it be that he chose to stop when he saw the car in your driveway?"

She looked startled by the suggestion, then smiled. "You know, that never occurred to me. Of course that means he has a habit of driving by here to check on me, but that wouldn't surprise me."

"What does he do?"

"I really don't know. He used to work as a financial officer in a couple of the businesses owned by Callaway Enterprises. My dad found some discrepancies in the books in both companies, but never said a word to me until after I'd asked Arthur to leave and filed for divorce. Then he fired him. Up until then, he'd put new checks and balances into place without saying anything."

"Could he prove Arthur was the cause?"

She smiled. "My dad doesn't have to prove anything to anyone. Once he's investigated and found out enough to be certain who the offender is, he gets rid of them and dares them to file a complaint with the labor board."

Sam nodded. "Somehow, that doesn't surprise me. Your dad strikes me as the kind of person no one would want to cross."

"I always thought that Arthur was intimidated by my dad, but in his efforts not to show it, he was almost belligerent whenever we were with my family. I'm fairly certain he didn't adopt that attitude at work, though, or he would have been fired, in-law or not." She looked down at her empty cup and said, "I've been yammering on about my past, no doubt boring you to a stupor. Let me get us more coffee."

He stopped her by laying his hand lightly on her arm. "You aren't boring me, Katie. Nothing about you—your past or your present—could ever bore me." He lifted the cup and saucer from her hand and set them on the table, then leaned toward her. Putting his arms around her, he gently eased her against him, then kissed her with a slow thoroughness that had his heart pounding in his chest.

When he finally raised his head, they were both breathing hard.

"You go straight to my head," he said. "I forget everything—your girls upstairs, the fact that we just met a few days ago. All I can think about is claiming you and making you mine." She started to speak and he stopped. "I know. It's too soon and you're still going through a tough adjustment. Just know that when you're ready for a relationship with another man, please think of me."

"Oh, Sam. Thank you for understanding. I never expected to meet anyone I wanted to get involved with once the divorce was finally over. Meeting you has created so many conflicting feelings." She bowed her head, unable to meet his gaze. "I'm very glad I met you, though. You've helped me to discover that my faith in men hasn't completely disappeared. I'm just afraid…"

"Afraid of what?"

"Of what Arthur will continue to do if he sees me spending time with another man. It isn't that he was ever possessive of me when we were married, but his behavior since the divorce has been out of character. Whatever he felt for me disappeared not long after we married, so why he's doing and saying all these hateful things now is beyond my comprehension."

"I don't want to make your life any more difficult." He glanced at his watch. "I need to get back, anyway. Let me hear from you when you're comfortable seeing me again, okay?"

The phone rang, causing her to jump. Nothing could have better shown how tense she was and Sam was irritated with himself. He had never before had trouble hanging on to his self-control. Look at what he'd done to her.

As soon as she answered the phone, he saw her stiffen. She wore the same look she'd had the night before. No doubt it was her ex-husband.

Her words confirmed his guess. "It's late, Arthur, and there's no reason for you to be calling me. I would appreciate it if you'd just leave us alone."

There was another long pause. Arthur's voice could be heard getting louder.

"How many times must we go through this?" she finally asked. "Please get on with your life as the girls and I are attempting to do."

He said something else, then obviously slammed down the phone. She winced and rubbed her ear before returning the phone to its cradle.

"You could get a restraining order, you know," Sam said quietly.

She rubbed her forehead. "I know. It may come to that, yet. I had hoped it wouldn't, but I can't take much more of this."

Sam stood and held out his hand to draw her to her feet. "I'm going to leave now and let you get some rest. Thank you for allowing me to spend the evening with you and your girls."

She stepped closer and cupped his jaw with her hands. "Oh, Sam. The pleasure was all ours. You have so much patience with the girls. You listen to them, speak to them with respect. I can't tell you how much that means to me." As if on impulse, she went up on her toes and kissed him. "I'll be in touch, okay?"

He kissed her back, lingering while he teased her

lightly with his tongue before reluctantly stepping away from her.

"Take care of yourself, okay? You're a very special lady. Don't ever forget that." He diplomatically ignored the sudden tears that filled her eyes. If he didn't get out of there right *now,* he wouldn't trust himself to leave before morning.

He let himself out the front door and waited to hear the dead bolt slide into place before he went to his car. Being with Katie was like a fantasy to him—nothing else in his life seemed real when he was around her.

Chapter 9

Clay and Pam left the condo in silence. They reached his truck and he waited for her to get inside before he walked around to the driver's side and got in.

"You didn't have to do this, you know," she said quietly.

He looked around at her in surprise. "Do what? Eat? Maybe not, but my stomach isn't one to suffer in silence."

"No. I meant take me out to eat. We could have ordered in."

"Yeah, I know. I was thinking about something different for tonight. I called Katie earlier today for some recommendations and she mentioned a couple of places that sounded good to me." He looked at her. "Unless you have an idea or two."

She shook her head. "I don't really care."

She said nothing more and the silence seemed to

grow. He thought about turning on the radio or making different comments, mostly about the work they'd shared all day, but he didn't want this outing to be work-related. He just wanted to be with Pam. So he remained silent, wondering if she was as uncomfortable as he was.

They reached the restaurant and were seated immediately. Their first course was delivered before he said, "You would think that as much as we've shared over the years, we could think of something to talk about."

She'd been toying with her salad when he spoke and she looked up, her eyes moist.

He blinked, wondering what he could have possibly done to cause her to tear up. It certainly wasn't something he'd said.

"Actually, I was thinking that it's because we've shared so much history that there's nothing to say at this point in our lives."

"How do you figure that?"

She lifted a shoulder in a slight shrug. "I just have trouble keeping my distance from you."

"Why should you?"

"Because you remind me of a part of me I've tried to forget over the years."

She looked down at her plate, then set her fork down. She reached for her water, took a sip, then raised her chin and looked at him. He'd waited for the eye contact before he spoke. "Why don't we forget the past? Pretend that we just met and go from there. We're both different people now. What's wrong with that?"

"I believe my best example of what's wrong with that is that it wouldn't work. Look what happened last night. Two people who had just met each other would not have behaved so recklessly.'' She shook her head. ''I don't know what it is about you that makes me lose my head. I've been on my own for years now, ever since I canceled the wedding and my father washed his hands of me, and I've never had any problem keeping my emotions in check. I consider myself a strong woman, intelligent, independent and in control of my reactions. Then all you have to do is to step back into my life and there I am in bed with you.''

The waiter appeared with their entrées. Clay waited until he left before he said, ''What do you mean, your father washed his hands of you?''

She glanced up from her plate in surprise. ''Just what I said.''

''I never knew that.''

''Why should you? It certainly wasn't your problem after I so effectively severed all communications between us by canceling our plans.''

He looked away, staring blindly at the view from the window of the restaurant. ''I was so caught up in my own hurt that I never thought about what it must have taken for you to change your mind.''

''Actually, I never changed my mind. If you'll recall, my father never gave either one of us a chance to discuss how we felt about getting married. You went back to college while he pushed all the plans so that as soon as you got home for the summer, the deed would be done. I didn't think I could explain how I felt in a letter to you. Unfortunately, you didn't get home until the day before the wedding.''

He stared at her in wonderment. ''Well, you certainly had no trouble telling me how you felt when you arrived at the ranch that night. By the time you got through, I felt as though I'd railroaded you into the most horrible situation you'd ever faced. Since I hadn't a clue about any of those feelings you expressed that night, I had to assume that you'd never cared anything about me, that it was just because you'd been friends with my family for so long that you'd bothered to continue to see me.''

"How can you possibly say that! Once we'd made love, I could never keep my hands off you. That's what I'm talking about. I have this sort of uncontrollable reaction whenever I'm around you, where my brain shuts off and all my hormones go into overdrive!''

"Well! That goes a long way toward easing my aching heart.''

"Oh, c'mon, Clay. Your heart was never involved. Teenage boys are even worse than girls when it comes to raging hormones.''

"So you think we would have behaved that way with anyone we happened to date at the age.''

"I think that *you* would have behaved that way. Yes.''

"I see. So you're the only person who can have finer feelings for a person, is that it?''

She rolled her eyes. "I didn't have a clue what I felt for you at the time. That's what I've been trying to tell you. There's this really strange chemistry in me that only you have the ability to trigger. It happened back then. It happened last night. For that matter, it probably happened last weekend in Dallas.''

"We were asleep at the time that started up.''

"Yes, I know. And you thought I was Melanie

Montez. I remember quite well. But what you don't understand is that I'd been dreaming about you. All my sexual dreams my entire life have been about you. By the time I woke up I knew very well who I was making love to, regardless of how you turned up in my bed. At the time I wasn't questioning why you were there. Don't you find something rather sick about that?''

"Sick?"

"Deranged! I should have been screaming my head off. There was a man in my bed!''

"I figured that you thought it was Adam."

"Adam?"

"Yeah, the guy you were with."

"Adam and I are friends. Not lovers."

"Oh."

"I don't happen to sleep with every man I date."

"The same goes for me. For your information, I have never slept with Melanie. Last weekend was going to be our first time together."

She clapped her hand over her mouth. "You're kidding," she whispered, her eyes wide. "Oh, my. Oh, Clay, that's horrible. Your first night together and you end up in somebody else's bed?"

Her eyes danced with laughter. Oh, all right, he thought. He still didn't find the situation amusing. Not in the least. But he could see how he might if it had happened to somebody else.

"I tried to apologize to her but I didn't have much luck." He'd thought about calling her but had decided that he'd already said everything he could say. He couldn't explain that Pam was part of the meetings, a part of his reason for being in Texas. Besides, what had happened was inexcusable. What if he'd gone to bed with a complete stranger? He could have been killed.

So no. He didn't find it at all amusing.

He forced a small smile. "Can we talk about something else, please? Let's just say that Saturday night was not one of my shining moments."

They ate without further conversation. Eventually they ordered dessert and over coffee, Clay said, "The worst part about all that happened between us way back when was losing you as a friend."

She nodded. "I not only lost my best friend, but all of your family as well. I was too ashamed to stay in touch with Kerry or your mom. If I hadn't had the trust fund from my mother so that I could go on to college without my father's assistance, I'm not sure what I would have done. I truly felt orphaned from everyone I loved, and had to face the fact that I'd brought it all on myself. I could have let everything play out and been married to you, living in College Station while you went to school, spent summers at the ranch with the family."

"I didn't realize that you didn't stay in touch with the family. Your name was never mentioned around me after that. I just figured everyone was being considerate of my feelings."

"I guess I felt that I deserved to be punished for waiting so long to stand up to my father." She eyed him for a few moments before she said, "Someday I'll tell you about the diaries I found written by my mother in the months before she died. I'd found them years ago in the attic but at the time was too young to realize that it was an opportunity to get to know the woman who gave birth to me. Those last few weeks before the wedding date I dug them out and spent night after night reading them. I realized how much of herself she had given up to marry my father.''

''And you figured that if you married me, you'd have to do the same thing,'' he finally said.

She nodded. ''Yes. It was almost as if I was giving my mother a second chance when I chose to take control of my life. I look back and wonder how in the world I ever had the nerve to stand up to both you and my father.''

''As I recall, I was in too much shock to give you any argument.''

''Well, my father certainly wasn't. He flew back to Washington the next day and told me he wanted me out of the house before he returned. I remember feeling grateful that he let me keep my car.''

The waiter brought the check and they left, neither one of them talking. Clay felt almost as stunned with these new revelations as he had the night she'd broken off their engagement. He'd assumed that her father had accepted her decision, since the man had never had much use for Clay, anyway.

They drove back to the condo without saying much. When they arrived, the place was quiet.

''Sam must be at Katie's again tonight,'' Pam said.

''Again?''

''Didn't you know? That's where he was last night. He said something about visiting with the girls as well tonight.''

''Now, that *is* interesting. My sweet little cousin never mentioned a word about seeing Sam tonight when I talked with her.''

''Maybe she's shy about discussing it.''

He stretched and yawned. "Maybe." He looked over at her. "I was wondering if my irresistible power over you is going to work tonight. I hate to think about lying in bed all night knowing you're just down the hall."

She laughed. "You're incorrigible. You know that."

"Part of my charm."

She shook her head. "I think we're both adult enough to be able to acknowledge the sexual attraction without acting upon it."

He walked over to her and slid his hand around the nape of her neck. "You do, huh?" he asked softly before kissing her.

She stiffened, but he didn't pull away. He massaged her tense neck muscles as he softly nibbled her lips, sucking on the bottom one, then licking it before taking possession of her mouth.

She let out a soft moan and relaxed against him, wrapping her arms around him and kissing him back without restraint. She made no protest when he picked her up and carried her into his room, closing the door behind them.

Sam received a call the next morning from Joe.

"What's up?"

"I'm not sure, but I thought you should know that I ran into Melanie Montez last night at one of the local cantinas. Come to find out, she was born here."

"Melanie Montez. Wasn't she Clay's date at the party in Dallas? I thought I heard someone mention that she was there."

"She didn't mention his name specifically, but

she appears to be nursing a grudge toward some man in her life—a boyfriend who 'done her wrong' kind of thing. I know that's really reaching, but if she is upset with one Callaway, maybe there's some connection.''

''You think that's possible?''

Joe sighed. ''Not really. I guess I was hoping that you might want to put her under surveillance. It would certainly liven up my existence down here.''

Sam laughed. ''Nice try. As a matter of fact, I think we've got strong-enough leads in this area to have you come back up. If you leave this morning, you should be here by evening. I think it's time to put all of you on the road to check out some of these people.''

''Sounds like a plan. I'll see you later today.''

Sam hung up the phone and looked at Clay and Pam. ''There are some addresses here that I'd like you to check out. From the map I would say these are in a hundred-mile radius. See if you can find out if any of these men are still in the area, if they're working, who for, and possible groups they belong to.'' He nodded toward Pam. ''I think you're on to something.''

''You know,'' Pam replied, ''I could get a car and we could divide the list. We'd get through it faster.''

Sam nodded. ''That's true. However, if either of you run across anyone who's involved in any of this, I'd like to think you have backup.''

Pam looked at Clay. Sam watched them both, but they weren't giving any thoughts away. ''You have a problem with working together?''

''No, sir,'' Clay immediately responded. He

looked at his watch. "We can be on the road within the hour."

"It may take a couple of days to cover the territory. In the meantime, the fellow from the drilling rig called and said he's coming in with his report and Joe will be here this evening. I'll team them up and have them check the addresses in the eastern sector of the state. I'll have my cell phone with me at all times, if you need to get in touch."

Pam said, "I'll throw a few things in a bag and will be ready in fifteen minutes."

Once she left the room, Sam looked at Clay. "Is this going to be too much for you? I can wait and send her out with Joe."

"No! I mean, I don't mind working with her. We had dinner together last night and were able to talk about what happened. I think it helped to clear the air. We each are very much involved in our careers. That's not going to change. I can deal with it. I know she can, too."

"Be careful out there. If this is the group responsible for the bombings, we already know they're dangerous."

"Don't you find it strange that no one has received word about who's behind this? It's been too quiet these past two weeks. Surely someone wants to take credit or make some kind of demands. I find the silence as ominous as anything else that has happened."

Sam sighed. "That's been on my mind as well. That's why I want my agents in the field with a partner to guard their back. We're still not sure who we're dealing with or what else they might do."

* * *

The phone rang Saturday morning, two days after Pam and Clay had left, a day after Joe and the other man had gone out into the field. Sam absently reached for his cell phone before he realized it was the condo telephone ringing. He grabbed it on the third ring.

"Hello?"

"Hi," Katie replied, sounding a little breathless. "I was beginning to think you'd already left for a day of playing tourist."

Sam felt a jolt of surprise and pleasure go through him at the sound of her voice. He hadn't contacted her since their last dinner date, thinking that he needed to give her some space. He was ecstatic that she'd reached out to him. Her comment reminded him that he was supposed to be on vacation. "I'd thought about it, but I've been too lazy to make plans for the day."

The truth was that her phone call was the first work break he'd had since dawn.

"I have a suggestion," she said a little hesitantly.

"Name it."

"Well, my cousin, Trisha, whom I named my daughter after, was here this morning and offered to take the girls with her. She's planning to take her kids and the twins to Fiesta Texas in San Antonio for the day, keep them overnight and return them tomorrow afternoon." She paused, then said, "So I was wondering…" Her voice trailed off with a hint of uncertainty.

"Yes," he said immediately.

She chuckled. "You don't know what I was going to ask."

"It doesn't matter. As long as it means seeing you again, Katie, I want to do it."

"Oh."

When she didn't say anything more, he wanted to hit the heel of his hand against his temple. How many times did he have to remind himself not to scare her off?

"I promised I wouldn't come on so strong and I just blew it," he muttered.

"The problem is," Katie finally replied slowly, "is that I feel the same way…and I'm scared."

Sam expected to hear anything but that. He wouldn't have been surprised if she'd hung up on him, but to admit that she was attracted to him? He idly noted that his hands were shaking.

"I'm scared, too, honey," he finally replied. "Like I told you—there haven't been many women in my life—and there's never been anyone like you."

"Well…I know you're just visiting our area…so I know I'm being forward about calling and suggesting we get together. But without the children, there are several places you might enjoy. Austin is known for its music. I thought I could introduce you to some of the nightlife."

He grinned, delighted that she'd called him. "I think that's a fine plan."

"I'll drive into town and meet you at the condo around one o'clock, okay?"

"Sure. Let's plan on eating, then you can show me around the area. I was getting bored on my own. This evening we might be able to find some of those music places I've read about in the paper."

As long as he kept his phone with him, he'd be fine.

She laughed. "You're so good for me, Sam."

"I'm glad. You've certainly added a sparkle to my existence, let me tell you."

"I'll see you soon."

He listened for her to hang up before he slowly returned the phone to the base. His heart was racing. He was acting as if he were facing one of his missions. Hell, he would probably feel calmer and much better prepared for a covert military assignment than he was at the idea of spending the day with Katie Callaway Henley.

Chapter 10

It was midafternoon when Clay and Pam turned into the tree-lined street of one of the small Texas towns scattered throughout the Hill Country. They had chosen this particular town because it was almost the center of the area they intended to cover in their investigation.

"Oh, look, Clay," she said. "What an adorable bed-and-breakfast place."

"Exactly what I was looking for." He wheeled into the parking area next to the large, rambling house and stopped the truck.

"We're going to stay here?"

"These places are perfect for our cover. We can ask all kinds of questions and the owners are full of local information and folklore."

"And just what is our cover?"

He grinned at her. "Why, just what we look like. A couple who wants to spend more time together.

Of course we'll have to pretend to be married, but I promise you, this is the closest you'll get to marriage with me."

No expectations, he reminded himself. No reason to think there would ever be a future for them, but he fully intended to enjoy every day he spent with her.

Clay got out of the truck and walked around to Pam's side. After helping her out, he retained her hand, leading her up the flower-trimmed sidewalk and stairs to the porch and front door.

He stepped inside and rang the bell on the desk. A short, white-haired lady came bustling into the hallway.

"Welcome. May I help you?"

"Hi. I'm Clay Ramirez and this is my wife Pam. We thought we'd get away together for a long weekend, but since our decision was sudden, we didn't take time to make reservations. Would you happen to have a room available?"

The woman smiled. "Why, yes, we do. Let me take you upstairs and show you."

The room looked out over the backyard. It was obvious someone enjoyed gardening from the looks of all the flowers. The room itself wasn't large, but certainly adequate to their needs, with a small bathroom available.

Once he signed in and paid for the two nights, Clay got their bags from the truck. Pam was waiting when he returned to their room.

"Ramirez?" she asked.

"I'm using Mom's maiden name. Callaway always gets people to asking if I'm kin to the well-known Texas family."

"So what do we do now?"

"I figure we've got the rest of the afternoon to check out the area and see what we can find with some of the addresses given." He eyed the bed, then grinned at her. "Unless, of course, you would prefer—"

She gave him a long look, before her lips moved into an amused smile that had always made his heart race. "In your dreams, cowboy," she drawled. "I know it's going to be tough for you and that one track mind of yours, but we need to focus on the job at hand. I don't know about you, but I left too many pending files back at the office to linger on this assignment more than is absolutely necessary."

He scratched his chin thoughtfully. "Now that you mention it, given the choice of making love to you or tracking down whoever is behind all of this, I'd immediately choose work. Yep. No doubt about it. Work wins, hands down."

"You're hopeless, you know that, Callaway?" she replied, turning away and heading downstairs. Clay followed her, pleased to discover that somewhere along the way they had both lightened up about their relationship. They could even joke about it.

The truth was that he would choose being with Pam over anything else he could name. Not necessarily making love to her, but being close to her, being able to see her every day.

He could no longer kid himself about his feelings where she was concerned. His pride over the years had probably kept him from admitting to himself how much he'd loved her. How much he still loved her. Why else would her rejection of him have hurt him so deeply?

Things were different now. They were older and, hopefully, more mature. Suddenly feeling more optimistic about his life for the first time in a long while, Clay found himself whistling as he climbed into the truck and settled next to Pam as they started their search for possible suspects.

Sam heard Katie's tap on the door and glanced at his watch. She was right on time. He hurried to the door and opened it, then blinked. She'd pulled out all the stops. She had on a green sheath that lovingly caressed her curving figure and complemented her dark red hair.

Katie certainly didn't look like anyone's mother today. It took all the control in Sam's possession not to pick her up and carry her to bed right then. Instead, he stepped back and motioned for her to enter.

"Wow," he murmured half under his breath as she walked past, her scent wafting seductively around him, luring him to follow her. "Double wow," he added.

She smiled up at him and said, "Thank you very much. It was fun to have the time to get ready without making sure the girls were occupied. Of course I miss them, but there are times when I like to think of myself as more than the mother of twins."

"I'll freely admit that wasn't the first thought that crossed my mind when I opened the door—aah, here's the mother of twins come to see me."

She laughed and waited while he closed the door before she ventured into the living room. "I love this place. It reminds me so much of my mother."

She looked around at him. "They mentioned getting together sometime this weekend. So if you're available..." She let her sentence trail off and watched him.

"I'll be here," he said. "Your dad mentioned that they live not far from Canyon Lake. Is that close to Austin?"

"It's about an hour's drive." She walked over to the window and peered out as though she'd never seen the view before. In a casual tone, she said, "I haven't told anyone in the family that I've been seeing you." She turned and looked at him. "I've rather enjoyed having a secret life that didn't include anyone else. However, I'd like for you to spend some time with them if you don't mind."

Sam wondered what Cole Callaway would think if he knew Sam was spending part of his time on this assignment with his daughter. He had a hunch Cole wouldn't be too impressed.

Sam wished he understood this overpowering need he had to see Katie as often as possible. His behavior was totally out of character and he knew it. He just didn't know what to do about it. He wasn't neglecting the mission he was on. He just ignored his need for sleep.

"I'd enjoy getting to know your family better," he replied.

She smiled, her face glowing. "I'm glad."

He knew if he didn't get her away from the privacy of the place, he would be in big trouble. "Shall we go?"

"Oh! Guess we'd better. I have a list of things to show you in and around Austin—the University of Texas campus, Barton Springs pool, some of the gardens, the state cemetery. If you want to, we could drive to Waco and go through the Texas Rangers museum. Not to be confused with the ball team."

"Lead on. We'll play tourist today."

"Or—if you want to drive into San Antonio, we could visit the River Walk, see the Alamo, that sort of thing."

He took her hand and stroked her knuckles with his thumb. "Whatever you want to do is fine with me."

When they reached the parking area, Sam helped Katie into his car, then followed her directions to the first stop on their tour.

Hours later they arrived back in Austin for dinner. Sam didn't pay much attention to the restaurant, once they arrived and ordered, or to the food placed in front of him. However, he could have described everything about Katie—

The way the fine hair around her face curled in ringlets;

the way her cheeks glowed with shyness or heightened in color when his gaze lingered longer than necessary;

the way her eyes sparkled in the candlelight;

the sound of her chuckle and, more rare, her irrepressible laughter.

It pained him to think that anyone or anything had ever caused her grief. She deserved to be loved and cherished.

Sam kept reminding himself during dinner that he lived in a different world from hers. He'd spent too many years alone to even contemplate changing and adjusting to a woman with two daughters.

None of his admonishments and reminders

seemed to be working. Instead, he agreed to her suggestion that they go somewhere where they could dance. Since he never danced, he knew that his willingness to make a fool of himself only showed how far gone he was.

Sam couldn't remember the last time he'd felt so lighthearted, laughingly following her instructions on how to do the Texas two-step, cotton-eyed Joe and other dance steps.

It was while they were leaving the dance floor some time later that Sam overheard someone mention the weather. He paused and asked, "Is there a problem?"

The man nodded. "We're under a weather advisory. One of those unpredictable spring storms coming this way—with heavy wind and rain, possible hail, predicted."

Sam turned to Katie and said, "Maybe we'd better head back home. I don't think we need to be out in something like that."

When they reached the car, he immediately headed toward Lakeway.

"My car's at the condo," she reminded him.

"Don't worry. We can always get it to you later. I'd rather not have you driving in weather like this."

Strong gusts of wind and splattering rain kept hitting the car. Katie peered through the windshield and shivered. "I'm the first to admit that I'd rather not be driving in this, but you'll be faced with driving in it on your way home." She gave him a worried glance.

"I doubt that it will last long. I can always wait it out at your place," he replied, then gave her a quick glance. "That is, if you don't mind."

The sound of distant thunder rumbled. "Actually, I'd like the company. Without the girls here, I don't have to pretend to be brave. The truth is, I'm deathly afraid of thunder-and-lightning storms. And we seem to have more than our fair share here in Texas."

No sooner than they reached the Austin suburb of Lakeway, lightning flashes were carving up the sky, accompanied by deep claps of thunder. When Sam pulled into the driveway, torrents of driving rain bounced around them. Hailstones added an ominous tone.

He stopped in front of the house. "Go ahead and pull around to the garage," Katie said. "I have the extra door opener in my purse, thank goodness." She reached into her small bag and lifted out the square box, pressing it. As they approached the three-car garage the middle door opened and he drove inside.

She punched the opener again and the door slid shut behind them.

Sam looked around. There were various tools and gardening implements inside. Otherwise the place was empty. "You have the one car?"

She nodded. "That's all I need. When Arthur lived here, he kept his SUV and his BMW here." She smiled. "At least we're dry. Shall we go inside?" she asked, opening her door.

The door into the house opened into a large utility room off the kitchen. This was a part of the house he hadn't seen. "You've got a very nice home here, Katie," Sam said, shutting the door behind him. "I'm impressed."

"It's more house than I need, but the only home

I've known, really." She paused by the counter. "Why don't you go on into the den and I'll make us some coffee." A loud clap of thunder pealed over them and Katie jumped. "I know I'm being so silly. The noise isn't going to hurt me."

"If you'd like, I can wait in here—"

"No. Please. I'll be all right." She took his hand and pressed it between hers. "I can't tell you how glad I am that you're here, though." With a grin, she let go of his hand and turned away. "Now, then. I'll have coffee for us in just a few minutes."

Sam wandered into the den where Katie had left a lamp on and walked over to the French doors. They had managed to arrive before the worst of the storm hit. As though thwarted by their escape, the storm's fury raged outside. Wind and hail swept across the back lawn, scattering the chairs and table on the patio. The hail quickly covered the ground in a layer of ice. Lightning blazed across the sky like a multitude of strobe lights, almost blinding him with the never-ebbing brightness.

The lights flickered inside the house, then went out.

He heard a crash in the kitchen. All at once the glow from the lightning was a saving grace as he dashed back into the hall and rapidly reached the kitchen.

"Are you all right?" he asked, pausing in the doorway. Katie was a shadow beside the counter.

"Just clumsy, I'm afraid," she replied, trying to sound unaffected by the storm. It wasn't working. "I—uh—dropped one of the cups just as the light went off. At least I hadn't poured coffee into it."

He walked carefully over to where she stood. "Where's the broom? I'll sweep it up."

"You can't see anything now. I'll find some candles." He heard her pull open a couple of drawers, then give a quick sigh of satisfaction. Within a couple of minutes she'd lit two round candles several inches in diameter.

Sam went into the utility room and spotted the broom and dustpan. He quickly returned and swept up the broken pieces of ceramic.

Katie poured the coffee into a carafe, placed it on a tray with two cups. "Here, I'll carry that," he said. "Why don't you grab the candles and lead the way."

"Thank goodness the coffee had finished brewing before the electricity went out." Her voice shook despite the lightness of her tone.

"From the sound of things, I'd guess that lightning hit a transformer nearby."

He followed her into the den and watched as she set the candles on either end of the coffee table. He slid the tray down between them.

"Oh, I was going to get some cookies to go with the coffee," Katie said. Sam gently took her arm and sat down, pulling her into his arms.

"We don't need anything else, Katie. Just relax."

She sighed and slid her arms around his neck. "I'm so glad you're here," she whispered, hiding her face in his shoulder. "I'm such a big baby."

He smiled, enjoying the feel of her in his arms. He slipped his hand down to her ankle and gently removed her shoe. She chuckled and held up the other foot so he could rid her of the other shoe as well.

"I'm glad I'm here, too. I really enjoyed tonight. As you could tell, I've never spent much time dancing."

She lifted her head, her eyes sparkling in the candlelight. "You're very coordinated, you know. Within minutes, you were dancing like a pro."

He laughed. "We won't try to figure out what profession, okay?"

"I can't believe I just met you a few days ago," she said quietly. "I feel as though I've known you forever."

"Maybe we were acquainted on another level, at another time. When I first saw you, I immediately recognized you as someone very important to me."

She leaned over and kissed him lightly on the mouth, then pulled back to see his expression. "I feel the same way, Sam."

Another loud clap of thunder crashed nearby, causing the house to tremble. Katie let out a little squeak and buried her head in his shoulder once again.

Later, Sam would look back and realize that his mistake had been in thinking he could comfort her, could distract her, without becoming unbearably aroused. If only he hadn't kissed her, then maybe he wouldn't have lost control of his emotions.

But he did kiss her, and nothing was ever the same again.

The storm hit the Hill Country west of Austin several hours earlier. Clay and Pam raced the storm back to the bed-and-breakfast, barely reaching the front door before all hell turned loose—wind and rain mixed with hail. They were laughing and breathless by the time they reached their room.

"It's a good thing I saw those dark clouds forming this afternoon. I wouldn't have wanted to be out on the highway through all of this."

Thunder crashed, shaking the house.

Pam looked outside at the limbs of the trees in the backyard wildly swaying. "So much for heading back to Austin this evening. I have no desire to be out in that."

"Well, we're paid up for tonight. I thought we might need the extra day just in case."

She turned to him, her eyes shining. "I really think we're on to something, Clay. We've found the thread that links all these men together."

He nodded. "Yeah. I think Sam will be pleased. I figure the information can wait until we get back, though. This will blow over in a few hours. We can head back by morning."

He walked over to the window where she stood watching the fury of the storm whip through the area. He slid his arms around her waist. "In the meantime..." he murmured, nuzzling her neck, "I have just the plan to keep us from getting too bored while we wait."

She turned and slipped her arms around his neck. "I'm certainly open to suggestions," she replied in a whisper.

There was very little conversation after that. Pam enjoyed the moment, but she knew their problems were far from resolved. What did the future hold for her and Clay?

Chapter 11

Pam lost track of time. The storm had settled into a hard, driving rain as the afternoon went by. She knew she must have slept for a while, but now she was content to lie on Clay's shoulder and watch the rain hitting the windowpanes while she stayed close to the man who'd had such an impact on her life. Did she dare to stay so close to him? It took courage to fall in love. Could she risk it?

Clay stirred, arching his back into a lazy stretch. She turned her head and kissed his chest.

"Are you hungry?" he asked.

"A little. It's difficult to think about having to leave our comfortable nest and go out into this weather to find nourishment," she replied.

"Maybe if we wait awhile, the rain will let up."

"Or we'll get hungry enough to brave the elements," she said with a smile. "I was lying here thinking about when we were kids. I was so surprised when I heard that you chose the military as a career. You always seemed to rebel against everything anyone ever told you as far back as I can remember. I have trouble picturing you taking orders from anybody.''

Clay shifted, propping his pillow under his head. ''I guess I was pretty wild as a kid. I figure that was because I had to fight to keep from being dressed in frills and treated like my sisters' baby doll when I was little.''

''I never have asked you what it was like having three sisters, growing up in a warm, happy family.''

''You were there. You saw what it was like. Noisy, as I recall.''

''What I saw was a loving family who enjoyed one another. The noise came from laughter and teasing and joy.''

''What was *your* home like?''

She shrugged. ''Very quiet. Dad was always busy when he was at the house. When he wasn't, the housekeeper preferred not to have noise of any kind. Not even music.''

''It was your house. Why didn't you ignore her?''

''Because then I would have gotten one of those sad-faced lectures from my dad, wondering why I was causing so many problems when it wasn't all that important.''

''No wonder you liked coming out to our place.''

She smiled. ''Yes. I'll never forget the first time Kerry took me home with her. I suppose your parents and my dad had discussed the length of the stay. All I knew was that I was to spend spring break with you. She had twin beds and we'd go to bed and talk for hours. It was what I imagined having a sister would be like.''

"How old were you, do you recall?"

"Eight. We were in the third grade. I remember your mother always picked you up after school, rather than let all of you ride the bus."

He nodded. "Yeah. I'd forgotten about that."

"You'd all go running to the car when she arrived, looking happy."

"Well, why wouldn't we? School was over for the day. It was playtime!"

"The man of the couple who watched over me when my dad was away would be there for me. It wasn't the same."

"I imagine you were lonely."

"It got better after my dad allowed me to stay with your family when he needed to be gone. I used to feel guilty about being so happy when he had to leave. I know he did the best he could, taking care of a child on his own. I've never blamed him for what he had to do to take care of me."

"Do you see much of him these days?"

"Not really. We're both busy with our own lives."

"I would hope that he forgave you for standing up to him and doing what you wanted with your life."

"He's never said. There's a cynical part of me that believes he's never forgiven me for not making the Callaway clan part of his extended family. I'm sure he thought it would be an asset to his political career."

"You're right. That is a cynical view of the man."

"I've never viewed him in quite the same light after I read Mother's diaries. I got an entirely different picture of him. I know she loved him, but she had to give up so many of her dreams in order to fit in with his. He'd gotten so used to getting his own way over the years that by the time I tried to reason with him, he'd become a tyrant, unwilling to listen to anything I said."

"He must have, or he would have forced you into marrying me."

"That's why I spoke to you first. By the time he knew about it, the damage had already been done. I knew you would never consider marrying me after that."

"You're right about that." He slid his hand up and down her arm in a slow, stroking movement. "If anyone back then had suggested that I would be spending a lazy, rainy afternoon in bed with you after all these years I would have thought he was out of his mind."

She turned so that she was facing him. "Maybe we're the ones who are out of our minds, have you ever thought of that?"

"I've considered it a time or two, yes."

"I'm not sure what we're doing here together."

"Circumstances brought us to this point. The rest was our own reactions to each other. The chemistry is pretty powerful."

"But what's going to happen when we've finished this assignment?"

He pulled her closer and began to kiss her. Between kisses he said, "We'll go back to our previous assignments with much better memories of each other."

Pam knew that was more than she deserved, but oh, how she was beginning to wish for so much more.

A lamp suddenly flashed on, waking Sam from a sound sleep. He blinked, looking around the room to get his bearings. He and Katie were curled together on the comfortable sofa. He glanced down and found that the light hadn't disturbed her. She appeared blissfully asleep, her arms wrapped snugly around him.

He glanced over at the anniversary clock on the mantel. It was almost three-thirty. Rain still beat heavily on the patio outside the French doors.

As though finally becoming aware of the change, Katie's eyes slowly opened. She stared blankly at him for a moment before her sleepy expression sharpened to surprise.

"Oh, my," she whispered, her face suddenly going a rosy hue.

"At least 'oh my,'" he responded wryly.

She gave him her enchanting smile, the one that had made him lose his head and pursue her. It was still as lethal to his peace of mind as ever. "I'm glad you didn't leave," she said.

He kissed the tip of her nose. "I'd be lying if I didn't agree with that sentiment."

"We'd be much more comfortable upstairs in bed."

"That's hard to imagine."

She sighed and absently stroked her fingers across his bare chest. "Well, at least there we might have a little more room. I must be heavy, sprawled across you like this."

"I like it."

She shifted slightly, causing his insatiable passion to stir. "Mmm," she murmured, her grin picking up a slightly impish and wicked slant.

"I have no control over the way parts of me respond to you. Just ignore him."

"Him?" she repeated, laughing. "You've given him a gender?"

"No, his gender is obvious. He just seems to have a mind of his own. If the decision had been left up to me, I would have remained a perfect gentleman and gone home at a reasonable hour."

"I see," she said solemnly. "I'm glad he overruled your decision."

He hugged her to his chest. "Ah, Katie, what am I going to do about you?" She slid to his side, then sat up beside him. Her bare breasts looked lusciously delectable. Without conscious volition he raised his hand and took the weight of one of them in his palm, caressing her with his fingers. "You are so beautiful."

"You make me feel beautiful, Sam. I've never felt so admired and treasured before." She stood and held out her hand. "Let's go to bed, okay?"

Without saying anything, he gathered his clothes, causing her to hastily pick up hers as well, and followed her upstairs to her bedroom.

A night-light shone through the bathroom door off her bedroom, giving off enough light for him to make out the furniture arranged in the room. She placed her clothes on a chair, motioned for him to do the same, then took his hand and led him into the bathroom.

Once inside she leaned into the glass-walled

shower and turned it on. She waited until the water warmed, then she stepped inside and, still holding his hand, coaxed him into joining her.

Sam wondered if he would wake up and find that he was back at the condo, and that all of this had been a dream. If that's what it was, he wasn't ready to wake up just yet.

He picked up the soap and began to lather her body, turning her as necessary, until she was covered in tiny bubbles. He stood with the spray hitting his back, blocking it from her. Her nipples had hardened at his first touch and now peaked precociously through the sudsy film. He groaned with the effort of restraining himself from lifting her and allowing her to wrap her legs around his waist.

"Now it's my turn," she said, sounding more than a little breathless. Unfortunately for his self-control she immediately started with the most obvious protrusion on his body.

"Uh, Katie, maybe you'd better begin somewhere else." She released him with obvious reluctance and he turned his back to her, needing the sensation of water hitting his chest to concentrate on rather than her delicate touch as her hands slid over his back.

By the time they had finally rinsed off, Sam was quivering. He shut off the water and stepped out of the shower. By the time she followed, he had a large towel in his hands and briskly dried her off. She reached for another towel, but he was too fast for her. He dried himself in record time, scooped her up in his arms and strode to the bed in the other room.

No sooner had they hit the surface than he was inside her, all restraint gone.

She didn't seem to mind. Not at all.

The doorbell woke them several hours later. Katie glanced at the clock. "Who in the world would be here this early in the morning?" she muttered, half-asleep. "It's barely daylight." She got out of bed and peered out the window at the driveway.

She gasped, causing Sam to come fully awake and sit up. "What's wrong?"

Katie turned around, her face pale. "I don't know. But there's a police car in the driveway. Oh, no! Something must have happened to the girls...or my parents!"

He threw off the covers. "Don't panic. I'll go down with you."

She'd already run to the closet and was pulling on a robe. He pulled on his pants and shirt, automatically tucking it in after years of military life. He found his socks and was already dressed by the time she had combed her hair out of her face.

"Good grief. How did you get dressed so fast?"

He shrugged. "Habit, I guess."

He followed her down the stairs and waited there while she went to the door. The bell had rung twice more by the time she opened the door.

"Yes?" she asked. Sam could see how tensely she was holding herself, braced for bad news.

"Are you Kathleen Henley?"

"Yes. What's happened?"

Sam stepped away from the stairs so that he could see who was at the door. There were two men—one in uniform, the other in a jacket and slacks.

"I'm sorry to disturb you so early in the morning, Mrs. Henley. I'm Detective Salazar and I need to ask you a few questions. May we come in?"

Sam knew the minute that Salazar spotted him in

the hallway. Sam waited to see what Katie would do.

"Uh, yes, sir. I don't understand. Is it my family?"

The two men walked in. Sam stepped forward and said, "Sam Carruthers. I'm a friend of Katie's."

The fact that they had found him in her home at six o'clock in the morning gave them plenty of evidence that the relationship was more than friendship.

Salazar shook his hand and said, "This is Officer Carter." The other man nodded. Salazar glanced around the hallway, then asked, "Is there a place where we could talk for a few moments, Mrs. Henley?"

"Oh! Yes, of course. This way, please," she said, heading toward the den. Sam hoped to hell they'd picked up all their clothing. This visit wasn't a social one. He would hate to have some intimate apparel lying in the den for these men to speculate on.

Once they were seated, Salazar said, "When was the last time you saw your husband, Mrs. Henley?"

"My husband? I'm not married, Detective."

Sam had sat down beside her to let her know he was there for her, but he made no effort to touch her.

"Arthur Henley is not your husband?" the detective asked.

"He's my ex-husband. We were divorced several months ago. Why? What has he done?"

He lifted his brow quizzically at her question. "His automobile was found abandoned on a rural lane about three o'clock this morning."

"Have you called his home? Maybe it broke down."

"Actually, we have checked his apartment. You see, Mrs. Henley, there was blood on the front seat of the car. Fresh blood. It seems that your husband—that is, your ex-husband, is missing. We're hoping you can help us determine what happened to him."

Chapter 12

The continual ringing of the phone finally awakened Allison Callaway enough for her to realize that Cole wasn't still asleep beside her. She crawled across the massive bed that she had shared with her husband for years and answered it with a soft hello.

"Mom? Is Dad there?" she heard Katie say.

Allison looked at the clock beside the bed. It was barely seven o'clock on a Sunday morning, not the time Allison would expect her daughter to be calling. "Uh, yes, honey. I believe he's in the shower. What's wrong?"

"Oh, Mom. Everything is such a muddle. The police are here and Arthur is missing and they must think that I——" Allison heard a soft sob from her daughter.

"Hold on, baby, I'll get your dad for you."

She threw the covers back and raced across the room. She heard the water shut off just as she pushed open the bathroom door. "Cole! Katie's on the phone. Something's happened to Arthur and the police are there asking all kinds of questions."

Cole stepped out of the shower and grabbed a towel, wrapping it around his waist. Allison followed him back into the bedroom and hovered while he talked to Katie. He asked terse questions, then listened as she made lengthy explanations.

Only then did Allison realize that she was standing there nude. She'd gone to bed in her nightie but Cole had been quick to remove it from her. She hadn't even missed it until now. She spun away and hurried to the closet. Whatever had happened, she knew that Cole would want to go to Austin immediately. Nobody messed with any of his children without his getting right in the middle of the situation…and Katie was his precious daughter. She almost felt sorry for whoever it was that had upset Katie.

Arthur was missing?

Normally, Allison could care less. She didn't like the man and was relieved when Katie had finally gotten rid of him. But what could be going on now that would involve her?

As soon as Cole finished the call, he put in a call to Cameron, tersely giving the details as he knew them and asking him to meet him at Katie's house. Next he called Cody.

Cody and Carina were sound asleep at their home in San Antonio when the phone rang. Cody caught it on the second ring.

"This had better be urgent," he muttered into the phone.

"It is," Cole replied, causing Cody to jackknife into a sitting position.

"What's up?"

"I just got a call from Katie. Arthur Henley's turned up missing and the police suspect foul play. They're at her place right now. They're putting her through a heavy barrage of questions. She says they're acting as if she's not telling them everything. I don't like the sound of this at all. I've already contacted Cameron. Thought you might want to be there, too."

"They don't actually suspect Katie of harming him in some way, do they?" Cody asked incredulously.

"I can't tell from what she told me on the phone. She was upset but trying to hide it. She kept saying she was glad the girls weren't there when the police arrived. She doesn't want them upset."

Cody rubbed his hand over his face. "Damn right I'll be there. I shouldn't be much more than an hour. I'm really sorry to hear about Arthur for Katie's sake."

"Yeah. Me, too. I know she loved him and he's still the father of her daughters, but he really is a worthless piece of cow dung."

"Spoken like a true protective father."

"Maybe so. But we're still finding discrepancies in the accounting systems he'd set up. When I can gather enough proof to show that idiot was skimming money from the companies, if he's still alive, he's going to wish he was dead by the time I get through with him."

* * *

"That's my uncle Cameron's car," Katie said, peering out the window of the dining room.

"Do you want me to stay?" Sam asked.

She turned to him. "I know you want to go home and change clothes. I can't thank you enough for staying with me while the police were here."

"Actually, I'm part of any case they attempt to make against you, Katie. I'm your alibi."

She put her arms around him and allowed her head to rest on his chest for a moment. "I'm so sorry to involve you in all of this."

He held her close, not wanting to let her go. But he knew that her family was gathering around her now. It was time for him to step back.

"I'll go get cleaned up, then stop and get some muffins and rolls, maybe some doughnuts for breakfast. I should be back within the hour."

She went up on tiptoe and kissed his cheek. "Thank you."

Katie followed as he went through the kitchen and into the garage for the car. So much had happened since they'd arrived the night before. For that matter, Katie's car was still at the condo.

He turned to her. "If you'll give me the keys to your car, I'll drive it back for you."

"I hadn't even thought about that." She reached for her purse where she'd laid it on the counter the night before. "Here. And thank you for remembering."

When Sam reached the condo he checked the time and decided to contact Clay. He needed to know about this latest development.

The phone rang several times before Clay answered in a sleepy voice. "Callaway," he said in a graveled voice.

"This is Carruthers."

Clay immediately sounded more alert. "Yes, sir. We're coming back in this morning. I must have overslept. We figured to report in person, but if you need the information before—"

"Whoa, soldier, slow down for a moment. That isn't why I called."

He was met with a silence that would have amused him under different circumstances. "I wanted to let you know that Arthur Henley is missing and the police are treating it as foul play."

"Why?"

"Because his car was found abandoned and there was blood. They found a letter in the glove compartment from Katie that contained some inflammatory remarks, so she was one of the first people they contacted. Their theory is that he was attacked and removed from the scene. The car was taken to an isolated area and abandoned in a ravine with heavy brush. It was sheer luck that a passing motorist caught the gleam of the reflector on the taillight some time after midnight and phoned it in."

"Well, this certainly puts a different light on things, doesn't it?" Clay said with irritation. "How did you hear about it?"

Sam didn't answer right away. There was no getting around that question. He'd already told the police. Everyone else would eventually know about it. He rubbed his hand over his face. So much for keeping a low profile with this family, he thought ruefully.

"Sam?"

"I'm here. I—uh—I was with Katie when the police contacted her early this morning."

Another silence replaced the conversation before Clay finally said with more than a hint of awkwardness, "Oh. Well. That's good to know. Katie shouldn't have had to face that kind of news alone. How is she taking it?"

"She's pretty shaken. I understand her dad and his brothers should be with her by now."

"Good. That's—uh—that's good."

"I'm going back over there, and I wanted you to know where I'd be if I'm not here when you return. You say you expect to come in this morning?"

"Uh, yes, sir."

"You feel the trip was worthwhile?"

"I sure do. The problem will be finding the evidence to prove what we've got. It's all pretty circumstantial at the moment."

"Give me a call at Katie's when you get here and I'll meet you for the conference. I'll check with Joe and see how he's made out. Maybe we can piece this thing out before the day's over."

"Sounds good to me," Clay said. "See you soon."

Clay hung up his phone and turned to Pam. "Well, that really tears it."

"What happened?"

"Our prime suspect has just turned up missing."

Cole Callaway sat in the study of his old home that now belonged to Katie, using the phone. He was more than a little frustrated that the police had already left by the time any of the Callaways had reached there. But maybe that was a good sign.

Maybe she'd given them satisfactory answers, despite what she'd felt was their attitude toward her. Just maybe they weren't hassling his daughter about any of this.

She seemed shaken, but calm enough by the time he arrived. Cameron had gotten the information he needed to go to the police and find out what he could.

Cody was still there, waiting in the den to see what he could do, if anything, to help. Cole had spoken to several people, including a private investigator he'd used from time to time, about tracing Arthur's steps. Somebody was bound to have seen him. There was a reason for his disappearance. Cole considered the fact that they hadn't found his body a good sign.

He might be being held somewhere. Maybe this was a simple kidnapping. Who knew? The phone might ring with instructions about payoffs. It didn't matter what he thought about Henley, the man was the father of his granddaughters. He'd do whatever was necessary to keep him from harm.

If the man was still alive.

Cole had just managed to drop the phone back into the receiver and look around the room with a sense of nostalgia when he heard the doorbell ring.

If that was another house call from the police, he was going to give them hell for harassment. Surely there was somebody else besides Katie who hadn't been totally enthralled by Arthur Henley. Why weren't they filling a stadium or two with the people who could see through all that smarmy charm?

He pushed back in the chair and stood, ready to defend his daughter from any more attacks on her veracity. When he stepped out into the hallway, Cole froze, unable to believe what he was seeing.

There…just inside the front hallway…was a scene he could never have imagined, regardless of any provocation. His daughter, Katie, his one and only daughter, the absolute love of his middle age, was wrapped in the arms of Lieutenant Colonel Sam Carruthers, kissing the holy heck out of him, if Cole was any judge. Mouth-to-mouth resuscitation couldn't have been more intense. They were kissing as though their very lives depended on it.

Every one of his protective instincts came roaring out to do full battle against the invading marauder of his daughter's castle.

He happened to know for a fact that the good colonel had been in Texas barely a week. In fact, the first coherent thought Cole managed to have was to wonder why he'd allowed the man on the company plane with his family in the first place, if this was the way he was going to treat his daughter.

A blind man could tell from that steamy embrace that they had done more during this past week than just meet. Hell's bells, he was wondering if he should dig out his shotgun right now and insist on an immediate ceremony by clergy.

Cole continued toward the front of the house, realizing as he did so that neither one of them had heard his approach. He doubted anything less than a hand grenade exploding at their feet would have gained their attention.

When he reached the foot of the stairs, he leaned against the balustrade, crossed his arms and loudly cleared his throat.

Now, that certainly got their attention, he noticed.

They sprang away from each other quite nicely— almost reacting as if that hand grenade had indeed gone off.

Both of them looked at him with more than a hint of unease in their expressions. Sam, especially, looked uncomfortable, but why wouldn't he, since there was no way in hell he could camouflage his arousal, or the fact that both of them were having trouble catching their breath.

Hell, at the rate they'd been going, it was a damned good thing he'd interrupted them before they'd gotten horizontal!

"Oh, hi, Daddy. I thought you were still on the phone," Katie said, brushing a wisp of hair from her face.

"Did you?" he asked softly.

"I want you to meet...uh...I mean, I believe you know Sam Car—"

"I've already met the colonel, thank you," Cole replied without changing his lounging position against the first baluster.

Katie gaped at him. "The colonel? Oh, you must be mistaken. Sam's just—"

Cole watched with a great deal of interest as Sam reached over and grasped Katie's hand—in what Cole considered to be a much too possessive manner—and said, "Your father's right, Katie. I'm a lieutenant colonel in the army, and I'm here in Texas doing more than just seeing the sights on a vacation."

"A good deal more, if that spectacle I just witnessed was any indication," Cole drawled.

Katie looked bewildered. Cole would have been glad to explain to his treasured daughter who Sam

Carruthers was, but she didn't give him the opportunity. No, she turned to Sam for answers, and Cole had a sinking suspicion that the man who could command his daughter's happiness and all her love had finally walked into her life.

Arthur Henley had never been that man. Cole really hadn't given the idea much thought before...until now, when he saw these two people together. Something had occurred, and he had a strong hunch that part of it may have been sex—but not all—that had bonded them together. He was witnessing something that humbled him. These two people had been joined as one without the help of formal rituals performed before doting family members.

For the first time since he'd held her in his hands as a newborn, Cole felt the loss of his daughter.

"I'm sorry I didn't tell you before," Sam was saying in a low voice to Katie. "I was ordered to tell no one of my reason for being here."

"But Daddy knows?" she asked in a puzzled voice.

Sam glanced at Cole before looking at her. "Yes. Your father is part of the reason I'm in Texas."

She dropped his hand as though she'd suddenly been burned. "I see," she said, stepping back from him.

His stern expression lightened slightly. "Actually, you don't, but after I've spoken to your dad, I'll explain everything to you, okay? That part of my life has nothing to do with you and me."

Cole could no longer play the part of the observer. "I take it there *is* a 'you and me,' as you put it?" Cole asked, biting off the words.

Katie's chin came up in a gesture Cole recognized as classic Katie with her back up. Allison always said that Katie had inherited her stubbornness from him, but since all of his was still intact, he had never been able to agree with Allison. But Katie *was* every bit as stubborn as he had ever thought of being when her mind was set on something.

This time it looked as if both her mind and her heart were set on the colonel.

"I'm in love with Sam," she said quietly.

Cole stoically watched as Sam put his arm around Katie. "The feeling's mutual," he said, watching Cole with a steadfast gaze that made Cole sigh.

"Well," Cole replied, "then the police should probably check to see where you were when Arthur Henley turned up missing. You've got a bigger motive to get rid of him than Katie does." Cole straightened and walked into the den, knowing they would follow him.

Cody glanced up from the television when Cole walked in. "What have you found out?"

Cole headed for the bar. He didn't care if it was barely the middle of the morning, he definitely needed a drink. "I think we're going to get an update from Sam on his deal," he said without turning around. "I haven't heard anything from Cameron yet. He was going to get a copy of the police report."

Cole kept his back to the room while he filled a glass with ice, then poured a shot of his favorite Scotch over it. He heard Sam and Katie speak to Cody, heard Cody turn off the television. There were the normal sounds of the couple settling into a seat-

ing arrangement, no doubt holding hands and thinking sweet thoughts about each other.

He wasn't certain why he felt so threatened by
the idea that Sam Carruthers was interested in his
daughter. He wanted her to be happy, and Arthur
Henley had certainly done everything he could to
ruin any chance of that during their marriage.

But Sam Carruthers? He was hard-bitten career
military and tough as old boot leather. Somehow
Cole couldn't picture him as a family man.

But it wasn't up to him, Cole knew, to decide
what was best for his beloved daughter. He couldn't
protect her from hurt like he had when she was a
child. He could no longer kiss her wounds and make
them better.

Maybe, just maybe, this man would be able to do
that for her. The thought caused his mood to lighten
somewhat. He took a long drink before he turned
around and faced them. Sure enough, they sat side
by side on the sofa. Sam held her hand between both
of his. Her chin was still slightly elevated, which
signaled to Cole that his daughter wasn't about to
take anything from him, father or not.

On the other hand, Sam's gaze communicated his
complete understanding of Cole's feelings at the
moment, which unnerved Cole a little. He didn't
particularly want anyone to know what he was feeling, because he wasn't particularly proud of his reaction to this unexpected news.

Allison would probably point out to him later that
he hadn't handled the matter well.

Knowing that she would be right didn't appease
him in the slightest.

"If you don't mind," Sam said to the two men,

"I'd like to have Katie sit in on what I'm planning to discuss with you. It's been difficult not being able to tell her of the ongoing investigation, but I was following orders. Since you chose to let her know who I am, then I believe it's now necessary for her to know why I'm here."

Cole sat down across from them near Cody in one of the comfortable overstuffed chairs and nodded for Sam to go ahead. But before Sam could say anything more, Katie spoke.

"For your information, Daddy, the police have already questioned Sam about his whereabouts last night."

Cole waved his hand in a deprecating manner. "I'm sorry, honey. That was a cheap shot and uncalled for." He looked at Sam. "I apologize."

She ignored his explanation with one of her own. "Just so you know, Sam was with me from one o'clock yesterday afternoon until the police arrived here shortly after daylight this morning."

All right, so she was going to wipe up the floor with her old dad's feelings, was she? He guessed he deserved that.

Cole took another sip from his drink before he said wryly, "Thank you for sharing, Katie, but that's way more information than I have any desire to know."

He noted with interest that Sam's lips twitched as if he was fighting to hold back a smile.

Cody didn't bother hiding his amusement. He laughed out loud.

Let him laugh, Cole thought to himself. Cody still had one daughter, his baby, who hadn't married yet. Cole had already seen how possessive Cody had been with his two older daughters. He hated to think what Cody would do when Denise decided to marry.

Cole took another sip of his drink and felt his tension slowly drain from his body. Despite everything he'd just learned, Cole knew that he liked Sam Carruthers. He couldn't fault him for falling in love with Katie. What father could? And he was definitely the kind of man Cole wanted on his side in a fight.

"So tell me what you've turned up," he asked, leaning forward and waiting to hear what Sam had to say.

Chapter 13

Sam hesitated a moment. He hadn't intended for Katie to hear his theories at this point in their relationship. If they proved to be accurate, then of course she would need to know, but he had hoped to protect her from any unnecessary pain.

Unfortunately, none of that could be helped now. When he saw her standing there in the doorway earlier, saw how she lit up at the sight of him—as if a high-watt bulb had suddenly been turned on inside of her—he had forgotten that her family was there, forgotten that someone might walk in and see them together. He'd forgotten everything but the look on her face. He'd never had anyone look at him like that before in his life.

Her reaction to him made him feel like a giant among men—that he could face and conquer anything.

Obviously.

Otherwise, a bit of sanity would have reminded him that her father was lurking somewhere in the house before he grabbed her.

"As you know, sir," he began, leaning forward and placing his palms together, "we've been doing a deep background check on all the current employees and recent former employees of the various companies owned and or operated by Callaway Enterprises."

Cole nodded. "Go ahead."

Sam glanced at Katie from the corner of his eye before continuing. "Several interesting items showed up in Arthur Henley's report."

Cole settled back into his chair and waited.

Sam continued. "He mentioned to me that he'd been in the navy and participated in part of the SEAL training."

Cole's brows rose. "I wasn't aware of that."

"He was particularly proficient during the explosives training. His instructor noted that he had an aptitude for underwater demolition as well as being able to rapidly set charges. His instructor was quite impressed with him."

"How interesting," Cole replied thoughtfully.

"With that knowledge, we felt it necessary to dig deeper into his life-style, his marriage—" Sam glanced quickly at Katie before he returned his gaze to Cole "—and the subsequent divorce. That's when we discovered that he'd been embezzling from your company."

Cole nodded once again. "Yeah. I had hoped that Katie wouldn't ever have to know about that, but it looks like his playing cutesy with the books was the least of his crimes. So you think he masterminded the explosions?"

"About three years ago he became involved with a disgruntled group of ex-military men here in Texas who think they could do a better job at running the government than the present administration. Various members of this group have been spotted near the areas where the explosions occurred at around the same time."

"There are always discontents around," Cody said, speaking up for the first time. "They do a lot of complaining, make threatening statements, then hide behind the idea of free speech. It really doesn't surprise me that Arthur would enjoy a group like that."

"It's my theory that this is where he got the extra manpower needed to set up a series of explosions all over the state at close to the same time. If we're looking for motive, I would say he's got a vendetta against the Callaways."

Katie had sat quietly through the conversation until now. "How horrible. You actually believe that Arthur was behind all of that?"

"It's a working theory, but it's the best one we've come up with so far. All the signs seem to point in his direction, at least until this latest news."

"Do you think one of his co-conspirators killed him?" she asked, her eyes reflecting her horror at the idea.

Sam took his time answering. "That's one possibility. Ever since I heard about his disappearance, and the letter found in the glove compartment, I've been thinking about several different theories."

Cody leaned forward. "What letter? I haven't heard about that."

Katie sighed. "It was an old letter I wrote to Arthur a couple of years ago. I was really angry with him and wrote this blistering attack, but I never gave it to him."

"Then what was it doing in his car?"

"Well, he found it in my desk not long before he moved out and asked me about it. I had no idea he kept it. I haven't the slightest idea why."

Sam said, "That letter was the reason the police showed up here so quickly. After Katie explained to them about when it was written and the circumstances surrounding it, I got to thinking about his reason for having it in the car in the first place. Why would he be carrying around something like that?"

Cole studied the melting ice in his glass. "Do you think he was trying to set her up in some way? That his disappearance was planned to implicate her?"

"I consider it a strong possibility."

Cole muttered an obscenity, then quickly apologized to Katie. "You know, you've got a good point. I wouldn't put it past him."

"If he is connected to the multiple bombings," Sam continued, "then all the state and federal investigators going over the various areas are bound to have made him and his buddies a little nervous."

"Surely they didn't think we would ignore what happened?" Cody asked.

"No, but I think something has spooked him. If that's the case, he's gone to ground with a last little salute to the family, by leaving a trail that might lead investigators to Katie. Because of his connections to your family with its high visibility in the state, it's my guess that if he is behind this, he's hoping the media will have a field day speculating on why he disappeared and what might have happened to him. It's my theory that he set the whole thing up and went to ground, hoping that Katie would be arrested at best, humiliated by all the speculation at worst.''

Cole nodded. "That sounds like something he's capable of doing, all right.''

Sam continued. "Over the past week, our team compiled a list of his friends—names and addresses, background checks, that sort of thing. If my theory holds up, then he could be hiding with one of them, waiting to see what havoc he can cause next.''

"What do you suggest we can do to help?'' Cody asked.

"At this point, we've got to wait and see what develops. When I spoke a few days ago to the group in Washington monitoring our progress, I told them the direction we were looking. None of their investigators had thought to check the man out because of his close connection to the family. He hasn't let many people know that he's no longer employed with your company or that he's been divorced.''

Katie asked, "What if someone else actually did this? Would they have killed him, do you think?''

"There's always that possibility,'' Sam replied. "He could have had a falling-out with these people. Now that he's served his usefulness, they may have considered him more of a liability.''

"In which case,'' Cody said, "having that letter found with the car would benefit them as much as it would Arthur.''

Katie shook her head. "I don't understand why

Arthur would have gotten involved with such a group.''

''I can,'' Cody said. ''To make himself feel important. He could brag about the connections he had, the inside knowledge he had. He could play the big man with them.''

Cole nodded. ''That would certainly fit with what I know about him.''

''Unfortunately,'' Katie admitted, ''it does.'' She closed her eyes. ''What am I going to tell the girls?''

Cole replied, ''Don't tell them anything until we know something for sure. From what you've told us, he doesn't see them very often, anyway. Wait until this matter's resolved, then we'll come up with something to say to them.''

''What is the next step?'' Cody asked, looking at Sam.

''One of the agencies investigating this situation will be given a list of the men we think are directly involved with Arthur. They're going to stake out various locations. My team is having a meeting at the condo this afternoon to go over that list and decide who needs to be watched. You might as well be there to hear it firsthand.''

Sam watched Cole and Cody take all of this in. They hadn't flinched, even though the news that a former member of the extended family might be behind all this must have hit them hard. He knew this couldn't be easy for either of them to hear. He didn't want to think what this must be doing to Katie.

Sam was relieved he hadn't needed to go into too much detail to back up the conclusions he and the team had drawn over the past few days. There was no reason to unnecessarily hurt Katie by revealing to her some of the less-savory aspects of the man's life they'd uncovered, including illegal behavior during the years he'd been married to her.

"When can they start the surveillance?" Cole asked.

"They hope to put it in place by tomorrow night at the latest, once we give them the places to watch. There are eight different suspicious people with whom he has been in close contact over the past several months. Two of them live in east Texas, one in south Texas, and the rest are here in the Hill Country."

"I'm surprised the government is willing to continue with the investigation if this turns out to be a grudge situation rather than a threat to national security," Cole said.

"Actually, they consider it both," Sam responded. "They've been keeping an eye on this particular group of quasi-military men for some time. Arthur may have played into their hands by joining the group. He was just what they'd been looking for—someone who knew the inside operations of many of your companies. Our concern is that they may be planning something even bigger in the future...unless we stop them now. If my theory is correct and we can find him alive, we're hoping to convince him to turn over evidence in exchange for a lesser sentence."

Cole reached for the phone. As he punched in a series of numbers, he said, "I need to tell Cameron about the meeting. He'll want to be in on it as well."

Sam turned to Katie and said in a low voice, "I've been hoping that I was wrong about all of this.

I'm so sorry that you're being dragged through anything more.''

"I'm already in the middle of it. So are the girls. If Arthur's involved in all of this, they need to catch him before anyone else gets hurt."

Cole was sharply questioning Cameron, then waiting in silence for some lengthy answers.

"I didn't want to lie to you, Katie," Sam said, speaking low. "The only thing that wasn't the truth about all I've told you about me is that I'm not retired military. I'm very much on active duty and here in Texas on assignment."

Her bottom lip quivered briefly before she managed a smile. "In the scheme of things, that's more of a fib, considering the kind of things Arthur used to expect me to believe."

"I didn't want to start out our relationship with your not knowing everything there is to know about me," he said.

"I'm afraid I don't understand why you'd want to have anything to do with me once all of this is over."

He smiled. "Then I guess I'll have to spend some time convincing you that I want to be a permanent part of your life."

Cole hung up the phone and looked at the two of them.

"Now that we have this situation moving forward, I think that maybe it's time you tell me what's going on with you two and where this relationship is headed."

"Dad! That's none of your business."

Sam smiled and said, "You want to know if my intentions are honorable, is that it?"

"You're damn right," Cole replied.

Cody stood and said, "Well, this is one conversation I don't need to be in on. So I'll see you later today at the condo." Sam and Cole had also stood. Cody shook Sam's hand. "I appreciate your diligence in this matter, Colonel." He turned to Cole and said, "Try to cut him a little slack, okay, bro?"

Cole watched his youngest brother leave the room, thinking, *That was one hell of a good exit line.* He'd better start back-pedaling pretty fast or Allison would have his head.

Chapter 14

When Clay and Pam entered the condo on Sunday afternoon, the first person he saw was his dad. He paused in the entry to the large living area and looked around in surprise. His uncles Cameron and Cole were also there.

"It looks like the gathering of the clan," Clay said with a smile. "I guess things are really heating up."

Pam said, "If you gentlemen will excuse me, there are some things I need to do in my office before we start our meeting."

Clay looked around. "Where's Sam?"

Cole answered. "He's in the dining room on the phone with Joe. Good to see you again."

Cody looked his son up and down. "You look a lot better than the last time I saw you—was it only a week ago?"

"Well, I've managed to get a little more sleep

than I'd had in a while before I managed to get to Texas." He sat down on the sofa. "Any news on Henley?"

Cameron answered. "No. I've been down to the police department and read all the reports filed in the matter, but until the lab work gets back on samples taken inside his car, there really isn't much to report."

"How's Katie taking it?"

"Quite well," Cole replied, "given the circumstances." He glanced toward the other room before adding, "Your leader seems to be giving her comfort through all of this."

Clay grinned. "And how do you feel about that?"

Cole shrugged. "I want to see Katie happy. I'm not too sure that Carruthers won't end up breaking her heart, but I don't see where there's much I can do about the situation."

Cody looked at his son. "How's your heart doing these days, son?"

Clay frowned. "There's nothing wrong with my heart. What are you talking about?"

Cody nodded toward the hallway. "Has it helped to see Pamela again after all these years?"

"I suppose. It helped me to understand that I'm no longer that kid who thought his life was over when she changed her mind about marriage. Nobody will ever be able to get to me like that again."

"Not even Pam?" Cody asked softly.

Clay's short laugh was a little harsh. "*Especially* not Pam. I guess what I've realized is what a favor she did both of us, calling off the wedding before the situation became intolerable."

"So you have no feelings for her now?"

Clay shrugged. "We've known each other since we were kids, so we have a lot of shared history."

"But you don't see a future together?"

"Hell, Dad, I don't ever look to the future for anything. My life is just the way I like it."

Pam was thankful that she had paused in the hallway to be sure she wouldn't be interrupting a family conversation. As it turned out, she would have. The fact that the conversation was about her would have embarrassed all of them if she had walked into the room.

She wasn't surprised by Clay's remarks. His attitude toward her this past week had already told her that once this assignment was completed, she wouldn't see him again. She tried to convince herself that she wasn't hurt by his attitude. She was a grown woman now. She was strong. Independent. She didn't need a mate to complete her.

Need wasn't the same as wanting, of course. There was only one man in her entire life that she had ever wanted. However, she had proved to herself and everyone else that she could get along without him.

The problem with their present situation was that it wasn't part of the real world. They were working undercover, pretending to be other people. None of it was real.

Except for her response to him. That was very real. Her feelings for the man had never changed. Even when she knew that marrying him would be the biggest mistake of her life, Pam had never kidded herself about her love for him.

Nothing had really changed this week. Nothing that she couldn't live with.

Pam leaned against the wall of the hallway, wondering when she could safely walk into the other room. She heard Sam say to the others, "All right, Joe will be here shortly. Let's go ahead and get started with the meeting."

That was her cue to enter this male-dominated meeting and hold her own.

It was dark by the time the meeting ended. New strategy had been set out.

The Callaway brothers had returned home to their wives. Joe had arrived without his partner, who had returned to his previous assignment. Now it was the four of them left in the condo, looking at the final plans.

After Clay's report of what he and Pam had found, Sam decided that before they called for reinforcements, the three men would do a reconnaissance of the area where a man by the name of Dirk Davis lived.

It was a ranch in the western part of the Hill Country and appeared to have too much security surrounding what should have been a sheep and cattle ranch. Clay and Pam hadn't lingered as they drove the narrow country road past the entrance, but they'd seen the armed guards at the gate.

Sam decided that he, Clay and Joe would maneuver their way onto the property to see what was being so closely guarded. Since they had no legal reason to be there, he thought it better not to get the authorities investigating the case involved just yet. He was counting on the fact that if they were discovered, whatever was going on at the ranch would stop the owners from turning them over to the local police. But just because they wouldn't turn them over didn't mean they wouldn't shoot them.

Sam assigned Pam the duty of staying with Katie while the men were gone. There was still hope that in the next several hours she might receive a phone call from either Arthur or, if he was being held somewhere, his abductors. Mainly, though, he didn't want Katie to be alone.

Allison, with Cole's blessing, had volunteered to pick up the twins at Trish's home and keep them until some news arrived about Arthur.

Pam was to go to Katie's house first thing in the morning. The men intended to catch a few hours of sleep, then travel west into the Hill Country. Once Sam saw the area, he would be better able to map out a plan and strategy for breaching the security of the place.

She recognized that the men were trained for this kind of operation and she wasn't, therefore she made no audible objection to the plan, even though she felt as if she'd been assigned a baby-sitting job.

She also recognized that she was terrified at the idea that Clay might be shot. She reminded herself of his present occupation. His assignments were always potentially life threatening—and he'd survived. So she told herself that there was no reason for her to worry about the man.

Her calm reasoning did nothing to prevent her worrying. She knew what it was like to lose someone she loved.

She heard him stirring around when she went past his room on her way to the kitchen later that evening. She got her glass of water and returned down the hallway to her bedroom. As she passed his door again, her hand, over which she obviously had no control, tapped lightly on the wooden frame.

He must have been standing nearby because the door immediately opened. When he saw her standing there, he nabbed her free hand and pulled her inside. Before she had a chance to speak, he removed the glass from her hand, placed it on a nearby table and pulled her into his arms.

The kiss he gave her wiped out any stray thoughts that might have been drifting around in her head. He always seemed to have this effect on her. Her knees gave way, but it didn't matter, since he held her tightly against him. Her collapse must have been a signal to him because he scooped her up, without lessening the searing kiss, and carried her to the bed.

It wasn't fair that anyone should have such an effect on her. Somehow she would have to devise a plan to guard against such a reaction…much later, when her brain decided to function once again.

In the meantime, her emotions and her body reigned supreme. They frantically pulled at each other's clothing. She dimly heard something rip, but didn't care as long as the offending article was no longer a barrier to their getting close to each other.

She couldn't seem to touch him enough, her hands sliding over his spine, then up his chest before moving to his back once again. They rolled until Clay lay flat on his back. They took care of protection, then Pam straddled him, breathlessly laughing as she enjoyed having control of their passion.

He arched and she took him to the hilt, riding him, her heart racing, her breathing staggered. He slipped his hands to either side of her hips, assisting her in keeping the fast rhythm they both seemed to demand. They shared the explosive climax, their mouths welded together to muffle their mutual cries.

Pam collapsed on his chest, wondering if she would ever be able to breathe normally again, or if her heart would be able to stand the strain of her racing heartbeats.

After what seemed like hours but in reality was probably five or ten minutes, Clay murmured, "Thank you for bringing me some water. I can certainly use it."

She raised her head and stared at him in surprise. Her shift allowed him to reach for the water and take several swallows before she grabbed it away from him. "I didn't bring that for you! That was mine!" she replied, laughing.

Pam straightened so that she was now seated vertically on him. He held her where she was with him still deep inside of her. "Where are you going?"

"To bed."

"You're here."

She slowly lifted away from him, causing Clay to groan his protest. She frowned at him. "You've got to get some sleep. Didn't I hear Sam say you'd leave at four o'clock?"

"I can sleep just fine with you right here."

"And what am I supposed to say if he finds me in here with you?"

"Why should he? He doesn't do a room check, you know. Besides, what difference does it make if he knows we're together?"

She lay back beside him and reached over and turned off the light. When he turned toward her, he pulled her into his curled body, her back against his chest, and sighed with unabashed contentment. He murmured something that sounded like "good night" and was immediately asleep.

Pam had to admit, at least to herself, that she felt quite comfortable with Clay's arm across her, holding her close. She smiled at the memory of his hauling her into his room and bed without a word. They were past talking about their reactions to each other. From what she had overheard him say to his father, he had no intention of discussing a future with her.

Perhaps she was taking the coward's way out by not broaching the subject herself. *Perhaps? Who are you kidding? You aren't sure which you would find scarier—that he might suggest marriage or that he might suggest you not see each other after this assignment is completed.*

She closed her eyes, unable to explore either option at the moment.

The following morning, Pam drove up in front of Katie's house in Clay's pickup. Katie came outside before she'd even turned off the ignition.

"Why don't you pull around back and put the truck in the garage. There's no reason to signal that someone else is here," Katie said.

"Good point."

Once in the garage, Pam got out with her bag. Again, Katie waited at the door into the kitchen. "I really appreciate your coming over like this. I always enjoy having the girls gone for a day or two, but after that the house echoes with silence until it drives me nutty."

Pam barely knew Katie. The eleven-year gap in their ages hadn't allowed Pam to get to know the cousin to the group of Callaways with whom she'd spent so much of her childhood.

Now she wasn't certain what to do or say.

Within a couple of hours she realized she needn't have worried about it. Katie treated her as though she'd known her forever, sharing tidbits of her life growing up as a Callaway, and telling stories she remembered of Cody's four children that Pam had never heard before.

Her relaxed manner came across so easy that Pam discovered that she, too, was finally able to sink back into her comfortable chair in the den and chat. She felt as if she'd made a new friend, or became reacquainted with an old one.

This must be what it feels like to have a warm, loving family around you, she thought.

The phone rang several times during the day. Katie spoke to her girls, as well as her parents. Other family members checked in. There were no more calls from the police, but Pam knew they were under no obligation to keep Katie up to date on their findings, unless they came to charge her with his disappearance.

The day crept by. They had a light lunch, then sat outside by the pool until its glistening blue water lured them into taking a swim about midafternoon. Pam couldn't keep her mind away from thoughts of Clay—what had happened last night, and the nights before—what might be happening now.

She mentally kept a time line going. Now they would have reached the town where she and Clay had stayed; now they would be deciding how close to get to the ranch before going on foot. Maybe it was just as well she didn't know exactly when they would be venturing onto the property.

By nine o'clock that night she was exhausted. When Katie showed her the guest room and left her for the evening, Pam realized that she had been on edge all day, waiting for word that something had happened.

She was being silly, she knew, and forced herself to shower and go to bed. Surely they would get in touch with her when there was anything to report.

The distant sound of the phone ringing woke her sometime later, and Pam propped herself up on her elbow to look at the time. It was a little past eleven o'clock, not a great time to be getting a call.

She threw back the covers and hurried to the door. Once it was opened, she could hear Katie's voice, but not what she was saying. She moved quietly through the hallway to Katie's bedroom door, which was open.

Katie sat on the side of the bed with her back to the door, speaking quietly but with an urgent undertone. Pam waited, unwilling to listen in and yet wanting Katie to know that she was available if she needed her.

Katie put the phone down a few minutes later, but made no other movement.

"Bad news?" Pam asked sympathetically.

"Oh!" Katie said, spinning around. "I'm sorry if the phone woke you."

"Don't be," she said, seeing the tears on Katie's cheeks. She walked over and sat down on the side of the bed. "Tell me what's wrong."

Katie reached for a tissue and hastily wiped her face. "It's actually good news, I guess. I mean, of course it is. It was Arthur. At least we know he's alive."

"What a relief!" Pam said, reaching for Katie's hand.

"Yes. At least I won't have to tell the girls that—" Her voice broke and she swallowed hard. "But as usual, he's in trouble and wants me to bail him out."

"How?"

"He wants me to meet him."

"When?"

"Tonight." She glanced at the clock. "In fact, if I'm to get there on time, I need to leave right away."

"But why tonight, of all times? Couldn't whatever it is wait until the morning?"

"My questions, exactly. He was scared, that much was obvious. He was practically hyperventilating. He kept saying that he needed me to come meet him at a place where we used to like to go. It's a state park west of here. I told him it would be closed, but he said it was the safest place for us to meet."

"What does he want from you? Why didn't he call the police?"

"Because whoever he's gotten involved with would kill him, or so he says. I'm wondering if he's just as much afraid of the police. When I mentioned them, he panicked and begged me not to contact them until after I meet him."

"Are you really going to go?" Pam asked in surprise.

Katie stared at her. "I don't know what to do. He told me not to tell anybody he called."

"Not even your family?"

"Especially my family. He also asked if the girls were here and seemed relieved to know they weren't. I don't know what to make of any of this except that once again Arthur has gotten himself into something he can't seem to get out of on his own."

"You don't owe him anything, Katie. You know that."

She nodded slowly. "Yes, I do know that. I also knew when I divorced him that he would continue to be a part of my life because he's the girls' father."

"Did he give you any reason why he needed to see you tonight?"

"No. He just kept saying over and over that he had to see me right away." She was quiet for several minutes. Pam waited, not certain what she should say. Finally Katie stood and went to her closet. "I'm going to go. I certainly won't get any sleep lying here tonight wondering what's going on."

"Katie, please stop and think about this," Pam said. "If he doesn't want the police to know, and he doesn't want your family to know, then this could be something very dangerous he's trying to involve you in. We already suspect him of having something to do with the explosions we're investigating. It was only his disappearance that made us wonder if we were wrong. And now he's calling you in the middle of the night? I don't like the looks of this at all."

Katie hesitated, looking torn. "But I can't just sit by and do nothing."

"At least wait until Sam and Clay get back. Give it a few more hours. Let them tell us the best way to handle the situation."

"But if we wait, Arthur won't be there. Don't you

understand? He needs help. Maybe he needs a ride somewhere. No doubt he's on foot, stranded with no way to go far.''

Pam frowned. ''I don't buy that. For one thing, how was he going to get there to meet you? And where did he find a phone to call?''

''He has a cell phone.''

''And whoever grabbed him was going to leave the phone with him? I don't believe that for a minute. There's something going on here that he isn't telling you. I vote that you stay here where you're safe until the men get back. Believe me, if you don't show up, Arthur will be calling you again.''

Katie didn't respond right away and Pam waited, hoping that her reasoned and logical argument would sway Katie from rushing off to meet her idiot ex-husband.

Pam wished she'd set up a contingency plan with the men, in case something happened while they were gone. They'd obviously expected her to handle whatever came up, but no one had anticipated a request from Arthur for Katie to leave her home and meet him somewhere.

Katie stirred. ''I'm sorry, Pam. I know you're probably right. I know I'm taking chances. But I've got to go.''

Pam didn't try to argue. ''Then I'm going with you,'' she said, striding to the door. ''I'll leave a message for Clay and Sam, and then meet you downstairs.''

Katie came out of the closet and said, ''Pam, you don't have to—''

Pam stopped and looked at her. ''I'm with you as protection, Katie. This is dangerous, and we probably shouldn't do it, but I won't allow you to go alone. You aren't leaving this house without me.'' She left the room and hurried into the guest room. Within minutes Pam dressed in dark clothing, quickly braiding her hair and wrapping it around her head. She pulled a black stocking cap over her head, covering her bright hair. She stepped out of her bedroom just as Katie came down the hallway.

Katie let out a squeak of surprise. ''My goodness, I didn't recognize you dressed like that!'' Katie wore jeans and a long-sleeved yellow cotton sweater.

''Do you have a darker top you could wear?''

''Why?''

''Since we don't know what we're getting into, it would be best to dress to blend into the shadows. I hope it doesn't become necessary that we'll need to hide, but I think we should be as prepared as possible.''

''Do you think this is some kind of a trap?''

''I have no idea, Katie. And neither do you.'' She made no mention of the small pistol hidden in the top of her short boots.

After Katie changed shirts, they went to the garage and got into Katie's car. Pam wished she had worked out a signal to Sam and Clay in case something like this came up. If they were already on the property, attempting to contact them now would put them in danger. Of course, they had probably left their phones turned off for that reason.

The women were silent on the drive that took them out of Lakeway farther into the Hill Country of Texas. They'd been driving west on the highway almost an hour when Katie turned south onto a

winding county road. Pam hadn't seen another vehicle on the road. Nor were there lights that would
indicate homes near the road.

Their headlights picked up the sign indicating a
state park a mile ahead.

Katie slowed even more as they approached the
turnoff.

"The park is closed, isn't it?" Pam asked.

"Yes. He said he'd meet us at the gate."

When they turned into the park, the lights made
an arc of the surrounding terrain. Pam was alert to
any movements, but she saw nothing. There was no
car parked there.

"Did he say what he would be driving?" she
asked.

"No. I didn't think to ask."

Pam had heard the doors to the car automatically
lock as soon as they had backed out of the garage.
At least no one would surprise them by attempting
to get inside.

"Now what?" she asked.

Katie turned off the lights and the engine. The
only sound was the ticking of the clock and the
sounds of metal cooling beneath the hood. "I don't
know," Katie replied. "We may be here a little
early. I suppose we wait for a while." She glanced
at her watch. "If he doesn't show up within the
hour, then we can chalk it up to a wild-goose chase
and go back home."

They sat there and waited. Eventually, Katie
asked, "I know it's none of my business, but what
happened between you and Clay all those years ago?
Do you mind talking about it?"

Because they were in the dark, Pam knew that

Katie couldn't see her roll her eyes. She could be rude and agree that it was none of Katie's business, but this was not the time to offend the woman she was protecting. She knew that Katie was trying to get her mind off her own situation. Pam didn't blame her.

She thought about the question for a few moments. "I'm not sure that I can explain, Katie. We were just kids back then. At one time I convinced myself that the only reason I thought I was in love with Clay was because I wanted so desperately to be a part of a warm, loving family."

"But now you're not so sure?" Katie asked.

"All I know is that we grew up, we went our own ways. There was no reason for our paths to ever cross again. I would have been fine with that."

"Who assigned you to be here?"

"My immediate supervisor, but he made it clear he was merely passing on orders. He didn't know where they came from. He had no information about any of it."

"Do you suppose Clay requested your inclusion?"

Pam chuckled. "I think he was as surprised and dismayed as I was to find out we were expected to work together."

"Has it helped to see him again?"

"Helped what?"

"For you to discover how you feel about him?"

Pam didn't want to talk about Clay. She didn't want to discuss her feelings at all. Finally, she said, "Yes, I think we've both been able to deal with the past and accept where we are today."

Katie waited. When Pam didn't say anything

more, she asked, "How well do you know Sam Carruthers?"

Pam almost sighed with the relief of discussing
anything other than her feelings for Clay. "I just
met him. He appears to be very knowledgeable in
his field."

"I wouldn't know about that." She shook her
head. "I just don't trust my judgment where men
are concerned, that's all. I mean, I thought Arthur
was so wonderful—and look how that turned out."

"I think that Sam is quite trustworthy, if that's
what you mean."

"All I know is that Sam makes me feel young
again, and attractive. He shows an interest in the
girls that seems more sincere than the way their own
father behaves."

"Has he said anything to you about the possibility
of a future together?" Pam heard herself ask the
prying question with surprise. Hadn't she just re-
acted to an equally nosy question earlier?

"Not exactly. We—uh—really haven't had much
time to discuss it. I mean, everything happened so
fast...the way we met, our time together. And then
Arthur's disappearance. I guess it's no secret that he
spent Saturday night at my house. He was there
when the police arrived early Sunday morning."

Pam welcomed the dark yet another time. She was
certain her surprise was written on her face. She
waited a moment before she cleared her throat and
said, "Actually, nobody mentioned it."

"Oh." Katie was quiet for a long while before
she said, "The thing is, I know I should be embarrassed, even ashamed, that I should become so in-

timately involved with a man I've known only a week."

"You don't owe me any explanations, you know," Pam replied.

"It's just that I've acted totally out of character for me. I can hardly believe I did it, myself. To be honest, though, I know that given the same choice, I would want to be with Sam."

"Did he tell you what he does, when he's not on special assignment?"

"He's stationed at Fort Benning, Georgia. I believe he's an instructor there."

"How would you feel about living a military life?"

"I have no idea. I've never lived far from my family. It's hard to imagine a life away from everyone I love."

After a moment, Pam said, "You're very lucky to be so close to your family...I don't just mean geographically, but emotionally."

Katie turned and looked at Pam. "I take it you and your father aren't close."

"No. He never really forgave me for deciding to make my own decisions about my life. He keeps up appearances, of course. He makes certain his secretary remembers to send me gifts and cards at the appropriate times throughout the year, but I seldom see him. Our schedules don't work together too well, even though we live less than an hour apart."

Because she was looking at Katie she caught a movement somewhere in the shadows behind her. "Katie," she whispered urgently. "Someone's out there."

Katie spun around and peered out the side window. They watched as the darker shadow of a lone figure separated from the wooded area and cautiously moved toward them.

"It's Arthur," Katie whispered.

"Are you certain?"

"Oh, yes. I'd recognize his walk anywhere." She reached for the door handle.

Pam grabbed her arm and slumped down in her seat. "Don't get out."

Katie looked at her in surprise. "But how am I going to talk with him?"

Arthur tapped on the window and said, "Katie, let me in."

Pam quickly took in the situation, then whispered, "Have him get into the back." She didn't think that Arthur had seen her inside the car. She reached up and flicked off the dome light that would ordinarily come on when a door opened.

Katie obligingly repeated, "Get in back."

He pushed the handle, but of course the car was still locked. He growled, "Unlock the damn door, Katie," and Katie immediately reached for the release. Pam tried to stop her from releasing all the locks but it was too late. She heard the simultaneous click of all four doors.

Arthur opened the back door just as both doors on Pam's side swung open. She spun around and saw two large, heavily built men standing there. The one at her side grabbed her elbow and yanked.

"Looks like your wifey brought along company, Henley. Man, you can't get anything right, can you?"

Chapter 15

Clay moved silently through the underbrush late that night. They had worked through the fence a couple of miles back. The three men were dressed in black, faces blackened, with night-vision goggles strapped to their heads. They were spread out, communicating through mouthpieces and earphones as they carefully checked the property.

The three of them had spent most of the day watching the entrance from a hill overlooking the roadway. Their powerful binoculars had given them a clear view of anyone going into or out of the property.

They had reviewed the photographs on file of each of the suspects. They spotted one drive up to the guard hut and stop about midafternoon. After a brief conversation with the two men working, he'd gone inside.

By the time it had grown dark, Sam felt they had

enough information to know they were on the right track. He had chosen to drive several miles beyond the ranch, finding a secondary road that eventually followed the fence line of the back of the property. He pulled Joe's rental car deep into the undergrowth where it couldn't be seen from the highway or the ranch area.

Now they moved through the hilly terrain, watching for any sign of people. Clay saw deer feeding, no doubt feeling safe with no moonlight to give them away. A rustle in the nearby bushes called his attention to an armadillo foraging for its supper.

Sam spoke in a whisper through Clay's earpiece. "I've found their main headquarters." He gave Joe and Clay directions to where he lay on the ground watching through binoculars.

Sam had found a clearing that overlooked a large cabin with several outbuildings. Several trucks were parked on the graveled drive. There was no noise coming from the cabin. Only one room had any light coming from it.

"Shall we move in closer?" Clay asked. "Maybe find out what's in the outbuildings?"

"Yeah," Sam drawled. "Let's go."

"Get your hands off me!" Pam said as the man dragged her out of the car. She heard Arthur say, "Who the hell is this, Katie?"

"She's a friend. She didn't want me driving out here alone."

"I've never seen her before."

"So what? I have lots of friends you don't know."

"Including that Carruthers character, right?"

''What do you want, Arthur?'' Katie said, staring at the two men who stood next to the driver's side.

Pam noticed that Arthur looked at the man beside him. The man looked at her across the roof of the car. ''Too bad you decided to be helpful, girlie. Looks like you get to go along on this little outing.'' He looked at the man who still held her arm in a strong grip. ''Put her in the back seat.'' Then to Katie. ''You might as well get in back, too. We'll have Arthur drive.''

''I don't understand,'' Katie said, getting out of the car. ''What do you want with us?''

''Not us. You. Dirk's waited a long time for this. Let's just consider this a family reunion.''

Katie turned and looked at Arthur.

The unknown man laughed. ''Don't look for any help from him, little lady. He's about served his purpose as far as Dirk's concerned.''

Arthur jumped in. ''Now, wait a minute, Sid. I've kept my end of our agreement. Getting Katie involved was never a part of any of this. We were getting back at Cole, remember?''

Sid shoved Katie into the back seat, where she fell against Pam. The man who had pulled Pam out of the car slammed the door and got into the front seat next to Arthur, who started the engine. Sid sat down next to Katie and closed the door behind him. ''Let's go,'' he muttered.

Clay, Sam and Joe had split up, carefully moving closer, each with a specific outbuilding to check out. Sam was the first to signal that there were guards near each building, unmoving in the shadows.

He'd almost tumbled over one of them before he

saw him. When he pulled back far enough to let the others know, he pointed out that the guy was asleep. It was obvious no one expected intruders.

The trio silently worked their assignments. Clay found the guard to his building awake and silently slipped behind him.

The storeroom was stocked with firearms, from pistols to automatic rifles. No doubt ammunition was in another location. Whatever these people were up to, they meant serious business.

He wished he knew why they had targeted the Callaway companies. Why declare war on the Callaways? Yet there were people who resented him for no other reason than that he'd been born into this particular family.

He'd never been able to understand that kind of reasoning; he'd just learned to live with it. Until now. Now he recognized that what he didn't understand could very well get him killed.

As soon as he'd gotten a rough count, Clay slipped out of the building, carefully made sure the door was secured behind him, then ran back to the designated meeting place.

He was joined within minutes by Sam and Joe. He reported in minimum detail. The other two had found ammunition and food supplies, enough to hold off an army for many months in case of a siege.

"So what are they up to?" Sam murmured, as if to himself. He glanced at his watch. "We need to get out of here."

"Hold on!" Joe whispered. "Vehicles are coming from the front gate." He trained his binoculars on the graveled road.

"Can you tell how many?" Sam asked.

"Two. Coming fast."

"Do you think we've been spotted?" Clay asked, raising his glasses.

"Negative," Sam growled. "But this is a hell of a time to be having visitors."

Clay looked at his watch. It was almost three o'clock in the morning.

They stayed where they were. They had a clear view of the cabin and the road approaching the cabin. Eventually the vehicles came into view. One was a late-model car, the other a large utility vehicle.

The three men waited and watched. Eventually the vehicles pulled up in front of the cabin and stopped. Two men got out of the sports utility vehicle. Three men and two women stepped out of the car.

Sam started cursing beneath his breath.

"What is it?" Clay asked.

"I just recognized that car," he replied.

Clay took a closer look, then brought the binoculars into close-up range. He didn't recognize the men, although one looked vaguely familiar. One of the women turned her head and he recognized the profile.

"That's Pam!" he whispered in shock.

"And Katie," Sam added angrily.

Clay panned the viewfinder back to the men. "Well, hell. That's got to be Arthur Henley. I've only seen a photo of him, but isn't that him?"

"Yep," Sam said with an irritated sigh. "It looks like he suckered the women into meeting him somewhere."

"And they walked into a trap," Joe concluded.

Clay could feel his body reacting to this new information with another burst of adrenaline. What the hell had happened? Surely Pam would know better than to allow someone to get the jump on her. Then he thought of Katie, who wouldn't have understood the possible dangers of seeing her ex-husband.

Had the men turned up at the house? How could Katie have allowed them inside? Pam would have warned her not to blithely open the door, even if Arthur had identified himself.

They watched as the group went inside the cabin. Within minutes other lights in the place came on.

"What do you want to do?" Clay asked Sam.

"We're moving in closer until we can figure out what is going on."

"What about the guards?"

"We're going to have to make damn sure they don't see or hear us. Come on."

They spread out and moved forward.

Clay wanted to know what was going on in the cabin. He circled the area, staying outside of the clear spot in the brush surrounding the buildings. The first he knew that he wasn't alone was Sam's soft voice asking, "Have you gotten a head count?"

"Seven so far. But there's no telling how many who haven't shown their faces."

"That's what I got. Let's move in closer."

Now it was time to get serious.

Pam had been taking a head count as soon as she walked into the cabin. It was obvious that none of the men saw her and Katie as threats. They didn't check for weapons, but she was well aware that her small pistol wouldn't do her much good with these odds.

When all the men gathered around to find out what the two women had been brought in for, she counted ten men, none of whom she would want to claim as close buddies.

She decided to stay quiet, unwilling to draw attention to herself until she decided what she needed to do to get them out of there.

Katie spoke to the guy named Dirk, who was obviously their leader. "What do you want with me?" she asked.

Dirk nodded to Arthur. "It was his idea," he replied.

Arthur exploded. "Are you crazy? Holding Katie would be the very last thing I'd decide to do. Her father is Cole Callaway. Don't you have any idea what he's going to do when he finds her missing?"

Dirk looked her up and down with amusement. "Well, little sister, I figured it was time for you and me to get acquainted."

Katie stared at him as though he had spoken a foreign language. "What is that supposed to mean?" she finally asked.

The half smile disappeared from his face. "You mean your daddy never told you? I'm the son Cole Callaway didn't bother to claim, at least to the world. Oh, yeah, I know all about your big brother Tony and how dear old dad never knew about him for years. Well, he sure as hell knew about me. He and my mother were an item at one time, but as soon as she got pregnant with me, he told her he never wanted kids."

"That's a lie!" Katie said indignantly. "My dad

loves kids. He loves to tell the story about how
thrilled he was to learn about Tony and to finally be
able to marry Mom and have a family with her. And
maybe he did date your mother before he found
Mom again and discovered Tony's existence. But if
you are his son, he would have claimed you, just
the way he claimed Tony!''

"I'm sure that's what he'd want you to believe.
But the truth is he paid my mother money to keep
quiet about me. Well, she may have loved him and
promised him never to admit that he was my daddy,
but I never made any promises to him. He's ignored
my existence all of my life. I've grown up watching
all of you with your high and mighty airs thinking
you're some kind of royalty, while I had to scrape
by on whatever I could make. All of you make me
sick. I decided to let him know that even if I don't
have the Callaway name, I'm just like him. I can
plan a war campaign against him and pull it off. I've
proved that well enough.''

She stared at him in disbelief. "What did you
prove? My father has no idea who caused the explosions or why. What did you hope to accomplish
with all of this? And why involve me in all of it?''

Pam wished that Katie would ease off her inqui-
sition. Studying the man and remembering what
she'd learned about him, she realized that regardless
of his possible parentage, and she certainly wasn't
buying his story, the man had developed a twisted
perspective of the Callaways and the world around
him. He was a dangerous sociopath. There was no
reason to antagonize him at this point.

Of course Katie had no way of knowing that this
was the area that Sam, Clay and Joe planned to re-

connoiter. Pam had recognized the ranch as soon as they had pulled up to the gates. With any luck, the men were somewhere close by, even though they were heavily outmanned.

She could only pray that the men were still on the property and would have seen her and Katie arrive. Otherwise, they were in a much more perilous situation than she wanted to be. If the men had seen them, she knew that Sam would call for reinforcements. What she had to do was to make certain that she kept Katie safe from any crossfire. Antagonizing the leader wasn't going to help her.

Dirk had stiffened at Katie's response. "You're here because I decided it's time for me to meet face to face with Cole Callaway. I figure he'll be glad to come visit if he knows his little girl is here!"

Arthur exploded. "Are you crazy? If I'd known what you were up to I would never have agreed to call her for you. It was one thing to get even with him by blowing up some of his plants and factories, but when you start messing around with his family, you've signed your death warrant!"

Katie turned to Arthur. "So you've been a part of this all along?"

"You're damn right I've been a part of this! They wouldn't have been able to do it without me. I met Dirk when we were in the army and we've been friends ever since." He looked back at the man and said, "But you never told me what you had against the Callaways. You never told me that you were Cole's son."

Dirk glared at Arthur. "There's a lot I haven't told you because I never trusted you after you married into the Callaway family. But then I realized I could use the connection to my advantage, which I have.'' He turned away from the group and started to pace. ''I noticed that you didn't mind disappearing like that, pretending that you'd been kidnapped, hoping your ex would be blamed, and you certainly didn't object to calling her and getting her out where we could grab her.'' He spun around and faced Arthur. ''But you must have been out of your mind to have brought the other one.'' He nodded toward Pam.

Everyone looked at Pam. She dropped her eyes and studied her feet. She wanted them convinced that she was no threat to anyone.

''C'mon, Dirk,'' one of the men who'd been with Arthur at the state park said, ''we couldn't let her drive back to town and call somebody.''

Dirk frowned. ''I don't know how I managed to get involved with a pack of inept people like this bunch,'' he muttered, as though talking to himself.

Pam risked a glance at Katie, who was much too pale. Weighing the situation, she decided to risk speaking. She cleared her throat before she said, ''Please, is there anyplace we could lie down to rest?'' She hoped she sounded pathetic and helpless.

It seemed to work. The other men looked around as if a lamp had suddenly spoken. Dirk glanced at Katie. ''I suppose until I figure out what to do with you. Arthur, take 'em into the bedroom and stay with them. I'll give dear ol' dad a call in the morning and see how eager he is to join our charming family gathering.''

''Dirk,'' Arthur said. ''You're making a mistake here. Everything we've done to the Callaways up until now was like a bee sting to Cole—annoying, that's all. He might be looking for the hive to take out the likelihood of more stings, but he'll be treating all of this as part of doing business. Involving his family is another matter, entirely.''

"The problem with you, Henley," Dirk replied, "is that you have no guts. I'm not afraid of any of them, including Cole. Before I'm through with him, I'll have him agreeing to anything I want. And what I want is for him to acknowledge me, and for him to give me my share of the family dough. With that kind of power, I can make a real difference to this country. I can teach those politicians how the country should be run.''

Pam turned and walked to the door Dirk had indicated led to the bedroom. She wasn't certain she could control her expression any longer. The man was a raving lunatic.

Katie followed her into the room. There were three sets of bunk beds. Pam immediately stretched out on the bed closest to the window and closed her eyes, but not before she took a good look outside.

The only light in the room came from the living area, which made it easier for her eyes to adjust. There was thick brush about ten feet from this side of the cabin, if she could figure a way to get them out of there. She was counting on the window as their escape route.

Katie picked the bed next to Pam.

Arthur walked in and closed the door. He grumbled as he felt his way in the dark to one of the beds.

As soon as the door closed, Katie said to Arthur, "I can't believe I was married to you for so long without knowing the kind of man you are."

Pam could hear Arthur's movements as he
stretched out on the bed and gave an obvious sigh
of relief at being horizontal. She could certainly
identify with the sentiment. He ignored Katie's comment and said, "You'd better get some sleep. Dirk
will have us up before the sun."

"You'll never get away with any of this, you
know," Katie said. "I hate to think what my dad's
going to do to you when he gets his hands on you."

Arthur chuckled. "Maybe you haven't noticed the
security around here, Katie. Nobody's getting on
this place without the guards knowing about it. For
once, your dad doesn't have the upper hand. I wonder how he'll handle that? Now shut up and go to
sleep."

Pam forced herself to take slow, steady breaths in
the hope of indicating that she had already dropped
off. She listened as first Arthur, then finally Katie,
quietened.

She continued to lie there, silently counting as
time passed. Once Arthur began to snore, she slowly
sat up and reached for the pistol in her boot. Moving
silently, she crept past Katie, careful not to bump
something. Faint light from the window guided her
to where Arthur lay sprawled asleep on his stomach.

With a steady movement she brought the grip of
the pistol down on his head, right behind his ear.

He gave a soft sigh and remained silent.

Katie sat up with a gasp. Pam whirled around and
faced her, motioning for her to be quiet. Then she
silently glided toward the window and checked the
lock. It turned easily, quietly, in her fingers. With
careful movements she lifted it up as high as it
would go.

She turned to Katie and found her immediately behind her. She motioned for her to crawl through the window, thankful they were both wearing dark clothing. As soon as Katie reached the ground, Pam got out and looked around.

The closest cover was straight ahead. She took Katie's hand and sprinted toward the trees. She kept moving, although by necessity had to slow down once they reached the underbrush. She waited until she heard Katie breathing hard before she slowed down, looking around for a sheltered place to stop and catch their breath.

She led Katie to a cluster of shrubs and knelt down in the midst of them. Katie collapsed on the ground beside her. Her first question stunned Pam.

"You didn't kill him, did you?" she asked, panting.

"No! I just knocked him out. He'll have a goose egg and a headache, but I wasn't going to waste time trying to convince him to let us go."

Katie's chuckle sounded more like a sob. "I've never been so scared in all my life. What do we do now?"

"I was hoping you weren't going to ask that just yet. I'm not sure. The main thing is not to get caught by those bozos. I'm hoping that Sam and Clay are somewhere in the vicinity and—"

"Then you're in luck," Clay drawled from right behind them, causing Katie to let out a tiny shriek before Pam clamped her hand over her mouth. Katie looked around and saw Sam next to Clay. She threw herself in his arms and tried to bury herself against him.

Pam looked at Clay. "Do I need to tell you how glad I am to see you guys?"

"Probably not. We called for backup, which should be arriving shortly. Joe's meeting them down the road so they move in by increments—taking out the entrance guards first. Then we were going to have to figure out how to keep from getting you two killed. You've saved us a great deal of time and effort."

"Just part of the job," she replied with a grin.

"Then will you explain to me how in the hell you managed to get yourselves picked up? That certainly wasn't part of the job."

Of course he would have to be a pain about it. Otherwise, he wouldn't be Clay Callaway.

"Can we wait to evaluate my performance until later? I'd really like to get out of here." She looked over at Sam, who held Katie and was whispering to her. Sam looked up.

"I think you're right. If you're up for the hike, we'll take you back to the car. I've already radioed Joe that you two are out of there and they can move forward. We don't need to be here for the mopping up."

Pam looked from one man to the other. "You mean we're through with this assignment after tonight?"

Sam nodded. "Our part of it, anyway. And if it's all the same to everybody, I would just as soon not let Cole Callaway know how we risked his daughter's neck tonight. I don't think it will help me win any points with the man, and frankly, I need all the help I can get."

Katie chuckled. Pam knew they blamed her for

this, but it no longer mattered. She'd gotten them out of there. Thank God the men had found them.

She heard a shout from the direction of the cabin. "Uh-oh. Sounds like Arthur may be awake by now, or someone else discovered we're gone."

Sam nodded to Clay. "Lead the way," he said. Clay started off, angling away from the buildings and back up to the ridge where they had first spotted the headquarters. Pam had no trouble keeping up. Sam helped Katie and moved her as quickly as possible through the thick brush.

Pam watched Clay move ahead of her. He was in his element and she knew it. She tried to stay focused on where she was stepping. The last thing she needed was a sprained ankle. However, she kept reminding herself that this would be one of the last times she saw him. She began to store up impressions to add to her memories of the boy and teenager she'd once known and loved.

Chapter 16

"I appreciate all you've done," Cole Callaway said to the members of the team the next afternoon. They were at the condo. He'd come to see them on his own. "I'm impressed with how quickly you took care of the matter."

Sam replied, "The government is pleased to know that it wasn't a planned attack aimed at them."

Cole made a face. "No, just more enemies of the family to contend with. Everyone has been much too discreet to ask me about Dirk Davis's claim that I'm his father. I have no problem telling you the truth. Helene Davis worked as one of our marketing officers years ago in Dallas. She'd worked late one night and was attacked in the parking lot on the way to her car.

"Her attacker was out on bail awaiting trial for a similar incident at the time. The courts put him away with a long sentence and he died a few years later in a knife fight in prison.

"Unfortunately, Helene became pregnant as a result of the attack. Because she was one of our employees, I felt responsible for the lack of security around the building at that time.

"We made certain that Helene had ample provisions not only to have her child but to stay home to raise and care for him.

"I don't know when her son got the idea I was his father. Knowing Helene I could almost swear she would never have made up a story like that, but I don't really know how she explained the circumstances surrounding his birth. Since the checks she received came from our office, maybe he thought it was a clue that I was involved because I generally signed them. I feel badly about the way things have worked out. I'm not even sure if Helene's still alive."

No one spoke. Pam could think of nothing to say to mitigate the damage done by Dirk's delusions.

She was glad when Sam brought up another subject.

"I understand that Arthur is being held with the rest of the men without bond."

Cole nodded. "The prosecutor thinks he'll be the one to lean on to get the full story."

"I'm glad he was found alive. Katie didn't need suspicion following her around." Sam looked over at Pam and Clay. "If you two will excuse us, there's something I want to discuss with Cole that really has nothing to do with our assignment."

Pam walked into her room. Her bags were packed and stacked on her bed. There was really nothing more to do except wait for a ride to the airport. She heard a sound at the door and glanced around. Clay stood in the doorway, his shoulder resting against the opening.

"Looks like you're ready," he said.

She nodded.

"Mind if we talk?" he asked quietly.

She swallowed. If she were honest—and cowardly—she would say no. Instead, she nodded and he walked into the room. He pulled out the chair in front of the desk. She sat down on the daybed and waited.

"It's obvious that there's something between us," he began, looking down at his clasped hands. "There's no point in my denying the fact that I can't keep my hands off of you." He raised his head slightly, peering up at her from beneath his brows before dropping his gaze once more. "Although you put that down to adolescent hormones when we were in high school, I believe that you know in your heart it was more than that, even back then." He straightened, so that he was looking directly at her. "I need to know how you feel about us now. We also need to discuss the very real possibility that you might be pregnant."

Oh, this was much, much worse than she'd thought it would be. She wasn't ready to discuss their relationship. She wasn't certain that she would ever be ready. What a coward she was.

"Clay, I—" she began, then paused. After a moment, she said, "I found out this morning that I'm not pregnant, which should be a weight off your mind. As to how I feel about us—I'm not sure I fully understand that, myself. I'm sure you'll agree that being thrown together on this assignment was a shock for both of us. There were a lot of unresolved issues we've been forced to confront in a very short time. I can't deny that we've always had a strong sexual bond. I've never responded to any man the way I do to you.'' She shook her head. ''That didn't sound right. The truth is I've never made love to any man besides you,'' she carefully stated, needing to acknowledge that truth. ''In a way, I guess what we had all those years ago ruined me for seeking possible substitutes.''

Clay looked stunned by her revealing admission, then slowly smiled. ''If you think I'm going to apologize, you're out of your mind,'' he said lightly.

''The thing is,'' she went on, ''that attraction continues to color my thinking to the point that I don't know how I truly feel about you.''

His smile faded, but he said nothing more.

''You need to understand that when my dad insisted on our getting married, I resented that attraction. I felt as though I was being punished because I couldn't control my reaction to you. I was angry...and confused...and felt so totally alone because there was no one I could talk to about what I was going through...no one who would have understood.''

''You could have talked to me,'' he said quietly.

''I tried, Clay. Don't you remember?''

He scratched his ear reflectively. ''Maybe you did. All I heard was how much you didn't want to marry me. That came across loud and clear. I guess it didn't matter too much at the time your reasons why. I was pretty devastated by the rejection, as I recall.''

She sighed. "I guess that's my point. I hurt you very badly, then saw nothing of you for years. Now we've been thrown back together as if fate decided it was time to heal the past. The problem is, I don't know how."

"I suppose my suggesting at this point that we get married doesn't much appeal to you?" he asked, his voice light. However, the look in his eyes was very serious.

She stared at him in surprise. "Until a little more than a week ago, we hadn't spoken to each other since we were teenagers, and now you blithely toss out the idea of marriage as though discussing a date for the senior prom. We don't know each other any more, Clay. I'm not so sure we ever did. I think like most teenagers we built our fantasies of the perfect mate around each other's image. But we're no longer kids. We've worked hard in our chosen careers. Neither profession offers much in the way of stability for a sound family life. Marriage at this point in our lives, in our careers, doesn't make much sense to me. Does it to you?"

He didn't answer her right away. In fact, his gaze had returned to his clasped hands. She waited, not sure what she wanted to hear from him, that he loved her so much that losing her a second time was unthinkable, regardless of the obvious obstacles. Or did she want him to agree with her and admit that marriage would never work for them?

Finally, he said, "So what I'm hearing you say is that you still don't want to be married to me."

She looked away from him. She knew this was the moment of truth between them. But she wasn't ready! Not after the roller coaster her emotions had been riding during the entire time they'd been together.

Did she love him?

Without a doubt.

Did she believe they could make a marriage work with everything that stood between them?

She honestly didn't know. Even worse, she was afraid to try.

"I can't see it working for us, Clay. I really can't. The pitfalls are too obvious."

He nodded slowly, then stood. "Well. I appreciate your honesty. I didn't want to leave here wondering if we still stood a chance." He reached for her hand and gripped it. "Take care of yourself, okay?" He spun on his heel and left her room. Moments later she heard the front door close. She wasn't sure whether Cole had left, or whether Clay was the one gone. She wasn't sure that she wanted to know if Clay had gone for good.

Pam leaned against her bag, wondering what was wrong with her. She should be feeling good about her decision. She'd merely confirmed the one she'd made so many years ago—to be free, to be her own person, to make her own way in life.

So why was she shaking so? And why were tears pouring heedlessly down her cheeks?

Now that Clay and Pam had left the room, Sam considered how best to talk with Cole.

Cole said, "You want to discuss Katie with me, don't you?"

"Yes, sir. I do."

"It's none of my business, whatever is going on with you two. I've already made that clear, I hope."

"I appreciate that, but I need your advice."

"My advice?" Cole echoed in surprise. "About what?"

"I love Katie, which is a little mind-boggling to me, considering the fact I've only known her a week or so. However, I feel that I might have taken advantage of her situation by coming on so strong when she's in such a vulnerable space."

"You do, huh?"

"Yes, sir. I do. From everything I can gather, Katie has always had her family's support and guidance. Before I ask her to marry me, I need to be sure that, if she accepts, she'll be able to adjust to the changes that would cause in her life."

"Changes," Cole repeated in a neutral voice.

"Not just the money, though that's an obvious change since my income bracket is nothing like what she's used to. But in addition to all that, I'm at the mercy of Uncle Sam. I live wherever I'm told, I'm assigned to wherever I'm needed. I'll admit that this latest assignment was out of the ordinary. My usual duties as an instructor keep me at Fort Benning most of the time."

Cole smiled. "I think you're talking to the wrong person about all of this, Colonel. I'm not the one to ask if Katie would be happy with you. Katie is."

Sam flushed. "I know that." He thought for a minute. "I mean, I really do know that, but maybe I'm hoping you'll convince me that she's better off where she is, so I can quietly take my leave of her and not do anything to hurt her."

Cole rubbed his chin thoughtfully. "Well, since you ask, and this is just my opinion, but for what it's worth, the worst way to hurt my daughter is to walk away without telling her how you feel.''

"She knows how I feel about her."

"Then it's time you tell her what you want to do about it."

"You think so?"

"I know so. Yes, Katie is vulnerable right now. She's worried about how the girls are going to deal with what is going on with Arthur. But she's a strong woman, Colonel. She knows her own mind. She's willing to take chances to get what she wants. And it's my hunch that it's you that she wants. You have absolutely no idea how it pains me to play cupid in this little scenario, but my wife and daughter would never forgive me if I didn't tell you the truth. Katie loves you. You're going to have to deal with that as well as all the fallout surrounding it. So you're welcome to stay here as long as you'd like." He got to his feet. "Now I'm going home and curse the day I ever let someone talk me into sending all you hotshot army guys over here to solve our little problem because now it looks as though you're going to move my little girl away from me. I better have your promise that I'll be able to see her and my granddaughters as often as possible."

Sam stood as soon as Cole rose. He held out his hand. "Thank you for being so fair with me."

"Just wait until you have kids of your own, Colonel, and you'll see just how possessive a person can get."

Sam took Pamela to the Austin airport before driving to Lakeway to see Katie. Clay had gone down to see his folks and drop off his truck before he went back to his overseas assignment.

Sam pulled up in front of Katie's large home and got out of the car. He acknowledged his nervousness to himself, but didn't let his nerves deter him on this particular mission.

As soon as he rang the doorbell, he heard the clatter of footsteps and chattering voices.

"I'll get it!"

"No, I'm here, I'll do it."

"No! I was here first!"

The door swung open and two pairs of sparkling eyes greeted him.

"Hello, Mr. Sam," Amber said with a grin.

"No," Trish corrected her officiously, "he's Colonel Sam."

"Hello, girls," he replied. He decided not to take sides in their bickering. "Is your mother home?"

"Sure," Amber said, racing toward the back of the house, yelling, "Mom, Mr. Sam's here," while Trish took his hand and tugged him inside the house.

Katie came from the den and saw him standing there holding Trish's hand. Her smile widened. "Hi," she said, sounding more than a little shy.

"Hi, yourself," he said, suddenly feeling totally inadequate for the mission he was on.

She turned to the girls. "Okay, gals. Outside. You promised."

The girls looked at each other and rolled their eyes. With muttered comments they disappeared into the den, presumably on their way to the back-yard.

"You're coming to say goodbye, aren't you?" she asked, leading him into the den. She turned and faced him, then motioned for him to sit down on the sofa, while she sat in the chair across from him.

"Yes and no," he said with some hesitation. "I hope it will only be a temporary goodbye."

Her eyes widened slightly but she didn't say anything.

"I know we haven't known each other long enough to be making any decisions about the future, but the truth is, I do have some leave time coming and I was wondering if you'd mind if I came back to Texas. I'd like to spend some time with you and your family, let the girls get to know me a little better, and talk to you about the possibility of a long-term relationship. The truth is, I don't know much about relationships. I've never been in a committed relationship before, but after meeting you, I'm certainly interested in learning more about them. If you're willing to teach me, that is."

"I'm not certain that you've chosen a very good teacher. Not with my track record, but I would love to have you back here for as long as you can stay."

"Your dad said I could have the use of his condo for as long as I want. I need to return east and file the necessary reports, but after that, I'll be putting in for my leave." They stared at each other from across the wide table that sat between the two pieces of furniture. "I guess I need to tell you that I loved making love to you and look forward to having the permanent right to be in your bed every night, but until then, I don't intend to allow our relationship to go there again."

"Is that why you're over there and I'm here?" she asked with a small smile.

"Uh, yes, that's exactly why. I don't trust myself when I'm around you."

"So you're just going to tease me with your presence, is that it?"

He eyed her uncertainly. "I don't know about that...." he began, with a hint of hesitation.

She laughed. "Well, I do. You give me a sample of what making love to you is all about, then let the memory entice me until...exactly what are you holding out for, Colonel?"

With utmost seriousness, Sam said, "Nothing less than marriage, Katie. The next time I make love to you, I want to know that you and I belong together permanently. But since it's too soon to be talking marriage, I figure we should cool it for the next few months. I'll visit you here. I hope to coax you into coming to Georgia for a visit. Then, and only then, if you feel like you'd be interested in my life-style, just maybe we can make some permanent plans."

Katie got up, walked around the coffee table and sat down in Sam's lap. Just before she leaned in and kissed him, she whispered, "You've got yourself a deal, Colonel, and I intend to do some enticing of my own."

Clay stepped inside the front door of his parents' home on the outskirts of San Antonio. "Hello? Anybody home?" he asked, closing the door behind him.

"In here, Clay," Carina called from the kitchen. He walked back to the sunny room that overlooked his mother's colorful garden. She was pulling a pan of cookies from the oven. "You're just in time for fresh cookies and milk."

He sniffed the air. "My favorite kind. You must have known I was coming." He looked around. "Where's Dad?"

"Actually, I only hoped you'd have time to come see us before you left the state. Cole called earlier and said everyone was heading back to his and her other assignments now that the men responsible for the bombings had been captured. As for your dad, he went out to the ranch early this morning. Cade had something going on out there he needed some help on. Can you stay long?"

He'd left his gear in the hallway. He walked over and pulled his mother into his arms, hugging her tightly. "I'm not leaving until I see both of you again. I'll check with the airbase and see if there's a military flight heading east in the next few days."

He sat down at the table and allowed his mother to wait on him. He watched her fill a giant glass full of milk, then she piled several cookies on a plate and set them both in front of him. "Mmm. Now, this was worth the whole trip," he muttered.

Carina sat down in front of him with a cup of coffee. "So everything's taken care of now?" she asked.

"Our part, anyway. The government agencies were more than willing to take credit for finding and capturing these guys. I'm glad we didn't need to be mentioned."

She studied him for a long while before she finally said, "Does it get in the way of your life sometimes, being a Callaway?"

He shrugged. "How would I know? I have nothing to compare it to. Some people react to the name and I see the reaction, but I figure it's their hang-up, not mine. They have to deal with whatever feelings are brought up.''

"I just wondered if that was why you no longer want to live here in Texas.''

"Good question. I only realized when I came back that what I'd been running from was memories more than the place.''

"Memories involving Pam?''

"Yep, those are the ones. I guess this trip has been good for me, made me face the hurt kid with too much pride. I wasn't willing to admit how much I'd been crushed by her unilateral decision. It was easier to deal with choosing my career and getting on with life.''

"Did it help to see her again?'' his mother asked.

He sighed. "Well, it convinced me that I'm not over her. That I'll never stop loving her. But it also taught me that you can't force another person to love you. She made it clear that she might be attracted to me, but that nothing will ever come of it.''

Carina reached for his hand. "I'm sorry, son. I had really hoped that this time you two could work this out.''

"I think she's scared, but I'm not sure about what. Maybe if she'd had a mother she could talk to about all her confusion, then maybe we would have had a chance...if not back then, then now.''

"I guess it would have been too awkward for her to attempt a discussion with me, considering our relationship,'' Carina said.

Clay stretched his arms high above his head. "Well, at least I know I tried. And I better understand her after this past week.'' He looked at Carina.

"Maybe you'll have to count on grandkids coming from my sisters."

Carina tilted her head slightly, studying him. "You don't think you'll get married?" she asked softly.

"I can't imagine being married to anyone else but Pamela McCall," Clay replied, getting up from the chair and wandering into the living room to wait for his dad to come home.

Chapter 17

Three months later

Pam came home from work late on a Tuesday evening, scooped up her mail where it had been pushed through the slot in her door, and carried the small stack to her table.

She quickly shuffled through the envelopes and pulled out a square one with an Austin, Texas, return address. Slipping off her shoes, she padded barefoot into the kitchen and poured herself a glass of water before opening it. She had a hunch she knew what it was.

She was right. When she opened the thick, creamy envelope she found an invitation to a wedding. Sam and Katie were having a small, informal wedding at her home in a few weeks, close friends and family only, and she was invited to attend.

Before she could stop her reaction, tears rolled down her cheeks. She'd become a watering pot over the past three months—everything reminded her of Clay, and every time she thought of him, she cried.

It had been one thing to decide that she wasn't ready for a relationship that might jeopardize her freedom and independence. It was another thing to discover that all the freedom and independence in the world meant very little to her without having the man she loved with all her heart be a part of her life.

So why hadn't she picked up the phone by now and told him that she'd been stupid and very short-sighted and that she loved him beyond anything else she could possibly imagine?

Well, part of the reason was because she had no idea where he was. Neither did anyone else she'd contacted, for that matter. She'd spoken to his parents. She'd spoken to Sam. She'd even attempted to get in touch with his commanding officer. Now, that had been a waste of time. As far as that office had been concerned, Captain Clay Callaway didn't even exist.

His mother was more sympathetic but had no more information to give to her. In fact, during the past couple of months she and Carina had gotten into the habit of talking to each other by phone every few days.

It was to Carina that Pam had confessed what she had discovered about herself during these lonely months back in Virginia. Part of the jolt of aware-ness came when she returned to her apartment, her empty apartment, after spending those days with the investigative team.

She was used to being alone. So why had a few days of camaraderie, not to mention the nights full of passion with Clay, effectively destroyed her serene existence on her own? Of course she'd never told Carina about their intimate relationship. Instead, she talked about her own feelings. What it had been like to see Clay again. How it had thrown her back into the past. How much of her time had been spent thinking about who she was, and how afraid she was to have a relationship.

At least she now understood that she was afraid. Had always been afraid. She barely remembered her parents' marriage. What she remembered was very different from the warm, loving relationship she'd witnessed between Cody and Carina Callaway.

One evening Carina shared with her the ups and downs of her early relationship with Cody. Pam had been shocked to discover the turbulent start of their marriage, which Carina laughingly referred to as one step removed from a shotgun alliance.

Carina, too, had wanted an education, and she'd moved away from Texas after the wedding to get it.

Why hadn't anyone told Pam any of this before? Would it have made a difference to her decision to call off the wedding? She would never know now. Instead, she began to see parallels in the situations, painful parallels. Only Cody and Carina had stayed together and worked out their problems.

Carina didn't condemn her, which made Pam feel even worse at times. Carina was very understanding and helped Pam to see how a motherless child might not have been equipped to work out all of her confused emotions at such an early age, particularly when faced with a domineering father.

What Pam had finally recognized during these past few weeks was that Clay was nothing like her father. He was a passionate, devoted man who had offered her his life if she wanted him. And she had rejected him. Again.

Now she was paying for that rejection by facing each day alone, with no relief in sight.

She'd just finished eating supper when the phone rang. It was Carina.

"I haven't heard from you in a few days. How are you doing?"

Even the warm sound of her voice made Pam weepy. Somehow, she had to get a grip on her emotions before she ended up with permanently red eyelids.

"Hi, Mama Cee. I worked late tonight. As a matter of fact, I intended to call you later. I just got my invitation to Katie's wedding."

"Really! I'm so glad she included you. She said neither she nor Sam wanted a big production. She had that with Arthur. She just wanted to make her commitment to him in front of loved ones."

"I'm honored that she included me."

"Does that mean you'll come?"

"If I can. I may try to take some extra time off. It would be nice to be home and just visit with you in person for a change."

Carina laughed. "We'd enjoy having you. Just let us know when you're coming and we'll meet you at the airport. You can ride up to Austin with us."

Pam hung up the phone feeling considerably better. It would be wonderful to see everyone again. And maybe, just maybe, Clay would be there, too.

*   *   *

The phone rang late one night, about a week later. Pam groggily felt for the phone and mumbled into the receiver.

"H'lo," she said softly.

"Pam?" a male voice asked.

She fought her way out of sleep and sat up, reaching for the lamp beside the bed. "Yes?" she said more clearly.

"This is Sam Carruthers."

She looked at the clock. It was two-thirty in the morning. Her heart started thudding with dread. "It's Clay, isn't it? Where is he?"

"I'm sorry, Pam, but I thought you'd want to know," Sam replied.

"He's not dead. He can't be dead."

"They transferred him to a military hospital not far from you. If you want to see him, I suggest you go as soon as possible." He gave her the address and she numbly wrote it down.

"Oh, no! He can't be—"

"I just got off the phone with his dad. They're making arrangements to fly from Texas to D.C. His C.O. contacted me as a personal favor, but officially none of this has happened."

"What do you mean, officially?"

"You know the kind of assignments he goes on, Pam. There's always a deniability factor built into them. Officially our government wasn't anywhere near this recent breakout of violence. From what I understand, out of a five-man team, Clay was the only one still alive when they got to them. They're not holding out much hope for him, but I've got more faith in his stubbornness than that. If anybody can pull through this one, Callaway can. I know how close you two are. I think it would do him good to find you beside his bed when he opens his eyes.''

If he opens his eyes, she thought, panicked.

''Will they let me see him?'' she asked, throwing back the blankets and reaching for her clothes.

''I gave them your name and told them to expect you momentarily.''

''Thank you, Sam.''

''It's the least I can do. I'm fond of both of you.''

They hung up and Pam raced around her room—finding practical clothing, brushing her hair and slipping a band around it to keep it away from her face. Then she was running down the stairs to her car, grateful for the light traffic at that time of night.

''Oh, please let him be alive,'' she prayed, forcing herself to observe the speed limits. ''Please don't let him die. I have so much to tell him. So much to apologize for.''

She hated herself for the wasted time that had gone by since she'd last seen him. Maybe they wouldn't have had much time together, but he would have known how much she loved him, how important he was to her. He would have been aware that she was waiting for him when he returned to the States.

After what seemed like hours, Pam pulled into the hospital parking lot, found an empty space and parked. She grabbed her purse and raced to the entrance, not pausing in her prayer for his continued survival.

She was stopped just at the front entrance by a military guard. ''I'm sorry, miss, but civilians aren't allowed here.''

"Colonel Sam Carruthers just called me. He told me that—"

He picked up a chart and scanned it. He paused about midway down. "You're here to see Captain Callaway?"

"That's correct."

He signaled to someone out of her range of vision. Another M.P. stepped into view. "Take her to room 403 in ICU."

She hurried to catch up with the long-legged corporal, who paused only long enough to call for an elevator. The doors opened and she stepped inside directly behind him. They didn't speak as they watched the numbers flash above the door.

Once on the fourth floor, the corporal escorted her past the nurses' station to a room with glass walls. She could see inside. There was no way to recognize the person in the bed. He was covered in bandages.

A nurse stood beside his bed, adjusting a drip into his hand, beeping machines behind her. At least the steady rhythm of the sounds told her he was still alive. The nurse turned around and said, "You can't—"

"I'm Pamela McCall. Colonel Carruthers—" She must have used the magic words because the nurse nodded and motioned to a chair. "He's stabilized somewhat since being transferred here. However, he's in a coma. There's no way to know when or if he'll regain consciousness, Ms. McCall. But Colonel Carruthers got clearance for you to stay here with him."

"How bad—" she began before her throat closed.

"He was hit several times by an automatic weapon. He underwent surgery overseas before he was stabilized enough to bring him home. There was extensive damage. We can only wait and see what happens," the nurse said.

"How long has he been here?" Pam asked.

The nurse checked her watch. "They brought him in a little more than an hour ago."

Then Sam must have gotten immediate notification and been on the phone to the family. And to her. God bless the man, Pam thought, walking over to the bed.

Clay was still unrecognizable, even up close. His face was swollen and discolored; his head swathed in bandages. Both arms were in casts as well as one of his legs. She touched his fingers of the hand without the drip taped to it.

Pam sank down into the chair and carefully took his hand in hers.

"Clay? I once heard that our hearing is the very last thing we lose. So even if you're deeply asleep you can hear me. I know you can. "

"I'm so glad that Sam called me. There's so much I want to say. Most important is that I love you. I've had all these months away from you to think—about you, about me, about us. I've had to face some really unpleasant truths about myself. I had to take a long look at all the walls I've built around me for most of my life.

"You were always there for me, Clay, do you remember? Even when I felt most alone, somehow you let me know you were there. For the longest time you managed to get inside those walls, to make me feel loved and treasured. You and your family made me feel special, even when my father seemed to forget I was around much of the time. You made loving someone appear to be so natural and easy. I discovered that loving you was easy, too easy for my peace of mind.

"Feeling so much love for anyone frightened me, Clay. I was afraid that it would consume me if I allowed it full rein in my life. So I ran from you. Ran from our wedding plans, used the excuse that I had to be independent and free in order to build those walls up again, this time with you on the outside."

Pam absently noted that tears streaked down her face while she spoke, trickling off her cheeks. She wiped them off with the back of her hand, but more quickly took their place.

"The thing is, Clay, I discovered the mistake in my thinking after spending time with you in Texas. I finally forced myself to face the prison that I'd built for myself—all in the name of freedom and my need for independence. That's when I realized what a coward I've been. I've been too afraid of being hurt, of being abandoned again. It was easier to choose being alone than risk losing another person out of my life.

"I've been searching for you these past several weeks in order to tell you what I've discovered about myself, but I couldn't find you. I've stayed in close touch with your mom, but she didn't know how to contact you, either.

"Oh, Clay, there's so much I want to tell you. So much I want to share with you. I am so very sorry that we've lost out on so much time that we could have spent together. I promise you I'll never leave your side again.

"Come back to me, Clay. Let's start all over. This

time we'll be so much wiser. We'll do it differently. I can't think of anything I'd rather do than to plan a wedding with you. We'll get married anywhere, at any time. We can plan a huge production or elope. I just want to be a part of your life. I want you to be a part of mine.

"Please hang on, love. For me. For us. For all those children we used to talk about having. We're all here waiting for you. Give your body a chance to heal. Let your mind adjust to this horrible shock to your system. But when you're ready to face the pain, I'll be here—right here—waiting for you to open your eyes."

She leaned down and carefully placed a kiss on the back of his hand and whispered, "I love you, Clay."

Hours later Pam heard the door behind her open. She turned her head and saw Carina with Cody close behind her. She left Clay's bedside and walked over to the couple. They both hugged her before going to stand beside Clay.

"We spoke to the nurses," Cody said gruffly. "They consider his condition stable, whatever the hell that means."

"He hasn't gotten worse," Pam said. "That's a very good sign."

Carina stood beside him, silent tears streaking her cheeks. She held his hand and spoke softly to him.

Cody looked haggard. "This is too much. I didn't try to talk him out of going into military service. We both knew the dangers, but it was his choice. But by damn! I never want to go through this again. Once he's back on his feet, he and I are going to

have a long talk about his future as a military officer!''

Pam smiled through her tears. She could tell that
Cody hated the feeling of helplessness at seeing
Clay almost lifeless in a hospital bed. Talking about
Clay's future made it less uncertain, somehow. He
would wake up. He just had to.

The hours crept by. Shifts changed, nurses came
in and out. Clay's three visitors took turns going to
eat, returning to Pam's to shower and change, but
there was always one of them beside his bed. When
Clay Callaway opened his eyes, they wanted him to
have a loved one by his side.

Eventually Pam talked Cody and Carina into going to her place for a few hours' sleep. She promised
to do the same once they returned.

She lost track of time, whether it was daylight or
dark or even what day it was. When she was there
alone, she sat and talked to him. She recited stories
about their years together as children, reminding him
of things they'd done together, pranks he had pulled
on his sisters, pranks they had pulled on him. She
reminisced about the parties, the holidays, the school
activities they had shared.

Most of all, she reminded him of how much she
loved him, missed him, and needed him.

By the time his parents returned each day she
would be hoarse. She knew that they, too, were letting him know of their vigil, talking to him, always
making certain that he knew he was not alone.

Pam had no idea how long it had been since her
world had narrowed to one hospital room, the route
between the hospital and her apartment, and her bed

and shower. She vaguely recalled notifying her supervisor that she would not be in to work for an indefinite period of time.

She was grateful that she and Carina had reconnected these past few months. They understood each other so much better. She had formed new impressions of the woman she had thought of as her second mom. This time, the impressions were made as an adult, not a child. She saw Carina's frailties as well as her strengths. She saw her as a woman and as a mother suffering because of her son's debilitating injuries.

Their mutual pain—and strength— had brought them closer than they had ever been before.

The three of them continued the vigil beside Clay's bed, bolstering each other's belief that he would regain consciousness.

Several days passed with little sign of change. They refused to discuss what his continued unconsciousness might portend.

Pam had just crawled out of the shower and was drying off early one afternoon when she heard the phone ring. She almost let the machine pick it up rather than listen to yet another telemarketing spiel, but there was always that chance that the call was news about Clay. She picked up the phone.

"Yes?"

"Pam?" It was Carina. "He's stirring. There was eye movement and his heartbeat has increased. The doctor is on his way."

"So am I," she said, tossing the receiver on the phone and racing to get dressed.

Chapter 18

Two months later

"Katie, you look beautiful," Allison said, stepping back from her daughter. She turned her slightly so Katie could see herself in the bedroom mirror.

Katie looked at herself and smiled. She felt beautiful these days. Sam had that effect on her.

The pale green dress she'd chosen to wear this afternoon made her eyes look brighter and her hair appear darker. She turned and hugged her mother. "I'm so happy," she whispered.

Allison nodded. "I can see that. You're the calmest one around here. So much for bridal jitters."

"Have you seen Sam today?"

Allison laughed. "Actually, your father called to say that he would bring him out in time for the wedding, but not too soon. I gather that he's having enough premarital jitters for both of you."

Katie nodded. "He's afraid he won't know how to be a father to the girls, or a husband to me."

"Valid concerns, I would think."

"He'll do just fine, Mom. The girls already love him to death. In fact, they're quite peeved that they have to stay here with you instead of going with us to St. Croix."

Allison smiled. "I know. You wouldn't believe all the promises I've made to keep them entertained. They will be thoroughly spoiled by the time you two get back."

"As if they aren't already." She touched her hair. "You really think I look okay?" she asked uncertainly, still finding it almost unbelievable that Sam Carruthers wanted to marry her. She could certainly empathize with any nerves he was having at the moment, taking on a wife and two children for the first time in his life.

"You look absolutely gorgeous," Allison replied. She peeked out her daughter's bedroom window. "There they are now. Let's get downstairs so he doesn't have to wait any longer than necessary." She straightened up and looked at Katie. "Honey, all you have to do is to notice Sam's expression when he sees you to know that you are glowing. Now let's go."

Katie and her mother were halfway down the stairs when her dad opened the door and ushered the pastor inside, along with Sam.

Katie only noticed Sam.

He was listening to the pastor, nodding his head solemnly, when he caught movement on the stairs and looked up. He froze in mid-step, their gazes locked.

Katie vaguely heard her father say to the pastor, "We better get these two hitched before Sam has a heart attack and has to spend his honeymoon in the hospital."

Sam and Katie laughed at the same time, breaking the tension. Katie continued down the stairs and walked into Sam's arms. He didn't kiss her. He just held her as though she were the most precious thing in the world to him.

Cole cleared his throat and Sam reluctantly released Katie, holding her hand as they followed the pastor into the den, which had been rearranged to accommodate the visitors who had been invited.

Katie had asked her cousin Trish to be her only attendant. The girls were waiting impatiently in their matching dresses. The room was full, which was easy enough to do with so many Callaways in the area. Katie spotted Pamela McCall, looking sophisticated in a royal blue dress.

Sam had asked Clay to be his best man, but Clay had initially refused. He'd been released from the hospital and presently lived with his parents, going for physical therapy every day at the military base, but he was still in a wheelchair. The final prognosis had not been made as to whether he would ever walk again.

But Sam had worn him down. Katie smiled as she saw Clay seated in his chair beside the fireplace, where the pastor stood with Trisha. When she caught his eye, her smile became a grin; she was rewarded with a half smile in return.

He was so thin…and very pale. From what she understood, they were lucky to have him at all.

She was glad that Sam had insisted he be there for this occasion.

Then someone put on the music and she and Sam walked hand in hand and stood before the pastor to say their vows.

Pam sat on the last row of folding chairs, feeling very out of place. She'd wanted to be there, of course, but looking around, she discovered that she was the only non-family member in attendance.

If Clay had his way, she would never become a member of the Callaway clan.

She recalled how relieved and thrilled she was when he'd first regained consciousness. He'd appeared surprised to see her there and had very little to say to her. Mostly he'd asked what had happened to the other members of the team. When the doctor had told him, he'd retreated back into himself, rousing only when questioned by the medical staff.

He'd ignored the presence of his parents and Pam. The doctor had explained that this wasn't unusual under the conditions. Clay would have to deal with the shock of losing so many of his comrades. There would be the guilt of having survived. The only positive the army doctor had been able to pass along was that they had accomplished their mission. The attack against them had happened on their way out of the battle zone.

The doctor—and the Callaways—hoped that would be enough to ease some of Clay's suffering.

Pam wasn't surprised when Clay's parents arranged to have him sent to a military hospital in San Antonio to recuperate and begin his physical therapy.

She'd tried to talk to him before the transfer, but he'd made it very clear that he had nothing to say to her. She was part of his past. He intended for her to stay that way.

Pam had gone back to work once the Callaways flew back to Texas. What more was there for her to do? There was no way to convince Clay at this point that she'd been trying to reach him within weeks of leaving him in Texas. For some reason, he insisted on believing that the only reason she had come to the hospital was out of pity, something he had no use for.

She continued to stay in touch with his mother, who kept her up-to-date on his progress. Carina had suggested that she wait a while before coming to see him, that he needed time to adjust to his situation.

No matter how well he healed, his career in the field was effectively over. Carina reported that Cody and Clay discussed what else he might like to do if he decided to take a medical discharge from the army and enter civilian life. His decisions hinged on how mobile he might become in the future.

Now he sat tall in the wheelchair, his face in profile as he waited beside Sam and listened to the pastor read the wonderful words uniting Katie and Sam.

At least the two of them had found each other. They both deserved the happiness they had discovered together. Katie was excited about relocating and beginning a life halfway across the United States.

She'd told Pam a few days ago that she'd convinced Sam not to get upset with her because she had the money to buy a comfortable home in Georgia. She'd been pleased that he hadn't allowed his ego to create a problem for them at this stage of their relationship.

He admitted that he saw no reason to have the family attempt to exist on his salary. He'd already faced that subject before he proposed to her. They both knew that he wasn't marrying her for her money—she'd already gone through a marriage like that!—and neither of them really cared what others might think.

If only she and Clay had come to some kind of understanding before he'd been injured so severely, maybe they would be married by now. She'd lost track of the number of times she'd replayed the scene in her mind where he came into her room to talk to her about their relationship.

What she wouldn't give to go back in time and change her response to him.

"I now pronounce you husband and wife...you may kiss the bride," the pastor said. Sam turned and looked at Katie. Pam had never seen so much love in one man's face as shone in his. He leaned over and gently kissed her. The pastor said to those watching, "I'd like to introduce you to Lieutenant Colonel and Mrs. Samuel Carruthers."

Pam watched Clay as he unobtrusively backed closer to the fireplace to get out of the way of the well-wishers who surged toward the happy couple. The girls dashed forward, throwing themselves at the couple, chattering. The din continued to climb as more and more moved forward.

Pam edged around the group until she reached Clay. Without saying anything she pushed his chair toward the patio doors. Those in the way hastily stepped aside with smiles and greetings. As far as she could tell, Clay didn't respond.

She wheeled him onto the patio, which had been set up for the reception being held after the wedding. It was still quiet out there, except for the caterers, who were putting the finishing touches on the food at the buffet table, and the musicians, tuning their instruments and testing the sound system.

She paused by one of the tables and Clay said wearily, "Thanks, Dad, for rescuing me from the mob." He turned his head as she stepped from behind him. His face froze into stone. "I'm sorry. I thought you were Dad."

Pam pulled out one of the chairs at the table and sat down beside him. "I hope you don't mind that it was me," she said lightly, smiling at him.

His expression didn't change. He looked around the fenced-in backyard. "They did a nice job back here, didn't they? Good thing it didn't rain."

"It wouldn't dare rain on a Callaway wedding. That's not allowed."

"Yeah, like the Callaways have so much pull with the weather."

"It's good to see you, Clay. Your mom tells me you're making real progress with your therapy."

"She does, huh? I didn't know she was reporting to you."

She kept a grip on her temper. "Actually, we've stayed in close touch since I was here last spring."

He looked around the yard again. "Well, at least they managed to hold off getting married until the weather cooled down some. It will be pleasant out here for the evening. The lights look nice, don't they?"

"Did you know that I tried every way I knew how to get in touch with you once we left here back then?"

He finally turned his head so that he was looking at her. "Why?" he asked starkly.

"To tell you what an idiot I'd been."

"About what?"

"Us. I wanted to tell you that I finally figured out how much of a coward I was for not admitting how much I loved you, how much I wanted to be a part of your life."

"You lucked out, then."

"How do you figure that?"

"Well, if you'd reached me, I might have been stupid enough to propose. Then where would you be?"

"Where I'd like to be—with you."

"Oh. Right. There's nothing you'd like more than to play nursemaid to me. Now tell me another one."

"What I'm saying is that I want another chance with you."

"No."

"Clay—"

"I don't know how I can make it any plainer, Pam. I don't want you. I'm not going to propose to you. I sure as hell am not going to marry you. So could we change the subject now?"

"I know things are rough for you right now, and—"

"And I don't need you around trying to make everything all right. I'm going to get out of this chair. I'm going to walk again. I'm going to find another career. I'm going to make it. Alone."

"You don't have to do it alone."

He smiled, but the smile put a chill through her. It was as cold as his eyes. "Then let me be blunt. I won't do it with you. Now, if you'll excuse me, I'm going to start celebrating my cousin's wedding by getting a drink at the bar. And no, before you ask, I don't need you to get it for me. Goodbye, Pam. Have a good life." He wheeled the chair away from her, his back and neck stiff.

Pam had a strong urge to push him into the pool. It was what he deserved, the fool. So he thought she was feeling sorry for him, did he? Not on his life. She knew that he would walk again because he wouldn't accept anything less.

So she would bide her time, because this time she wasn't going to allow Clay Callaway to get away from her.

Chapter 19

Six months later

Pam was at the office when her phone rang. Because of the type of work she did for the bureau, she rarely received outside calls.

"Pam McCall," she said, still more intent on the printout she was studying than the intrusive phone.

"Hi, Pam, this is Carina."

Pam froze. "Oh, my God, what's wrong?"

Carina laughed lightly. "Not a thing and I'm sorry for bothering you at work, but something has come up and I thought it might turn into an opportunity for you."

"Okay," she replied slowly, waiting.

"Cody and I have been invited to go with Cole and Allison to visit Sam and Katie. They want to leave this afternoon. So I wanted to mention to you that Clay will be here at the house alone, besides the housekeeper, of course, in case you wanted to drop by.''

"Drop by? Flying from D.C. to San Antonio is hardly a drop-by situation.''

"You think not? Well, of course, if you can't get away—'' she began.

"I didn't say that, Carina, and you know it. You're still playing matchmaker, aren't you?''

"Well, I hate to see my one and only son pining away like he is. I figured that seeing you again might be just the thing he needs.''

"He's still depressed?''

"No, just frustrated. Now that he's walking, he's irritated that he still needs to use the cane, even though the doctors have told him that if he continues to improve in the next few months as he has in the last few, he'll be almost as good as new.''

"Does he know you've called me?''

"Surely you jest. He would tear me limb from limb if he suspected we're still in touch.''

"I don't know, Carina. He's made it very clear that he wants nothing to do with me.''

"Yes. So he says. Do you believe him?''

"Well, he's pretty darn convincing.''

Carina sighed. "The one thing I know about my son is that he's deeply loyal. I've never known his feelings to change toward anyone. I know that he loved you with all that was in him. In fact, he readily admitted as much the last time he was home before he was hurt so badly. I don't think his feelings have changed…just his circumstances. He's touchy about them. Looking at his situation from his point of view, I can see why he wouldn't feel he has much to offer you."

"His injury certainly hasn't lessened my feelings for him."

"Then maybe you might want to take this opportunity to convince him of that. The housekeeper leaves around seven. You know where his bedroom is, and where we hide the extra key. Just let yourself in whenever you get here. We'll probably see you when we get back from Georgia." With that, Carina blithely hung up, as though suggesting that she seduce her son was nothing out of the ordinary.

Well, what did she have to lose? Besides her dignity and what little pride she'd managed to salvage after their last encounter at Katie's wedding.

She stared blankly at the printout she'd been studying so intently before Carina's call. She could no longer make anything of it. With a groan she went to find her supervisor. She needed some time off, effective immediately.

This was no way to build a career with any future. But now Pam no longer cared. She would do what she had to do to convince one very stubborn male that they were a match made in heaven...even if it had taken her several years to discover that for herself.

Clay turned off the news and slowly made his way down the hall to his bedroom. He'd been surprised when he got home from his therapy session to find a note on the kitchen table from his mother, telling him that his parents were going to Georgia to visit Sam and Katie.

Not that he saw anything wrong with it. Cole and

Allison generally flew up in the company jet about once every week to ten days. Sam must have figured by now that when he married one Callaway, he'd married them all. Now he'd also have Cody and Carina there. Clay smiled, wishing he could have gone just to see the look on Sam's face when he got home tonight.

According to Katie, Sam seemed to walk around in a state of shock, particularly after she informed him a few weeks ago that he was going to become a father. At forty-three.

It was hard for Clay to believe that next month would be a year since the benefit held in Dallas that had brought them all together. Quite a lot had happened in that year. Arthur had spilled his guts to the authorities, but was still resting nicely in a federal pen where Clay hoped he stayed for many a year.

Colonel Carruthers, now a full-bird colonel, had become part of the extended family—something that Clay would never have dreamed of during the time he trained under the man. And Clay was no longer a part of the military.

In fact, he'd been recently weighing a job offer from the intelligence community, which would make it necessary for him to leave Texas once again, and move to D.C. Or thereabouts.

Where Pam lived.

He didn't want his thoughts to go there. He refused to think about her, speculate on what she was doing, whom she was seeing. Instead, she visited him every night as soon as he fell asleep. He figured he should be used to it now.

Clay headed into his bathroom and took a long shower, feeling the hot water soothe his battered body. Every muscle in his body ached, he could swear. But he refused to complain. He still dreamed of that night when his team had been discovered. He still heard the sounds of automatic weapons, felt the bullets strike his body. His sergeant had inadvertently saved his life by falling across him, his body shielding Clay from further hits. They'd been left for dead. The only reason he survived was because sympathizers found him and carried him back across the border and into friendly territory.

There were nights when he woke up smelling the smoke from the ammunition, smelling the blood—his own and his team's—and he would think he was back there.

The dreams were coming less and less, just as the dreams of Pam came with more frequency. As his body healed, his mind wanted to re-create the physical union the two of them had enjoyed all those months ago.

Almost a year ago.

He hadn't been too polite the last time he'd seen her. Her appearance at the wedding had come as a complete shock to him. He'd been told it was for family. Of course he could understand why Sam and Katie would want to include her, considering how their romance had come about. Pam had been there at the beginning of their relationship. She might as well enjoy the culmination.

If Clay had known at the time that she'd been invited, he wouldn't have gone. He had a hunch that Sam had suspected his attitude and deliberately stayed quiet.

He'd tried to get out of it as it was, but Sam was persistent and he'd finally found it easier to give in than to argue. He hadn't been out in public before that day. He hadn't been ready for the stares from people. Sam had reminded him that this was family.

She had stayed the whole evening, but hadn't come near him again. She'd danced with his male cousins, visited with their wives and girlfriends, and in general acted as if he wasn't there. Which was just the way he'd wanted it, of course.

The water started cooling and he turned off the shower and stepped out in front of the fogged mirrors. By the time he dried off, the mist was lifting and he could see himself.

His body looked pretty chewed up, all right. He had scars on his shoulder, his chest, his thigh, his arms and legs. But he'd regained his weight and built it into muscle. He hadn't had much else to do with his days except work out. His leg was finally filling out. He'd probably always have the limp, but if he took the job that had been offered him, it wouldn't matter.

He understood it was with the same outfit where his cousin Clint worked. Now, that would be interesting. He wondered if the agency could handle two Callaways at a time.

He'd probably accept the job. He was certainly getting bored around here with nothing to do all day. Which meant that he'd be looking for a place to live around D.C. He might buy a house. Who knows? There could be worse things than owning a home.

He might surprise Pam and give her a call... maybe take her out to dinner. He'd wait until he took her home before telling her that he'd be moving to the area. Wonder what she would do? He smiled at the scenario.

His body stirred and he frowned. Couldn't he even think of the woman without getting aroused? Obviously not, he decided with disgust.

Tossing his towel, he limped into the bedroom and crawled into bed. Man, oh, man, he was tired. It didn't take him long to fall into a deep sleep.

Sometime during the night Clay realized that Pam had invaded his dreams once again. He needed her tonight. He ached for her.

She seemed to understand. She knelt beside him, kissing and caressing him, lightly touching each scar with her fingertips and her mouth before exploring the next.

When she found the one on his thigh, he shifted slightly, wanting more than her soft caresses. Wanting—ah. Yes. Wanting her to love him as she was now doing, with the tip of her tongue and her soft, luscious mouth, stroking him, bringing him to the brink of completion.

He reached for her and she flowed upward into his arms, sheathing him in one fluid movement, moving over him with a steady rhythm and causing him to explode into a million tiny particles of pleasure and release.

When she tried to pull away from him he clasped her tightly to his chest, searching for her mouth with his, kissing her with unleashed passion, relieved when she returned his kiss with equal ardor.

She felt so good in his arms, so real. This was one dream from which he never wanted to awaken. By the time that kiss had become several more, he wanted her again. He lifted his hips slightly and she followed his movement with one of her own.

As though teasing each other, they slowly and

sinuously came together, then moved until they were almost separated before once again sliding together. They had always known how to pleasure the other. They had always been such a perfect fit.

Clay had a moment of clarity when he was thankful that his body had healed enough to be able to pleasure her as much as she pleasured him.

She sat up so that she could ride him, using her knees to move up and away from him, then down, accepting him to the hilt. It was a lazy movement, as though they had all the time in the world.

In his dreamlike state, Clay was content to enjoy her until that time when once again, he would awaken and find himself alone.

Pam had felt like a thief, slipping into the house late at night. Thank goodness that Carina had warned her to check the alarm system. Sure enough, Clay must have set it before going to bed. That would have been all she needed, the alarms going off while she was sneaking inside.

Now that she was here, she knew the next step was to find Clay's bedroom. On the plane flying to San Antonio she'd been reminded of the time, almost a year ago, when he'd crawled into *her* bed late one night. All at once she decided there was no reason for her to feel apologetic for what she was about to do.

Now she could get even with him.

There was a night-light in the hallway so that she could see the doorways. She counted to the room where Carina said he slept and opened the door.

He was sprawled across the bed on his back. The dim light gave her a clear view of how much he had healed. He must have spent considerable time in the sun, as well, because he was as dark as she'd ever seen him, a golden-brown that she'd always found extremely attractive.

His musculature was also more defined. It was obvious that he'd been working out extensively. Mm-mm, but he looked good.

Pam carefully stripped out of her clothes, folding them neatly and placing them on a chair nearby. Next, she sank down on the side of the bed and waited for him to wake up. But he didn't.

Okay. Now we'll find out what it takes to wake him up, she decided, then leaned over and began to lightly kiss and caress the scars she'd never seen.

Clay slowly surfaced the next morning to the muted sound of the vacuum cleaner in some other part of the house.

He lay there with his eyes closed and realized that his body hadn't awakened him with aches and pains for the first time since his injuries. He felt as though he were floating on a cloud somewhere, dreaming of Pam.

He smiled to himself. He'd managed to dream about her again. This time the dreams were much more vivid than usual. He could still smell the scent of her, still feel the brush of her hair against his cheek. Perhaps he was still dreaming. Not even in his dreams had he experienced so many sensations. He'd made love to Pam—well, actually, she had made love to him—in so many new and different ways.

He stretched, his arms reaching high in the air,

then dropping to hit the—soft skin of someone lying beside him.

His eyes flew open and he stared at the woman lying next to him, sound asleep. Her fair hair partially covered her face as it also draped across his shoulder.

That hadn't been a dream last night. How could he possibly have thought—for one minute—that it was?

Oh, she was sneaky. Very sneaky. He wondered how she had known that he would be there at the house alone? Could his mother have mentioned to her that she and his dad...? Nah. Not his moral, upstanding mother. Not his uptight, straight-as-an-arrow father.

Maybe Pam had his room bugged. She was an FBI agent, after all. He grinned at the ridiculous thought. He didn't care why she was there. He was delighted that she was.

He leaned up on his elbow and gently smoothed the hair away from her face. She didn't budge. He leaned over and kissed her cheek. There was a slight flicker of her eyelash, then nothing.

Neither one of them had bothered with the sheet. In fact, he now saw that it was lying on the floor on his side. The temperature in the room was comfortable and they hadn't needed it. If his memory served him right, they'd probably raised the temperature of the room by several degrees last night. And this morning.

He cupped her breast in his hand and leaned down, pressing his mouth around the tip. She shifted her legs slightly, restlessly, and he knew that he was getting to her. For that matter, he was getting to himself as well. He was already swelling as if this were his first scent of a woman in months and months.

Instead of mere hours. Wonder-filled hours. Loving hours.

Pam had come back to him.

Despite his rudeness.

Despite his anger and resentment.

She'd come back.

This time, he would make darn sure she never left him again.

He tugged harder at her nipple, then slid his hand down her side to her hip. Applying a little pressure, he managed to ease her over onto her back. He moved over her and knelt between her legs, finding all kinds of delectable places to explore.

She came awake with a jolt. "Wha...!"

He patted her belly without pausing from stroking her delicate folds with his tongue. "Shh...didn't mean to wake you...just go back to sleep," he whispered between touches.

"Clay!" she groaned, grabbing his head between her hands.

"I'm glad you recognized me," he said, glancing up to meet her dazed expression. "You never know who you might wake up in bed with these days. Just can't be too careful."

Then there was no more talk. He loved her until she came to a screaming climax, which he muffled before the housekeeper decided to see who he might be torturing in his bedroom. He waited until the ripples deep within her slowed before he slowly pushed inside her, taking his time, loving the feel of her, the heat of her.

This time he joined her when she went over the edge, smiling to himself as he held her close, breasts flattened against his dampened chest.

He must have dozed back to sleep. The next thing he knew Pam was nudging him. "Clay?"

"Mmm?"

"I'm starving. Do you think we could get up for a while?"

He opened one eye and peered at the clock. It was a little after two. From the sunlight coming through the closed blinds, he figured it must be afternoon. He'd missed his physical therapy appointment.

Darn.

He stretched. "I suppose."

"Aren't you hungry?"

"A little."

She slid out of bed and went into the bathroom. He waited until he heard her little shriek as she crawled into the shower—it took forever for the hot water to reach the pipes—then he walked into the bathroom and joined her in the shower.

By the time they finally got out and dried off, both their legs were trembling. "You're insatiable," she muttered, wrapping the towel around her body and going into the other room.

"Yeah, well, maybe I overdid it a bit," he admitted, his limp more pronounced than it had been. "But I figure if I'm dreaming, I want to enjoy you all I can before I wake up."

She started dressing. He pulled out a drawer, found his shorts, socks and a T-shirt. After putting them on, he grabbed a pair of barely worn jeans and slid them on.

He happened to glance up and realized that Pam was standing there, watching him. "What?"

"You're looking great these days. You know that?"

He glanced down as though seeing his body for the first time in months. "Really?" He rubbed his belly. "Think I'm putting on too much weight?"

She shook her head. "You know better—all those rippling abs could turn a gal's head." She waited a moment, then asked, "Are you still having a lot of pain?"

He grinned. "Honey, at this point in time, I'm feeling no pain at all." He could see that she had grown serious. He wasn't real sure that he wanted to get too serious right now.

He and Pam had always had this wonderful physical relationship. It was when they tried to put their feelings into words that everything turned to crap.

"No, really, I'm doing okay. My knee's still a little stiff, although you wouldn't believe it the way I've been carrying on with you. I use the cane to help me keep my balance, but otherwise, the rest of my wounds have healed. I was lucky that the first surgeons who got a hold of me did such a good job of sewing me back together."

She went to the door and opened it. Without looking back at him, she said, "I'm going to make us something to eat," and disappeared down the hallway.

Clay stood there with his hands on the front of his jeans, ready to fasten them. Somehow, he'd managed to upset her and he didn't have a clue why.

So what else was new?

* * *

By the time he finished dressing and went to the kitchen, Pam had bacon frying, coffee brewing; bread in the toaster, and was cracking eggs in a bowl.

"You want to tell me what's wrong?" he asked, walking into the room.

She gave him a quick glance. "Nothing's wrong. I told you. I'm hungry."

He shrugged. "Okay."

He went over to the coffeepot, where the machine was dripping its last drops into the carafe, and poured himself a cup. He filled another one and set it beside her. Then he went over to the cabinet and pulled out plates, found silverware in the drawer and quietly set the table.

He watched her scramble the eggs, drain the bacon, butter the toast, then bring all of that over on a platter and put it between them.

"Thank you," he said politely.

"You're welcome," she replied, equally politely. They ate in silence.

Clay waited until they'd finished eating everything on the platter and he'd refilled their cups before he said, "So what are you doing here?" He thought it was a sociable-enough question.

"I thought that was fairly obvious," she finally said.

"Let's just say that I need to have it spelled out to me."

She picked up her cup and looked at him through the steam. "You know, the last time I saw you I came very close to shoving you into the swimming pool, wheelchair and all." She took a sip of her coffee.

His mouth twitched. "I probably deserved it," he admitted.

"Oh, you definitely deserved it."

"Would it help if I apologized?"

She thought about that. And continued to think about it.

"Groveled, maybe?" he suggested.

She nodded. "I like that idea."

"All right." He sat there as the silence stretched between them. Finally, he said, "I acted like an unmitigated jerk and I'm sorry. You didn't deserve that kind of treatment, from me or anyone else. Mom mentioned that you were at the hospital the whole time I was in a coma, talking to me, calling me back, loving me. It was a sorry way to treat you after all you did for me. I have no excuse for my behavior."

She leaned back in her chair and looked at him appraisingly. "Wow," she finally said, "when you decide to grovel you do a fantastic job of it." She leaned closer. "Do you remember anything about your coma?"

He shook his head. "My memories about the night of the attack were really hazy. It took several people to help fill in the blanks. Some of them may never be filled in. The next thing I remember is seeing you and the folks standing there by my bed. I wondered how the hell you'd found me in Europe."

"It was a very scary time, Clay."

"So my parents keep telling me...over and over."

"Your mom told me that you've been medically discharged from the army."

"She's just a regular on-the-spot reporter, isn't she?"

"She knows how much I care about you."

"Care about me?" he carefully repeated, as though tasting each word.

"All right. She knows how much I love you," she said almost belligerently, "how's that?"

He grinned, enjoying the way her eyes flashed when she was irritated. He sometimes wondered if he didn't deliberately goad her at times just to see that look in her face. If so, his motives didn't speak very well of his character.

He leaned over and took her resisting fingers. "I think it's a powerful coincidence, since I love you, too."

She eyed him uncertainly. "You do?" she asked.

He rolled his eyes. "As if you're surprised."

"Well, I wasn't sure, after the way you've been treating me."

"I've already apologized for my behavior at the wedding. And I thought I treated you quite well last night...and this morning...and later this morning." He watched as the color came up from her neck and flooded her face. "Did you really try to contact me after we left here last spring?"

"Yes."

"I'm very glad to hear it. And if you're considering marriage, I accept," he replied.

Now what? He thought, watching her eyes fill with tears. Had she hoped he would turn her down?

"Oh, Clay, I was afraid you'd refuse. I didn't dare hope that you would forgive me enough to marry me."

"Refuse! On the contrary, I think it's about time you made an honest man of me, don't you? I mean, what would my parents think if they were to walk in here and find you in my bed? You have no idea how lucky you are that they happened to be out of town.''

''That's true,'' she said demurely, studying their clasped hands.

''Which one told you they were going to be gone? Just out of curiosity.''

She flicked a quick glance at him before returning her gaze to their hands. ''Your mom.''

''It was her idea for you to come crawl into bed with me?'' This really was getting interesting, he decided.

''No, of course not.''

''I'm relieved. I wouldn't want to think that the grandmother of our children was lacking in moral fiber.''

That brought her gaze back to his face. He smiled. ''You really want children?'' she asked.

''We talked about that. Years ago. Of course I want children.''

''But I thought that—well, after so much time— that maybe you'd changed your mind about things.''

He stood and pulled her up from her chair, then wrapped his arms around her. ''Nothing in my heart has changed where you're concerned, not from the time I was eight years old. And frankly, I'm getting tired of waiting around for our happy ending. So when are you going to marry me?''

She laughed and threw her arms around his neck. ''Whenever you think you can support me and all my kids, big guy. I understand you're presently unemployed.''

''I guess it's time I catch you up on my prospects, Ms. McCall.''

Chapter 20

Pam focused her gaze on the sight of Clay's strong, capable fingers wrapped around the steering wheel of the car. Clay was all she wanted to concentrate on, as well as the fact that they were together again at long last. What could possibly be more important than her plans to finally marry Clay Callaway? She reminded herself.

Nothing. Absolutely nothing.

He reached for the key and turned off the ignition. "Well, we're here," Clay said lightly, turning to look at her with a grin.

She forced herself to gaze outside of the coziness the car represented to her at the moment. The carefully tended landscape was familiar enough. Not a weed in any flower bed, not a blade of grass daring to be a fraction of an inch taller than its neighbor.

The sweeping driveway formed a horseshoe shape in front of the large redbrick home.

"Are we going to stay here in the car for the duration of this visit, or shall we go knock on the door?" he asked in a friendly voice.

She took a deep breath and reached for the handle. "We're here. We'll go talk with him."

Clay joined her on the steps and took her hand. "It's going to be okay, Pam. Really."

"If he's rude to you, I swear I'll get up and walk out, right then and there."

"Don't be silly. The man's a professional and you're his only daughter. Why would he be rude to the man you're engaged to marry?"

She looked at him with a raised eyebrow. "Surely you jest. My father could care less about my feelings in any of this." She jabbed at the doorbell and listened to its soothing chimes echo in the high-ceilinged foyer.

"It isn't as though we need his permission to get married, Pam," Clay reminded her.

"I know that!" she said, aware that she was behaving badly and yet unable to get a grip on her feelings.

The door swung open. An elderly gentleman stood there. As soon as he recognized her, the man smiled and said, "Welcome to Havenhurst, Miss McCall. It's good to see you again."

With Clay's hand firmly grasped in hers, Pam stepped inside. "Good afternoon, Forrest. I believe that Father is expecting me."

"Yes. He's in the study. I'll have coffee for you in a few minutes."

"Thanks," she replied and moved toward the back of the foyer with a steady pace. The door to the room stood open. She paused just inside, feeling Clay's comforting warmth against her back.

"Hello, Father," she said.

The tall, lean, silver-haired man standing beside the empty grated fireplace turned at the sound of her voice. She had to admit that he looked very distinguished in his suede sports jacket and twill pants. The blue of his cotton shirt matched his eyes, the same color he'd passed on to his daughter.

"It's good to see you, Pamela," he said, moving toward her and holding out his hand. If there was a pause in his step when he recognized Clay, he managed to cover it quite nicely. "Forrest was just going to bring coffee. Please have a seat." He took her hand and squeezed it gently before looking past her shoulder. "Clay Callaway, isn't it? You're the spitting image of your father at that age. My God. I wouldn't have recognized you, otherwise." He held out his hand to Clay, and Pam let go of the breath she hadn't been aware she was holding.

It was going to be all right, she finally allowed herself to hope.

"So what brings you young people out this way?" Jason asked, once again motioning for them to sit. Pam chose the love seat so that Clay would be close by. She was being ridiculous and she knew it. The truth was that she wouldn't be here at all if Clay and his mother hadn't gently insisted she should come.

So here they were...and both men were looking at her as though she was supposed to say something. Oh! Her father's question.

"Well, it's been a while since I was here and—"

"Christmas, to be exact," her father said smoothly.

She nodded, jerkily. "Right. Christmas. And so I thought—" Her mind went blank. Absolutely blank. If she'd ever had a thought in her head it had deserted her in her time of need. "We, uh—that is, I, uh—" she looked at Clay in desperation.

He took her hand and slid it between both of his, forming a nice warm pocket of security to help calm her nerves.

"What she's trying to say, sir, is that Pam and I are engaged to be married. We wanted you to hear it from us before news filtered back to you from other sources."

Jason had seated himself across from them in his comfortably overstuffed chair. Being the consummate politician that he was, he knew she had absolutely no way of knowing how he felt about that tidbit of news. "I see," he finally said, then looked up with what might be considered relief when Forrest walked in carrying a tray filled with various items of food and drink. "Here, just set everything on the table, will you?" he instructed.

As though the man would have had no idea what to do with the tray otherwise, Pam thought with irritation. Or—the thought suddenly hit her—maybe, just maybe, her father was as nervous about this meeting as she was. Now there was a whole new perspective. She leaned back and felt Clay's arm resting along the back of the sofa. With a silent sigh, Pam forced herself to relax while Forrest efficiently filled cups and plates with a selection of cookies and tiny cakes, and handed them to each of them.

Once Forrest left, Jason smiled and said, "I won't

pretend that your news doesn't come as a complete surprise, Pamela. I wasn't aware that you and Clay had stayed in touch over the years."

"Yes, well, we hadn't until about a year ago. Actually, we ran into each other at the benefit the Callaways held in Dallas last year."

"Hmm. And it was love at first sight again?"

Clay chuckled, which made Pamela want to drop her steaming cup of coffee in his lap.

"Not exactly, Father. As you say, it had been a long time since we'd seen each other. Plus we've been quite busy with our own careers. Neither of us has been thinking about marriage until recently."

Jason focused his attention on Clay. "Exactly what do you do, Clay?"

"I work for one of the intelligence agencies."

"The FBI?"

Clay smiled. "No. One in the family will be enough, I think."

"I wondered if you would give me away at the wedding, Father?" Pam blurted out, getting to the point of the visit.

Jason stared at her, making no attempt to mask his surprise. Then he smiled. "Why, Pam, I would be honored to escort you down the aisle. Thank you for asking."

His sudden warmth and unexpected response stunned her.

"Oh," she finally said. "Well. That's good. I guess I wasn't sure if you'd be—" She stopped. There was no point in going further with that thought.

Jason leaned forward in his chair, resting his elbows on his knees. "There is nothing that would give me more pleasure than to see you marry the man you love. Although you managed to convince me that Clay would never be that man, I'm more than willing to accept the fact that you've changed your mind.''

"You never forgave me for breaking our engagement. I know that.''

"It wasn't a matter of forgiving you. I didn't understand, either then or now, what it was that you wanted, what would make you happy in life, what I could do to make your life better...easier.'' He got up and walked over to his desk, where he picked up a pipe and began to fill it. "I don't remember a time in your life when I didn't feel completely inadequate and hopeless in the role of father. I'd spent very little time with children and certainly knew nothing about little girls.''

He returned to the chair and sat down. "It didn't help my peace of mind to watch you grow more and more into your mother so that you became a constant reminder of the woman I so desperately loved and lost much too soon. Well meaning friends suggested that the best thing I could do was to remarry and provide a two-parent home for you once again. It was selfish of me, I know, but I couldn't do that. It wouldn't have been fair to the woman who would have attempted to fill the void in my heart left by the loss of your mother.''

Pam stared at her father in astonishment and dismay. She had never in all her life heard her father mention her mother. Not once. He had behaved as though her mother had never existed in their lives, as though there had always been just the two of them.

She'd interpreted that to mean that he had never really cared about his wife. Only now did she understand that he had cared too much, and had been devastated with grief by her passing.

Impulsively, Pam moved to her father's side and knelt beside his chair. "I'm sorry. I didn't understand."

Puzzled, he asked, "About what?"

"How much you loved and missed her, just as I did. As a child I thought you were so busy you soon forgot her."

"Never that, child. Never that. I couldn't discuss her without breaking down. It was just too painful to bear."

Pam wrapped her arms around her father's neck and held him tightly. She couldn't remember the last time she'd hugged him, or told him she loved him. When his arms held her with equal force she no longer fought the tears that slipped quietly down her cheeks.

Somehow in finding Clay, she managed to find her father again, as well.

Three months later she and her father stood waiting in the small anteroom of the church, waiting for the signal to go down the aisle.

"You look just like your mother did on our wedding day," her father said, his eyes moist. "You are simply gorgeous."

"Thank you for saving her dress for me, Papa," she replied, the name she'd called him when she'd been very small slipping from her lips. "I had no idea you still had it."

"I was too angry with both you and Clay about

the first wedding you planned. I didn't feel you deserved to wear this dress and so I never mentioned it. Looking back, I realize that it was just as much my fault as anyone's that I'd allowed you too much freedom, and that you'd become intimately involved with him much too soon. I think I was trying to punish you by forcing you to marry so young. If I was thinking at all. Mostly I was reacting. My baby had grown up when I wasn't around. I didn't know how to handle the situation and made a complete hash of it."

She went up on her toes and kissed his cheek. "That's behind us now. Today we start a whole new chapter in our lives. We've waited long enough to be together, Clay and me. And we're talking about a family as soon as possible. Think you can handle the role of grandpa?"

Jason chuckled. "I'm certainly willing to give it my best shot. All I've ever wanted was your happiness, baby. From the look on your face, you've found it in the young man waiting in the church for you."

She nodded. "You've added to that happiness, Papa. Thank you for sharing so many of your memories these past couple of months. I feel as though you gave me my mother back."

"It's been good for me, too. After all this time, I realize how important it is to keep her alive in our hearts and minds. She'll always be a part of both of us."

The organ music shifted into the signaled march.

"It's time to go," Pam said.

Jason opened the door and ushered her into the foyer of the church. They watched as the bridesmaids entered the church one by one. Kerry winked at her just before she started down the aisle as Pam's matron of honor.

And then it was their turn—hers and her father's.

Very soon it would be time for Clay and Pam to begin their life together.

She'd learned so much about herself and her loved ones since she'd first recognized her love for Clay so many years ago. She hoped that with her newfound knowledge would also come wisdom.

Before, she'd been too young to understand that sometimes love wasn't enough to make a person whole. Now that she'd found the necessary parts of herself, Clay's love for her and hers for him was more than enough to last a lifetime.

With her gaze firmly fixed on Clay's eyes, Pam walked down the aisle to her future with a steady heart and a calm resolve, determined to express her love each day with gratitude to the man who waited so patiently for her at the altar.

Epilogue

DALLAS, TEXAS, June 21

The social event of the season took place in Dallas, Texas, yesterday when two prominent families of the state attended the wedding of their offspring.

Senator Jason McCall gave away his daughter, Miss Pamela McCall, to Mr. Clay Callaway, only son of Cody and Carina Callaway of San Antonio, Texas, at a lavish wedding that will be talked about for years to come.

The bride wore an elegant Parisian wedding gown of exquisite lace and satin with seed pearls sewn along the sleeves, around the scooped neck and scattered along the train.

The matron of honor was the groom's sister, Kerry Callaway Malone. The groom's best man was Colonel Sam Carruthers from Georgia. The flower girls were the twin daughters of the groom's cousin, Mrs. Sam (Kathleen) Carruthers.

The large church was packed with friends and family of the McCalls and the Callaways. Senator McCall briefly spoke to reporters after the wedding, explaining that the couple had been childhood sweethearts and were merely solidifying a tie between the two families that had existed for years.

The wedding reception was held at the Anatole Hotel. Guest favors and souvenirs were plentiful and tastefully done.

After a three-week trip to Scotland for their honeymoon, the couple will make their home in Virginia.

* * * * *

Don't miss the incomparable
Annette Broadrick's next marvelous book—
an anniversary collection of her
first three Silhouette Desire novels:

HUNTER'S PREY, BACHELOR FATHER and
HAWK'S FLIGHT

In a 3-in-1 keepsake edition

MAXIMUM MARRIAGE:
MEN ON A MISSION

On sale October 2000

And to celebrate Silhouette's twentieth
anniversary, Annette has penned an
unforgettable love story that brings together
the families from *HUNTER'S PREY* and
BACHELOR FATHER! Watch the emotion
flow and the passion sizzle as the son and
daughter of these two families find themselves
stranded together...and falling in love?

MARRIAGE PREY
On sale November 2000
Silhouette Desire

Now, turn the page for a tempting look at the
novel that launched beloved Annette Broadrick's
sparkling writing career, *HUNTER'S PREY*.
You'll love it so much you'll want to read the
fifty love stories that came after....

One

She saw him cross the hotel lobby, his boots clicking a staccato rhythm on the marble surface. From her vantage point near the dining area, she watched when he paused at the cavelike entrance to the lounge, removing his Stetson as he surveyed the room. Only after he had disappeared into the gloom did Kristine Cole discover she'd forgotten to breathe when she saw him. Jason McAlister had always had that effect on her.

His appearance miles from where she expected to find him temporarily banished all thoughts of food from her mind. With a start Kristi registered the weary patience on the hostess's face as she waited to show her to her table. Kristi smiled her apology and followed the elegant woman to a small table tucked between potted palms.

The hotel was Holiday Inn's contribution toward the growth of the small southwest Texas town near where Kristi grew up. It was built at the cloverleaf of the interstate highway that skirted Cielo, and neither the highway nor the hotel had been there when she left Texas five years before.

Jason McAlister was the reason she had not returned sooner. He was also responsible for her being there now.

What should I do? she wondered, chewing on her bottom lip. She'd driven her Triumph TR7 from New York, taking her time, enjoying the freedom of being on her own after years of restrictive schedules and demanding deadlines. She had stopped at the hotel on impulse. A night's rest before driving the final fifty miles to her brother's ranch had seemed like a good idea earlier in the evening. Now she wasn't so sure.

Of course, Kristi intended to contact Jason—she just hadn't counted on seeing him quite so soon. Why should she be nervous? She'd mingled with the rich and royalty, politicians and playboys. Why should one particular rancher in an obscure part of Texas cause butterflies to flutter up under her ribs? Why indeed?

What should I do? she asked herself once more. The dignified waiter standing with pencil poised implied that she could order her dinner as far as he was concerned.

Good idea. Without glancing at the menu, she said, "The dinner salad, please." His blank face almost registered an expression of surprise as his eyes scanned her slender figure.

Of course I'm thin, she thought with irritation. *That's because models go around half-starved most of the time.* She gave him her dazzling smile as an apology for her waspish thoughts.

"Will there be anything else?"

"A glass of chablis, please." Hang the calories, I need a drink. Her insides continued to quiver like jelly in an earthquake. Of course she didn't *have* to face him tonight. She could stick with her original plan to visit with Kyle and Francine for a few days, then call Jason and arrange to meet with him.

The waiter returned with her drink and it was only when she caught sight of her trembling hand as she reached for the glass that Kristi faced how unnerved she was. Lifting the glass to her lips, she managed to spill a drop or two on her muted green ultrasuede dress. She ineffectually dabbed at the spots with her napkin, her appearance the least of her concerns at that moment.

No one in her family could explain the genetic accident that gave Kristi her striking good looks. High cheekbones created mysterious shadows, and slanted eyes tantalized with the glitter of emeralds. Rioting waves of fiery hair held a shimmering life all their own, and when photographers discovered how her translucent skin glowed under their powerful lamps, her career was off and running. Her face now gazed from countless magazine covers in the States as well as in western Europe.

Kristi Cole was a celebrity—but not in southwest Texas.

Would Jason find her changed? She bore scant resemblance to the teenaged tomboy who preferred Levi's and horses to satin and symphonies. However, inside she was the same person who'd spent her life in love with Jason McAlister.

FOUR UNIQUE SERIES
FOR EVERY WOMAN YOU ARE...

Silhouette ROMANCE™

These entertaining, tender and involving love stories
celebrate the spirit of pure romance.

Desire

Desire features strong heroes and spirited heroines
who come together in a highly passionate,
emotionally powerful and always provocative read.

Silhouette SPECIAL EDITION®

For every woman who dreams of life, love and family,
these are the romances in which she makes
her dreams come true.

INTIMATE MOMENTS®
Silhouette®

Dive into the pages of Intimate Moments and experience
adventure and excitement in these complex
and dramatic romances.